Deadly Deception

Alexa Grace

This book is a work of fiction. Names, characters, places and incidents are products of the author's imagination or are used fictitiously.

Although Bloomington, Indiana, Indiana University and Kramer, Indiana are real places, any resemblance to actual events or locales or persons, living or dead, is entirely coincidental.

Copyright © 2012 Alexa Grace

All rights reserved.

ISBN: 1477584609
ISBN-13: 978-1477584606

DEDICATION

To Mom

ACKNOWLEDGMENTS

A special thank you to Sgt. Adrian Youngblood of the Seminole County Sheriff's Office, Major Crimes Unit, who patiently answered my questions and reviewed passages for accuracy as I wrote this book.

Thank you also to Christine L. Snyder, Brian M. Bentsen, and Robert W. Golden, Jr. who shared their expertise from forensics, automobile accidents to firearms.

Any mistakes here are entirely mine.

Thank you to Wendy Ely who edited this book and to Christy Carlyle at GildedHeartDesign.com for the cover design.

Much appreciation goes to the Beta Reader Team who devoted their personal time to review each page of this book: Carolyn Ingham, Vicki Braun, Melissa Bourne, Angie Hunt, Elizabeth Queen, Nate Kitts, and Amy Wendt.

Thanks also to Melissa McGee, Megan Golden and Karen Golden-Dible for their help and support.

I also want to express my appreciation to my family and friends. Without their love, encouragement and support, this book would not have been possible.

CHAPTER ONE

Mandy Morris was the kind of girl a man would want to take home to meet his parents. But that was not a sentiment shared by *her* man. When the college sophomore told the man she thought was the love of her life she was pregnant, things got ugly. He'd even suggested the baby wasn't his before he'd walked away.

It was the toughest decision she'd ever made, but she had given her baby away. What else could she do? She had no parents, no baby-daddy, no job and two more years of college on a scholarship that was barely enough to cover *her* expenses. How could she possibly support a baby?

So why was she standing outside the office of the adoption agency that had supported her financially and adopted out her baby to a loving, wealthy couple who could give her baby everything?

Mandy had changed her mind about giving her baby away and wanted him back. She'd decided she'd move heaven and earth to support and care for him. Mandy had wasted four long weeks using conventional methods to get an appointment to talk to someone, anyone at the agency, about her change of heart. She wanted her baby back and nobody could talk her out of it now. He was almost six weeks old now. Mandy didn't want to miss another second of his life.

So she'd resorted to desperate measures. She'd Googled his home address then staked out Dr. Eric Caine's swanky home outside of Bloomington, Indiana, and then followed him to his office this morning. She slung her small purse over her shoulder, took a deep breath, and then pushed open his office door. He was sitting at a huge, L-shaped glass desk in front of a floor-to-ceiling window working on his computer. She walked inside and stood at his desk, and cleared her throat when she realized he had not heard her come in. He whirled around in his chair, his eyes wide with surprise.

"I didn't hear anyone come in. I thought the building was empty."

She noticed his eyes scanned her as if trying to remember her name.

"I'm Mandy Morris. I was your patient during my pregnancy."

"That's right, I remember. What can I do for you, Mandy?"

Mandy sighed and sat in one of his guest chairs. "I want you to know how much I appreciate how your adoption agency has supported me during my pregnancy."

"That's our job and we're glad to do it." The doctor looked at the door as a man with long, shaggy blonde hair entered the room. The man nodded to Mandy and sat at the round table in the back of the room.

"I know that I will need to repay you the money you gave me and I will." She glanced at the man at the back of the room, then said to the doctor, "I want my baby back."

The doctor glared at her, gone was his friendliness from before. "Mandy, we explained during your orientation, that once you give up your baby to the agency, there is no turning back."

"I want my baby back," she insisted.

"You signed our documents relieving yourself as the child's legal guardian. He is living in a wonderful home with loving parents." He was noticeably impatient now and began tapping his foot.

"I said I want my baby back." Was he hard of hearing or what?

"You're twenty years old and a college student. Babies have expensive needs. How can you support a baby?"

"I'll get a job. I'll find a way."

"This is not an emotional decision to make. Think about it. Consider this rationally. Can you give him the kind of life his new parents can? I think not."

"But he's mine. I carried him inside of me, I gave birth to him, and I need him. And if I need to involve the police, I will." She was tired of listening to his crap. She ached for her baby and she would get him back no matter what she had to do.

"It seems your mind is made up. There is only one thing I can do. I'll call the parents." He picked up his cell phone and headed to the hallway outside the office. The man with the long blonde hair followed him. Several minutes later both men returned.

"Mandy, this is David," the doctor said. "He's my driver. I've asked him to take you to the home of the couple who adopted your baby boy. They've agreed to give him back to you."

"Oh, thank you so much, Dr. Caine." Tears flowed down her cheeks. She threw herself into his arms to hug him. "I promise to pay you back every penny. I promise. Thank you so much for doing this for me."

Dr. Caine patted her on the back and guided her out of his office where she followed his driver.

It was an uneasy ride, both of them silent and seemingly deep in thought. They were hours and miles away from Bloomington before Mandy asked, "How much longer?"

David glanced at her for the first time since they started out and said, "Not far."

"So how long have you worked for Dr. Caine?" she asked, trying to fill the silence in the car. He didn't answer. He kept his attention on the road as he drove. That was fine with her. She wasn't looking for a new BFF so she ignored him and imagined herself holding her soft, cuddly little boy to her chest. She smiled at the thought.

It wasn't long before they left the interstate and were driving a country road leading through the rich farmland

4

the Midwest was known for. They drove for another hour then David slowed the car and turned onto a dirt lane that led into a wooded area. There wasn't a house in sight. Why did he pull over here? What the hell was going on?

"Why are we stopping here? Where's the house?"

"This is where the couple agreed to meet us." He walked around the car to open her passenger door and helped her get out.

"Might as well get out and stretch your legs. They won't be here for forty-five minutes."

She stretched her legs and arched slightly to ease the dull pain in her back. She hated long car rides. She disliked being cooped up in any small space for long.

"It's a beautiful day, isn't it?" She glanced at him as he leaned against the car.

"Yeah. I grew up around here. I used to know every inch of these woods," he said. He pointed to a dirt trail that wound through some trees. "See that path over there? It leads to one of the most beautiful fishing ponds you've ever seen."

"Really?" Not that she cared, but this was the first friendliness he'd shown her and she wanted to keep things pleasant for the drive back.

"Hey, we've got time." He headed to the path at the edge of the woods then looked back at her to see if she was following. "Come on, I'll show you." When he saw that she was, he waited for her to reach him then turned to walk ahead. "It's this way."

They'd walked for what seemed to her to be a couple of miles when she asked him, "How much farther is it?" As if the drive wasn't tiring enough, this hike to the pond was exhausting.

"Almost there," he said.

She trudged forward, clutching her small purse to her side. He stopped suddenly and she almost slammed into him. Her head jerked up. His expression was odd, his eyes dark and flat. She had a queasy feeling in the pit of her stomach. Something was very wrong.

He pulled out a revolver. "End of the road, Miss Morris. Turn around."

"What in the hell are you doing?" She turned away from him, her body trembling so hard she feared her legs would give out. "Why are you doing this?" The bullet slammed into her head with a loud explosion and darkness clawed at her as she sank to the ground.

David walked to the car, but had to stop several times to throw up. He attributed his physical reaction to the fact that it was his first kill at close range. He hadn't counted on the blood that sprayed onto his face, clothes, and shoes. In the army, all his kills had been done at distance. He'd found his target through the scope of his rifle and shot.

It was part of his job, he told himself as he wiped his face and shoes with a towel from his trunk. This was what he signed up for ten years ago when he assumed bodyguard duties for Dr. Caine. Serve and protect. Of course, when he signed up he didn't know he'd have to kill to protect the lucrative business the doctor had built.

He pulled his cell phone out of his pants pocket and pushed a button on his speed dial. "It's done." He'd be meeting with Caine very soon. This turn of events would mean a higher percentage of the profits, whether the doc liked it or not.

Frankie Douglas sat under the white wedding tent with the other guests. It was a beautiful spring day. The breeze caressed her face and blew through her long, blonde hair. The sweet scent of the roses in Anne Brandt's rose garden was incredible and reminded her of the times Anne taught her how to tend the bushes with exquisite care and love.

She'd been to weddings where the bride looked beautiful; but Anne was breathtaking. Her long ivory gown was silk with hand-sewn pearls. It had an empire waist with a long train. She had a glow about her that seemed to radiate from within. Michael Brandt, the groom, hadn't taken his eyes off her since she'd arrived at the altar to join him and the minister. His focus remained on his bride while he seemed unaware of the hundred or so guests watching the ceremony. Frankie had never seen a couple this much in love.

Although the happy couple had eloped last November, the groom's mother and Anne's friend, Daisy, had their own ideas about the celebration of matrimony. The two *would* have a formal wedding — period. Both women loved Anne as the daughter they didn't have. So the young woman who'd lost her mother years before ended up with two. They planned the wedding with zeal, enjoying every second of the planning.

7

It's funny how things happen, she thought. She was in the hospital last November with a gunshot wound that cut through one side of her shoulder and out the other when Michael pushed Anne in a wheelchair into her room. After he introduced them, Anne clasped her hand, thanking her for protecting her from a serial killer who had her pegged as his next victim. She had explained to Anne that it was her job as a private investigator to protect her but Anne would hear none of it.

They'd become fast friends, which was surprising to Frankie. She never had a female friend before nor had she wanted one until Anne. She and Anne had gotten together at least once a week at Anne's wind farm or at the Front Page Bar for drinks ever since. She'd found that she and Anne shared the same off-the-wall sense of humor, a love for Lady Gaga, as well as cravings for junk food when stressed.

The ring bearer pranced up the aisle holding the handle of a basket in his mouth. Tucked inside the basket was a black velvet jeweler's box. Harley, Anne's Giant Schnauzer, aimed for Michael and sat in front of him as Michael removed the ring from its box. Harley then took his place with Hank, Anne's farm foreman who sat at the end of the first row.

After the usual wedding vows, the minister pronounced them husband and wife. The couple kissed and then turned toward their guests. Frankie watched Michael kiss Anne again as he briefly rested his hand on her baby bump, and the guests erupted with applause. She had never met a couple who wanted a baby more.

Frankie joined the rest of the guests as they made their way inside the house for the reception. She scanned the crowd and saw Lane Hansen, the star of her erotic dreams. Her stupid heart slammed against her chest.

Lane had the dubious distinction of shooting her the year before. Guns drawn, they'd been creeping down some rickety storm cellar steps to stop a serial killer from killing Anne. One of the steps gave way under Lane. As he tumbled down the stairs, his gun went off, piercing Frankie's shoulder.

It had been six months since she'd seen Lane and seeing him now didn't exactly make her day. In fact, it pissed her off.

Last November, after three days of unconsciousness, Frankie had awakened to find six foot five, decidedly gorgeous Deputy Lane Hansen asleep in the chair next to her hospital bed with his hand clasped around hers. He had spent three days in her hospital room watching, okay more like hovering, over her before she woke up.

When she was released from the hospital, he dropped by her apartment for five straight days equipped with enough food to feed an army. After dinner each night, he'd ignored her protests and insisted on looking at her bullet wound and changing her bandaging. They'd relaxed on her sofa; played music, watched television, or just talked.

By the third day, though she'd never have admitted it, she was looking forward to his visits. On the fifth day, after he changed her bandaging, he'd kissed her. She'd played it in her mind a million times. She remembered the moment as if it had just happened.

He'd taken her lips tenderly, tentatively exploring her mouth with his tongue. Breaking off the kiss, he'd looked into her eyes as if asking for permission to kiss her a second time. She'd responded by snaking her arms around his neck and pulling him to her. Then she was kissing him and he was kissing her back as he swept her off the couch and onto his lap, stroking her with his wonderfully large hands. His mouth had tasted like the wine they'd had for dinner and his intoxicating scent was a mix of musk and man.

The kiss deepened. His tongue had explored the inner recesses of her mouth, sending a surprising, urgent need that flowed through her veins like molten lava. She'd leaned into him, tightening her arms around his neck and pressing her soft breasts against the hardness of his massive chest.

A heat swept through her as she remembered how he'd carried her to her bedroom and gently eased her down onto the bed. They'd made wild, turbulent love for hours and hours that night and then she'd slept in his arms. In the morning, he was gone. Just like that. No good-bye. Nothing. Like a ghost, he'd disappeared; leaving her like a victim of a one-night stand.

Frankie was so angry she'd punched a pillow then screeched as pain from her shoulder wound shot down her arm. Damn him. She'd broken her own rule of not dating cops and look what had happened. Hadn't she learned the hard way cops found it way too easy to lie? And obviously, this one found it quite easy just to screw her and leave.

She glared at Lane who stood talking to a familiar looking cop. Lane was dressed in a navy suit, white shirt, and red tie looking like he'd just left a photo shoot. Her stupid heart leapt. Her first instinct was to leave, but she'd promised Anne she'd stay throughout the reception and dinner. It was going to be a long night.

Lane didn't see Frankie at first, but rookie Deputy Edward Smith pointed her out. "Isn't that your sister, Frankie, over there?"

His eyes followed Ed's index finger that aimed at one of the most gorgeous women he'd ever seen standing next to Anne Brandt in a low cut, lavender silk dress that provocatively skimmed over her body. The garment ended at her knees, revealing her endless long legs. Damn, had he really forgotten how sexy she was? He started counting to ten and prayed his arousal wasn't obvious.

"I told you before. She's not my sister. She said that at the crime scene so she could get information out of you."

"Are you doing her? Because if you're not, I'm going to be all over her like a dog on a sausage salesman at a dog park." He stared at Frankie across the room.

"I don't kiss and tell. Anyway, I heard she was in a relationship." Okay, that was a lie, but he found he didn't like the idea of Ed Smith or any other man making a move on her.

"I don't care if she's in a relationship or not. He's not with her right now, so she's fair game," he said as he moved toward her.

Lane clenched his jaw and scowled as Ed now stood next to Frankie pulling her into a conversation. She crossed her arms across her chest and looked more uncomfortable than pleased and looked toward him. When their eyes met, she sent him an icy glare. He needn't wonder whether or not she was angry with him. That glare said it all. Damn it. He'd screwed up badly with her and had no idea how to fix it. And he *did* want to fix it, because awake or sleeping, he couldn't get her out of his head. He'd relived making love to her a million times in his mind and taken as many cold showers.

If she was haunting him, it was his own damn fault. What kind of a bastard had he become? Leaving her after a night of mind-shattering sex? The truth was, he'd never experienced the emotions she made him feel before and it scared the crap out of him. Figured that he'd take the easy way out by walking away. And now there was nothing he regretted more.

It was the bottom of the eighth inning and Detective Lane Hansen was up to bat. The pressure swirled around him like a thunderstorm. The bases were loaded with two balls and two strikes. The Cop Team needed a hit or there was a good chance the Fire Fighter Team would win the game. The Fire Fighters hadn't beaten the Cops for five years and he certainly didn't want to be the reason his team lost.

The pitcher unrolled a curve ball that surged past him and clapped in the catcher's mitt. Ball three. A cell phone went off in the dugout and Ed Smith announced it was Lane's. The pitcher aimed another one and Lane's bat cracked like a whip. The ball sailed over left field and out of the park. Lane flew to first base, raced to second and then third following his teammates before him. The crowd in the bleachers stood up to let out an ear piercing cheer. He slid into home base creating a cloud of dust that coated his eyes.

"Safe!" called the umpire. Suddenly his team surrounded him, patting him hard on the back. Lane rubbed his eyes and noticed Ed running toward him from the dugout with *his* cell phone in his hand.

"It's the sheriff. A couple of hikers found a body in a wooded area near State Highway 55 off of U.S. 41 close to Kramer. He said for you to get your ass out there ASAP. The crime scene techs are there and the medical examiner is on his way. Call dispatch for the exact location."

Lane grabbed his cell out of the deputy's hand and raced toward his county sheriff department issued SUV. He turned on his lights and sirens as he sped out of the parking lot. His adrenalin shot into high gear as it always did when a possible homicide was assigned to him.

The flashing lights ahead let him know he'd found the crime scene. He pulled up behind a patrol car, threw his county sheriff investigator jacket on over his baseball uniform and pushed his small notebook in his back pocket.

Karen Katz, a crime scene technician, stood near the crime scene investigation van. Striding toward her, he asked, "Hey, Karen, what do we have here?"

"See for yourself. Enter over there." She cocked her head toward the entry a few feet away. "And stay in the woods and off of the path we've got secured with crime scene tape. Other than the hikers' shoe impressions, we don't want any more made. The rain storms we've had for the past week washed away any chance of getting the victim's and the killer's shoe impressions. Same goes for tire prints."

"Thanks," he said as he started toward the opening of the woods.

"Where's your partner?" She called after him.

"Jan is out on maternity leave."

"Already? I thought she had a couple of months to go."

"Triplets. Her doctor put her on bed rest."

Lane hiked through the brush and soggy earth, his boots making a squishing sound with each step. He walked as close as he could get to the narrow dirt path which was more mud than dirt. Although it was early evening; there was still enough light so he didn't need his flashlight. Lane noticed two sets of shoe impressions, which were undoubtedly those of the hikers. Pressing onward, he hoped he wouldn't get a raging case of poison ivy like he did the last time they found a body in a wooded area.

A few feet away farther into the woods, a pair of teenaged hikers sat on a log talking with a deputy named Sam Hillsen. They looked like they might around fourteen years old. One was holding his stomach and looked like he'd either been sick or would vomit any second.

"Your parents are on the way," explained Sam as he gave Lane a nod.

Lane made a mental note to get their names from Sam and schedule an interview with them after their parents arrived. Judging from the terrified expression on their faces, he also needed to call in one of the victim advocates or counselors.

Bob Goldberg, another crime scene technician, took photos of the entire scene. He cautiously inched around the body of a fully clothed young girl lying face down in the dirt careful not to disturb the scene. He eyed a small leather purse lying near her. He fought the temptation to search it for identification. Touching anything before all pictures were taken and the medical examiner arrived was a violation of the rules.

He moved closer. The bullet wound at the back of her head was unmistakable. The gun shot appeared to have been taken at point blank range. Lane could see stippling had burned onto her skin around the wound. The killer could have been as close as three feet from the girl when he had fired. He looked around for any sign of a bullet in case it went through the victim. He saw nothing and assumed the bullet lodged itself in her skull. If so, the medical examiner would recover it from the body during the autopsy.

"I won't be able to get blood spatter," said Bob as he swatted a bug away from him. "Did Karen tell you that we can't get shoe or tire impressions either?"

"Yeah, I know, thanks to the rain." He inched closer to the body and bent down to examine her hands and wrists. There were no defensive wounds on the delicate, white skin nor was there any damage to her long, painted fingernails. He checked the wrists for ligature marks to determine if she came to the scene voluntarily. There were none.

He walked to the path. There were no drag marks. From what he could see, there wasn't a single sign of a struggle, nor were there signs she'd been dragged here. For what reasons would she willingly follow her killer to this remote area? And why would someone want to shoot her at point blank range?

Footsteps trudged through the mud behind him. He turned to see his supervisor, County Sheriff Tim Brennan, had finally arrived.

"What's your initial assessment?"

Tim studied Lane's face as he asked the question. He'd had been promoted to detective just five months before and he knew the sheriff still considered him a rookie.

"There are no defensive wounds or physical signs that she fought back, nor are there any signs she was dragged here. By what I've viewed so far, I think she knew her killer. Also her killer lives in this area now or has lived here in the past. How else would he even know this place exists? I don't think it was a random decision that he lured or brought her here to kill her."

"Wouldn't the rain have washed away the drag marks?" The question was to test Lane. Even with rain, there would've been drag marks if there was a struggle to get the girl to where the killer wanted to go.

"Not if there'd been a struggle. The drag marks would've been deep enough so that the rain would've filled the indentations in the ground instead of washing them away. None of the surrounding plants have been disturbed either."

"Agree. Find a bullet or casing?"

"No, sir. Chances are good that it's still lodged inside her skull."

Doc Meade arrived and shot a glance over to Lane and Tim before he bent to look at the body.

Lane slipped on his latex gloves as he watched Doc Meade open the girl's purse while Bob took photos of the contents. Doc handed the purse to Lane, who withdrew a small wallet. A bank debit card, driver's license, library card and Indiana University identification card were inside.

"Victim's name is Mandy Morris, 19 years old, and a student at I.U. There's a dorm address on the ID. The driver's license lists an address in Bedford that may be her parents' residence. I'll do a computer search for the phone number and contact them first." Lane jotted notes on a small pad he'd retrieved from his pocket. Contacting a victim's parents was his least favorite thing to do, but the task had to be done.

"Shit. She goes to I.U.? My daughter, Jennifer, is a junior there." Tim cringed and pulled his jacket collar up as if he was trying to fight a chill rushing through his body. "This murder hits too close to home. My wife, Megan, and I have worried about my daughter's safety since she'd moved out of their home to live in a dorm in

Bloomington. You know what they say about crime statistics related to coeds on college campuses."

"Yes, I do. On college campuses there are large concentrations of young women who are at greater risk for rape and other forms of sexual assault than women in the general population or in a comparable age group."

"That's why Jennifer's safety remains on my worry top ten list."

"There's a cell phone." Lane took out a plastic sandwich bag and placed the slim, silver cell phone inside. He'd examine it later for recent calls. There were no car keys, but that was not a surprise if Mandy Morris lived on campus. Many students at I.U. walked to their destinations or used public transportation. Mandy might be one of them.

The deputy and the crime scene technician gingerly loaded her body on a gurney and headed for the M.E.'s van. Doc Meade turned to follow them and said, "Lane, I'll do the autopsy at ten o'clock tomorrow morning. I'll see you there."

Lane had stopped by his apartment to shower and shave. As he found his cubicle in the bull pen at the Sheriff's office he felt almost human again. A smile spread across his face as his gaze took in streamers and colorful confetti littering his cubicle to celebrate the Cop Team's win over the Fire Fighters.

After pushing the small pieces of confetti from his desk into the trash can, he turned on his computer then searched for the home address listed on Mandy Morris's driver's license and found the name of Nelle Morris as the homeowner. He'd go to Bedford in the morning after the autopsy to talk to Nelle Morris in person, and then to Bloomington to talk to Mandy's friends.

At 10:00 a.m. sharp, Doc Meade made the initial Y-shaped incision in the body of Mandy Morris. Lane didn't think Doc would find anything of interest in his examination of the victim's organs. She was nineteen years old, for Christ's sake. Lane's interest was in the skull where he'd seen the entry of the bullet.

Queasiness swirled around in his gut. He cursed himself for meeting with some buddies from the baseball team at Mom's Cafe for his usual farm-style breakfast which included everything from the kitchen except the sink. It wasn't the smartest move just hours prior to an autopsy but it wasn't his first one and he didn't think eating all that food would matter. Until now. It was the combination of the formaldehyde smell and the sickening ripening of the dead body that had the contents of his stomach doing acrobatics. The Vicks VapoRub he'd smeared in each of his nostrils hadn't helped a bit. He would have walked into the hallway for some fresh air, but his boss stood beside him and Lane didn't want to reinforce the rookie impression his supervisor already had about him.

The fluorescent lights were old and periodically crackled and blinked. The medical examiner went through the motions of removing and examining her organs as he spoke into his tape recorder. Lane's mind wandered and thought about how young the victim was. He was startled when Doc plunked a bullet into a stainless steel bowl and handed it to him.

"I'm no bullet expert, but that sure looks like a .38 hollow point to me." Doc wiped the sweat from his brow and glanced at Lane. "It'll be interesting to find out what ATF has to say about what kind of gun it was shot from."

Lane put the bullet in a padded envelope to send it to ATF for analysis. He, too, was curious about the make of the gun the killer used. It would be one more piece to a puzzle he intended to solve in order to bring justice for the victim and her family.

He pulled up to the house and rechecked Mandy Morris's home address on his notepad. This was the right place. The house looked like it was overdue to be condemned with grass and weeds that went to his knees and house paint peeling down to raw wood in places. There was an ancient sofa on the front porch with a can of cigarette butts lying on a table beside it.

He knocked on the front door several times. The porch creaked beneath his weight as he turned toward the stairs. A female voice on the other side of the door asked, "What do you want?"

Not the friendliest greeting, but he could deal. "I'm Detective Lane Hansen and I'm looking for Nelle Morris." He held his badge up to the peep hole.

"Yeah, well what do you want with her?" She barked through the door.

"I have news about her daughter."

The door flew open and a middle aged woman with scary, wiry gray hair, and yellow teeth stood in front of him. She held a glass of what smelled like bourbon.

"That's funny. I don't have no daughter," she said. "I've got a good for nothing niece that my brother left me when he died. But she ain't here."

"Are you Nelle Morris?"

"Who else would you be talking to at this address?" She scowled at him and took a drink of her bourbon.

"Is your niece named Mandy Morris?"

"Yeah, so what?" She slid out a cigarette out a pack of Camels and pulled a matchbook from her pocket and. She lit the end of the cigarette and took a drag.

"I'm afraid I have some bad news."

"Then spit it out. Can't you see I'm busy?"

"Mandy Morris was found dead yesterday."

"No kidding. That's what she gets for going to college when she should've stayed here to support her aunt. She needed to get a damn job to help pay for things around here. But no. Her mother filled her with all these ideas that she could be anything she wanted. And she sure didn't want to turn out like her dear Aunt Nelle."

Lane just stared at her. He'd just told her that her nineteen year old niece had lost her life and this is her response? She was most definitely one of those women devoid of maternal instincts. He clenched his jaw and asked, "When was the last time you saw Mandy?"

"A couple of summers ago. Just before she got that scholarship and left for college." She slurred the word "college" like it was a dirty word.

"And you haven't heard from her since?"

"Nope and I didn't expect to hear from that ingrate. After all I'd done for her too. Who else would have taken her in after that car accident killed her parents?" She took a last drag on her cigarette then threw it into the yard.

"Do you know anyone who would want to hurt Mandy?"

"Nope. If you're done with your questions, I'm busy," she said as she pulled the pack of cigarettes out of her dress pocket again. She then stumbled back a couple of steps and slammed the door in his face.

Lane folded his notebook and crammed it into his pocket. With clenched fists he stalked back to his car. Mandy Morris was only nineteen years old. She'd been so young with her life ahead of her. Her mother had been right. She could have been anyone she wanted to be. That her young life was cut so short and her only living relative didn't give a damn sickened and saddened him at the same time.

His cell vibrated in his jacket pocket. He pulled it out and checked the display. "Hi, Mom."

"Hi, sweetie. How's my handsome boy? Just calling to see if you can come for supper tonight. Your dad caught some catfish yesterday and we're having a fish fry."

"Not tonight. I'm in Bloomington on a case. I may be here for a couple of days."

"Lane, there's another reason I called. You remember Nancy? I work with her at Dispatch. Well, Nancy has a pretty daughter and I thought..."

"Don't go there again, Mom. You're not fixing me up. I thought we had that settled. I don't need your help in that department." How many times in the past had she tried to fix him up? How many times did he have to say no?

"Honey, I respectfully disagree. You should've made me a grandmother years ago."

"Seriously, Mom? This is why you called me? Because I'm at work and I have a lot to do today."

"I love you, Lane."

"Love you too, Mom. Good-bye."

Lane smiled. Love was never in short supply among the Hansen family. What his mother didn't know was the only woman he wanted haunted his dreams. The one he'd probably never have again. Not that he'd stop trying. Seeing Frankie at the wedding had only deepened his resolve. Now he just needed a plan to make her forgive him and let him back in her bed.

He'd turned the ignition to start his car when the cell buzzed again. "Hansen," he answered.

"This is Dr. Meade. After you left the autopsy, I discovered something that may help in your investigation."

"What's that?"

"Mandy Morris had given birth within weeks of her death."

Lane disconnected the call and leaned back in his seat and felt anger wash over him. He had two immediate thoughts. The first was how could anyone have killed this girl? The second was this sick bastard is going down.

Like most cops, he knew the leading cause of death for young women is homicide at the hands of the husband or lover. So finding the baby-daddy jumped to first on his to-do list.

Lane checked into the Comfort Inn, ate pizza and spent the rest of his evening hunched over his laptop making interview plans and appointments for the next day. He wanted to talk to Mandy's dorm roommate as well as visit area hospitals to find out where she'd given birth. He vowed the name of the baby-daddy would be his by the end of the next day.

He pulled out the information he'd gotten from the college earlier in the day. He learned that Mandy Morris was a good student who was on a scholarship that paid all her expenses as long as she stayed enrolled in college, taking classes and maintained at least a B average. Student records revealed perfect attendance had diminished. She had missed numerous classes this term, which fit precisely with a pregnancy timetable.

He turned on his laptop to view her bank records. There were direct deposits of $500 to her checking account every two weeks from F.H.A.A. Since she was not working and had a scholarship, these deposits made him curious. Mandy made debit transactions to a grocery store, a pharmacy and small amounts for cash from the ATM. No payments were made to a physician, which he found odd since she was pregnant. In addition, there were no payments for rent. Something that popped out was a direct deposit of $10,000 from F.H.A.A. that had been made six weeks prior to her death. Who the hell was F.H.A.A. and why were they paying her this much money?

Her phone records revealed she'd made multiple calls to F.H.A.A. The last call was made the day before her murder. Other than that, the only calls she made the month before she died was to a pharmacy, a Pizza King, and a Chinese restaurant. It seemed odd to him that someone her age didn't call or text any friends.

It was close to midnight when he closed his laptop and turned on the television. Exhausted, he fell asleep watching a *Seinfeld* rerun.

He awoke on fire, panting and aroused. Damn it. Not again. He glanced at the time on his phone — 4:00 a.m. The dreams had started again. Not that they'd ever stopped. This one was in erotic Technicolor and started with the back of a blue dress Frankie was wearing. He pulled on her stuck zipper, his knuckles rubbing against her satiny skin, the sexual electricity sharp between them. He plucked a tiny piece of fabric from the zipper teeth and the zipper flowed down easily.

Lane slid his hands inside her dress and around her waist, pulling her closer to him until he could feel her heat. He pushed the dress to the floor to reveal her perfect, naked body. Turning her around, he possessed her mouth in a deep kiss that sent fire shooting through his body down to his toes. Beads of sweat formed at his temples, the heat becoming unbearable as he pushed her onto the bed, her soft body beneath his hard one.

The dreams were his punishment for leaving her like he did. One night with her and he experienced a sexual explosion like no other. He'd had sex with a lot of women but none who made him feel like he had died and gone to heaven. He always had the control, but with Frankie, he didn't give a damn who took charge as long as he was having mind-shattering sex with her.

Lying next to her that night, the realization had branded him that she was the one he might not be able to leave behind and it terrified him. So he'd held her while she slept. At dawn he slipped out of her bed and out of her life.

When had he become such a bastard? Why in the hell did he do that to her? That was a stupid question with a puzzling answer. She scared the crap out of him. With the SWAT team, he'd crashed through a well-known and armed drug dealer hideout and had not blinked; but this gorgeous, spunky woman and her effect on him made him shake in his boots.

Now he'd lost her. He knew he had. It was his own damned fault. He cursed and threw a pillow across the room. He then got out of bed and headed for the shower — a cold one.

.

CHAPTER TWO

It was the first time Lane had been in the Indiana University Memorial Union, but the Starbucks was easy to find. He simply followed the mass of students who were cursed with 8:00 a.m. classes to the coffee shop. He ordered a double espresso, sat down at a table and waited for Mandy Morris's roommate who promised to meet him. He scanned the crowd for a young woman wearing a red I.U. t-shirt with white letters and jeans. Christie Allen described herself as being 5'5" tall, blue eyes, with long brown hair she liked to wear in a ponytail. Unfortunately, he'd seen at least a dozen girls matching that description within the last five minutes.

A girl, he assumed to be Christie Allen, plopped down in the chair across from him. "You didn't say you were a hottie over the phone." She let her gaze travel over the length of his body in a sexually explicit way.

Shooting her a glare, he said, "I'm a detective, not a hottie. I want to talk to you about your roommate, Mandy Morris."

"I'm not sure how much I can tell you. Are you buying me a latte?"

"That depends on how valuable your information is."

"Mandy's been my roommate since the spring semester of last year."

"Are you friends?"

She rolled her eyes. "With that homely dork? No. She was my roommate, if you can call her that. She spent most of her time in the library so she wasn't around much, which was fine with me. It gave me more alone time with my boyfriend."

"Did Mandy have a boyfriend?"

"I thought so, but I never saw him. She started staying out all night starting last April. I thought maybe she was out with a boyfriend."

"What's his name?"

"I don't know," she answered with a huff. "We didn't exactly run around in the same circles, if you know what I mean."

Lane shot her another glare. The more he learned about Mandy Morris, the angrier he became about how badly people had treated her.

"Was she friends with anyone in your dorm?"

"I don't think so. She kept to herself."

"You're not much help."

"Does that mean you aren't buying me a latte?"

Lane gulped down the rest of his espresso and rose to leave. "That's right. Your information is not all that valuable."

He walked away and wondered how someone could be so self-involved as to not even wonder why a detective was asking questions about her roommate. Did Mandy Morris have anyone in her life who cared about her?

Lane purposely waited until midnight to visit the hospital where he thought Mandy delivered her baby. He knew there were fewer employees on the night shift and he might get one of them to talk about Mandy Morris. In addition, if he could find a birth certificate, he'd find the baby's father.

He headed toward the nurse's desk where two nurses worked on a computer. They were so intent, neither saw him approach their area. He watched the nurse closest to him. She looked like she was in her thirties with highlighted brown hair shaped into a bob. She wore glasses that kept sliding down her nose as she typed. Finally, she noticed him and jerked slightly in surprise. She rose and approached him. Her name tag read Danielle.

"I'm sorry I didn't notice you. I'm afraid visiting hours are over."

"Not a problem. I was enjoying watching you work, Danielle." Lane gave her his best flirtatious smile and was pleased to see her blush. He needed information from her that she was not supposed to give him and waiting weeks for a subpoena for Mandy's medical records was not an option. Lane pulled out his badge as well as Mandy Morris's photo.

"Do you remember this young lady? She gave birth about six weeks ago?"

She glanced at his badge then the photo. She lingered more than a second as she eyeballed the photo, frowning slightly, and biting her lower lip. In that moment, he knew from her body language she remembered Mandy. She looked nervously over her shoulder at the other nurse who was ending a phone call. A buzzer sounded from a patient's room and the other nurse responded she'd take care of it, and headed down the hall.

"Danielle, I think you recognize Mandy Morris. Why don't you tell me about it?"

"I'm sorry..."

"I'm Detective Lane Hansen. But you can call me Lane." He reached for her hand to shake and squeezed it gently sending another blush to her face. He shot her a reassuring smile. "Tell me about Mandy."

She glanced nervously over her shoulder obviously looking for the other nurse who was nowhere in sight. "I remember her. She had her baby boy here. One night I overheard her crying and I went to her room. I held that poor girl for fifteen minutes as she sobbed. She wanted to hold her baby and she said the day nurse told her it wasn't a good idea since she was giving him up for adoption. I went down to the nursery and brought him back to her. She rocked him back and forth on the bed for hours. I told her she could change her mind and keep him. She said she didn't think the adoption agency would let her."

"What's the name of the agency?" Lane asked as he pulled out his notepad.

"Forever Homes Adoption. They're a new agency here with their own clinic and everything."

"Did you see the baby's father? Did he visit her?"

"I don't think that poor child had any visitors."

"Danielle, I need the name of the baby's father."

"I can't give that to you. The privacy laws prevent me from..."

"She was murdered. The killer dumped her body like garbage in a wooded area. The baby's father may be her killer. I need to find him." He knew he was screwed if she didn't give him the name. A subpoena for the records could take time he didn't have.

Just as she was about to respond, the other nurse returned and sat in front of her computer. Danielle moved to a filing cabinet and pulled out a manila file folder. She looked at him with her index finger pressed against her lips, her eyes pleading with him not to say anything. She placed the file on the counter near him, opened it and pulled out a white sheet of paper. With her finger, she pointed to a section of the birth certificate that listed the baby's father — Billy James. Lane jotted the name in his notepad and smiled at her.

"Lane, it was nice talking to you." She patted his hand and glanced at the file as she closed it. "I hope you find what you're looking for."

Back at the Comfort Inn, he threw his jacket on the bed and opened his laptop to search for Billy James. He opened his driver's license database and found a Billy James, twenty years old, who listed an apartment address not far from the I.U. campus. Bingo. This had to be him.

He then went to Google where he spotted the entry that listed Billy James, I.U. student on Facebook. The profile photo matched the one from the driver's license database.

Lane clicked on the link and entered the Facebook world of Billy James. He looked at his photo albums, most of which included an intoxicated Billy toasting beer cans with his drinking buddies. Another album held several photos of Billy with a raven-haired young woman who wore a lot of makeup. Definitely not Mandy Morris.

He jotted down Billy's apartment address and planned a surprise visit. He'd learned that unexpected interrogations elicited the most information. He grinned. He was looking forward to it.

Frankie Douglas sat in her red sports car in a business parking lot next to a pizzeria on Kirkwood Avenue in Bloomington, watching the building with her camera within reach. Insurance scam assignments were lucrative for her small private investigation company and this one was turning out to be a gem. Her focus was Jerry Richards, a man who hadn't worked in three years and was living on his insurance company's disability checks. Her mission was to discover whether Mr. Richards was indeed physically disabled. Thus far, she had taken photographs of him mowing his lawn with a push mower, jogging around his neighborhood, playing basketball with his son, and wrestling with a large dog in his front yard. She'd followed him to Bloomington for some additional photographs before she met with the insurance company.

Frankie yawned and stretched as much as she could in her small car and daydreamed about the bills she'd pay off with the hefty check she'd get for this job. She poured a cup of coffee from her thermos and listened to the birds chattering to each other in oak trees lining the street. She pulled out the newspaper she'd plucked from her front porch earlier, and began reading a story on the front page about a young girl's body found in a wooded area near Kramer. It was a strange place to dump a body. The wooded area was near the old and the reportedly haunted Mudlavia Hotel located near Kramer. The hotel and spa had been built by a natural spring and in its day and served as a popular place to stay for the rich and famous. It was destroyed by fire in the 1920s, but haunted or not, that didn't stop curiosity seekers from visiting it throughout the years.

She noticed movement outside the restaurant and saw Jerry Richards lifting a keg of beer from the back of a Budweiser truck. She grabbed her red digital camera and got several shots of Jerry carrying the keg into the restaurant. Poor Jerry, too disabled to work, but able to lift and carry heavy beer kegs. Right. She chuckled to herself and went back to her newspaper. A couple more photographs and she'd head home. Not bad for a day's work and it wasn't even noon.

Taking another sip of coffee, she flipped to the local section. Suddenly her car door ripped open, and a large hand squeezed on her arm.

"Ouch, you're hurting me."

"Who are you?" A livid Jerry Richards leaned in just inches from her face. "Why are you taking pictures of me?"

"I don't know what you're talking about. Let go of my arm." She tried to pull her arm out of his grip, but he just squeezed harder and pulled her out of the car then pushed her against the side and waved his finger in front of her face.

"Who the hell do you think you are?" He rammed his index finger into her shoulder, pushing her against the car.

"Sir, please calm down." Though she was angry he was touching her, she used a soft tone of voice and spoke slowly in an effort to calm him. "I can see that you are upset about something."

"Damn right I am. I saw you taking pictures of me. I saw you!"

"Sir, if you must know, I'm a bird watcher and I was taking a photo of a White-Breasted Nuthatch that is nesting in that tree," she said as she pointed.

"Bullshit!" He screamed.

Lane steered his SUV down Kirkwood Avenue en route to Billy James's apartment. He'd just choked down two sausage and egg McMuffins and was toying with his GPS when he noticed a red sports car that looked just like the one belonging to Frankie Douglas. He shook his head. Great. Just great. *When I sleep, she haunts my dreams, now I'm imagining her while awake.* Why would she be this far from home? As he got closer, he saw a tall blonde woman being pinned against her car by a guy who looked like he'd been eating way too many donuts. The woman was gorgeous. The woman *was* Frankie.

He flipped on his emergency lights, squealed his brakes, shifted lanes, and did a U-turn at the next traffic light and raced back. By the time he slid his SUV behind her red sports car the guy was screaming and hammering her with his index finger. No freaking way.

He eased out of his car, removed his navy suit jacket, loosened his tie, and moved toward them. Frankie was talking calmly and seemed to have the situation somewhat in control so he paused when he reached the back of her car.

"Hand over the camera, bitch!"

It became obvious to Frankie that her calming methods weren't working and Mr. Jerry Richards was heading to the land of out-of-control.

"I am *not* giving you my camera."

Richards pushed her to the ground, then reached into her car, snatched her red digital camera off the passenger seat, and shoved it in his jeans pocket.

Frankie dusted herself off and stood to face him. "Unless you want to get arrested for theft, you'll give my camera back to me."

"Go to hell!" Richards shouted before he pushed Frankie hard against the car.

Before Lane could move, Frankie grabbed Richards's thumb bending back his wrist until he shrieked with pain. She jerked Richards's arm behind his back and dropped him to the ground. Still gripping his arm, she pushed her knee into his back to hold him in place.

Lane eased up next to her dangling a pair of handcuffs on his thumb. "Need these?"

She grabbed them from him and snapped them around Richards's wrists. "What are you doing here, Lane?"

"I'm on a case and I might ask you the same thing."

"On an assignment. Mr. Charming here has been bilking his insurance company for disability for the past three years. Does he look disabled to you?"

"No, I don't think so. And I think you can get off him now." Trying not to grin, he held her arm to help her to her feet.

"He has my camera in his pocket," said Frankie as she pointed toward his front jeans pocket.

"Sounds like theft. Do you want me to call it in?"

"Not sure."

"Let me up, you bitch, or you'll regret it." Richards squirmed and tried to roll over.

"Shut up!" Both Lane and Frankie barked in unison.

Lane pulled her to him with his arm around her waist and started picking leaves and sticks out of her hair.

"Do you mind?" she asked as she backed up. The close proximity of his body to hers was unsettling and made her stupid heart skip a beat.

He headed back to his SUV and returned with a first aid kit.

"Hold still or we can go back to my hotel to do this."

The thought of being with Lane in his hotel room caused an electric volt of lust that sent a shock through Frankie's system. Getting turned on at this particular moment was beyond inappropriate. Besides, this was Lane Hansen, the guy who dumped her six months before.

He placed the first aid kit on her trunk, and then leaned her back against her car. He pulled out some antiseptic swabs, ripped open the foil, and wiped at a cut near her lips.

"Ouch. That stings!" She slapped at his hand.

"Sorry, sweetheart." He kissed her forehead.

"You're *not* sorry and stop calling me sweetheart." She pushed at him, but he was as immobile as a boulder, all hard muscle pressing against her.

"I'm sorry it hurts, but you don't want an infection, do you?"

"Right, like you're concerned. I think you're getting turned on playing doctor." She pushed at him again but he refused to move away from her.

"Sweetheart, everything you do turns me on." He leaned dangerously close to her mouth and she stomped angrily on his foot, sending him back a step.

She was beyond pissed. Was he serious? He'd stayed away from her for months. Obviously, everything about her did *not* turn him on. What kind of sick game was he playing with her anyway? She moved toward Jerry

Richards intent on getting her camera back. He was cursing and flopping on the ground like a fish out of water so she pressed her knee on his back to stabilize him so she could pull her camera out of his front pocket.

"Frankie, if you want I'll stay here with him until back-up arrives," said Lane.

She got in her car and shot out of the parking lot. The sooner she could put some distance between Lane Hansen and herself the better. Richards, she could deal with. The feelings she still had for Lane, she could not.

Lane watched her car until it disappeared in the distance. Then he pulled Jerry Richards into a standing position. Lane walked him back to his SUV where his emergency lights blinked wildly. He pushed Richards so hard against the vehicle that his head knocked against the doorframe.

"I'm going to offer you the deal of a lifetime, asshole."

"What's that?" Sweat beaded across Richards's forehead and dripped down his cheeks as he had to look up to see Lane's face.

"You don't *ever* come in contact with the blonde that just kicked your ass and I won't use you for a punching bag. Understand?" Lane shoved him against the SUV again. He leaned in so close to Richard's face he could smell his breath. Lane used his most intimidating glare, the kind that worked on gang bangers and drug dealers.

"Yes, sir." Richards's body trembled.

"I don't want to even think about what I'll do to you if you ever hurt her. I'd hunt you down and when I caught you..."

"I agree. I won't go near the blonde. Hell, I don't even know who she is."

Lane jerked him around, unlocked the handcuffs, and then pushed him toward the restaurant. Lane watched Richards as he bounded like a rabbit to the building and scurried inside.

He got in his SUV, slammed his hands against the steering wheel, and thought about what a major screw-up he was. He'd give anything for a do-over with Frankie. What was he thinking trapping Frankie against the car like that and trying to kiss her? All he'd accomplished was to make her angrier and now he'd have to work that much harder to get her back.

The apartment house where Billy James lived was a converted gray Victorian with white shuttered windows and a porch that wrapped around the front. Lane had liked old houses since his parents fixed up a Craftsman cottage years ago. He liked the beauty of the woodwork inside and out as well as the small design details that were missing in modern homes.

According to the mailboxes inside the entry way, Billy lived in 2B on the second floor. As apartment houses go, especially those near a college campus, this one was very quiet. There was no loud music with the bass pounding through the walls. Lane slipped up the stairs and knocked on Billy's door. No answer. He put his ear near the door and thought he heard music or a television. He knocked again. Still no answer. Just as he placed his hand on the doorknob and twisted, the door jerked open. A young, raven-haired woman in a pink t-shirt and cotton sleep pants appeared holding a flat iron.

"May I help you?" She looked him up and down. "Can you make it fast? I'm getting ready to go to class."

"Yes, my name is Detective Lane Hansen and I'm looking for Billy James." He pulled his suit jacket back to show her his badge.

"He's my boyfriend. Has he done something wrong?"

"Is he here?"

"Yes, he's sleeping. I'll get him." She headed toward the back of the apartment.

Although she didn't invite him in, Lane followed her into the living room. While she disappeared into what he guessed was a bedroom in the back, Lane took the opportunity to look around. There was a flat screen TV hanging on the wall, and white sheets, instead of curtains, covered the windows. A worn sofa and chair sat next to a small bookcase filled with textbooks and CDs. A few framed photos featured the young woman with Billy James in various happy poses for the camera. Nowhere in sight were any photos of Billy James with Mandy Morris. A stack of letters lay on the coffee table and Lane leafed through them — bills, letter from an aunt, and junk mail. Footsteps came down the hall toward him. He dropped the mail back on the table and turned to see a disheveled Billy wearing a wrinkled white t-shirt and jeans walk into the room.

"Hello, Billy. My name is Lane Hansen. I'm a detective and I'm here to talk to you about Mandy Morris."

When Billy heard the name Mandy Morris, a flash of panic crossed his face as he glanced at his girlfriend.

"Marianne, aren't you late for class?"

"Mind if I sit down?" Not waiting for his answer, Lane claimed a spot on the sofa and sat down. Billy sat on a nearby chair.

Marianne looked at her watch and ran into the bedroom. Moments later she reappeared dressed and clutching a stack of books to her chest. She kissed Billy on the cheek then rushed out the door and down the stairs.

"I take it you didn't want your friend to overhear our conversation?"

"She's my fiancée. We're getting married in June."

"Fiancée? Really? I bet she wasn't too happy last year when you told her about Mandy Morris being pregnant."

"She can't know about that." There was an urgency in Billy's voice.

"Interesting. So she doesn't know." This could be good leverage if Billy decided not to cooperate.

"Listen, I'll answer your questions and tell you anything you want to know, but don't tell Marianne about Mandy and me."

"Well, that depends on how honest you are with me. Doesn't it?"

"So what's going on? Is Mandy trying to say I'm the father and going for child support?"

Lane leaned back in his chair and stared at Billy for a long moment. It's curious how just a stare, if timed correctly, makes people very damned uncomfortable.

"Mandy Morris was murdered and her body was dumped in a wooded area near Kramer."

"No way. Seriously? Mandy *can't* be dead."

"Someone put a bullet through her head."

"Oh, my God," said Billy as he put his head in his hands. Lane watched him carefully. He looked upset, but Lane had seen subjects give Academy Award winning performances before to escape detection.

"Ever been to Kramer?"

"Where? Hell, no. Never heard of it."

"Tell me about your relationship with Mandy."

"She was in one of my classes and helped me with a term paper. We just sort of hooked up. She was lonely and Marianne hadn't started school here yet. The thing with Mandy just sort of happened. Before I knew it, she was staying here more than at her dorm."

"Were you in love with her? Did you have a relationship with Mandy?"

"No way. I didn't tell her about Marianne and I never told her we were in love or in any kind of big relationship either. I couldn't believe the idiot got pregnant. I thought she was on birth control."

"So you weren't very happy about the pregnancy?" Lane frowned at the kid and thought about what a colossal asshole he was.

"Hell, no. I didn't want to be the father of Mandy Morris's kid. She was a freak. Everyone I know made fun of her. I told her I'd pay to get an abortion, but she said it was too late. I told her I didn't care what she did as long as she left me out of it. I just wanted her out of my apartment and my life before she screwed things up with Marianne and me."

Lane scowled and leaned as close to Billy's face as he could get. By now his fingers had formed a fist and he tried to control the urge to hit him. "Did you want her out of your life enough to kill her?"

"No way. I did *not* kill her. I couldn't do that."

"Do you own a firearm, Billy?"

"Yeah. My dad got me a Glock 21 for Christmas last year. He was worried about me living in the apartment without protection."

"May I see it?" Lane watched as Billy headed for one of the back rooms for the gun. He didn't like Billy one bit. But that didn't mean the kid was a killer. In a murder like this one, the baby-daddy is usually the prime suspect. But something didn't feel right about accusing Billy of the crime yet.

He was hoping the gun was something other than a Glock; a gun that was capable of shooting a .38 hollow point bullet like the one found in Mandy Morris's skull. Billy returned with a shoe box that he handed to Lane, who pulled out a black Glock 21. Lane examined the gun and discovered it not only hadn't been shot recently, but had never been shot, period.

He handed the gun in the shoe box back to Billy. "Do you know anyone who might have wanted to hurt Mandy?"

Billy shook his head. "She was kind of a loner. Not many friends."

Lane slipped one of his cards out of his pocket and handed it to Billy. "Call me if you remember anything that might help."

Later, he sat outside Billy's apartment house. His gut told him that Billy James didn't kill Mandy Morris. But if Billy didn't kill her, who did? And if she'd moved out of Billy's apartment and her dorm, where did she go?

Lane sat at the small round table in his hotel room with the contents of Mandy Morris's investigative file folder strewn across the table and taped on a nearby wall. His heart clenched as he glanced at the photo he'd enlarged from her university identification card. She was so damn young and full of promise. She wasn't beautiful, but she wasn't ugly either. She had the girl-next-door look with pale skin and a scattering of freckles, large green eyes, and a strong, determined jaw. She was a young, smart woman who didn't deserve the lack of respect or love in her life. That someone extinguished this girl like the way one would ground out a cigarette butt was reprehensible to him and made him that much more determined to get her justice.

He pulled out her cell phone records again, hoping they'd provide a clue as to where Mandy went after she moved out of her boyfriend's apartment and her dormitory. Where could she have gone? She had no family to rely on. He used a yellow highlighter to mark the calls she'd made to the Pizza King delivery then dialed their number. The kid who answered the phone was clueless so he identified himself and asked for the manager. He waited a good ten minutes before the manager sifted through his records. It was worth the wait. The manager gave him an address on East 19th Street near the Memorial Stadium. His call to the Chinese restaurant revealed the same address.

He slipped his notepad back in his pocket, grabbed his jacket and left for his car. He turned onto East 19th Street and noticed a bus stop. Since Mandy didn't have a car, this must be the bus stop where she waited for the bus. He pulled up in front of a newer looking brick apartment building and noticed a woman with a pronounced baby bump pulling a shopping cart filled with packages into the building.

As he approached, he noticed the building was much larger than it initially appeared, housing at least ten or more apartments. Mandy Morris' apartment was listed as 3B so he headed up the staircase. A very pregnant, but tiny woman answered the door. She couldn't have been more than five feet tall. She moved back to let him in after he showed her his badge. She introduced herself as Connie and led him to a small living room where he sat on the sofa. She slowly lowered herself to a chair nearby and looked very uncomfortable.

"What do you want to know about Mandy?"

"Did Mandy live here?"

"Yes, Mandy was already living here when I moved in. She was farther along in her pregnancy than me. Why are you asking questions about her?"

Lane paused for a second, unsure whether to tell the woman bad news like her roommate's murder. He didn't want to shock some poor woman into giving birth on the spot. The last thing he needed was to be the one to deliver the baby.

"I'm afraid I have bad news. Mandy Morris was murdered and I need your help to find her killer."

"That's terrible." She paled a little but didn't overreact like he feared she would.

"I'd like to ask you some questions about Mandy."

"Sure, anything I can do to help."

"Did Mandy have any visitors?"

"No. It was so sad. I don't think she had any family or friends. She talked a lot about her boyfriend. She seemed to think he would show up any day and rescue her. Of course, the bastard never did."

"So he didn't visit her?" Dumb question. Of course, the little self-involved asshole never visited. He wanted Mandy out of his life.

"No."

"Did Mandy socialize with any of your other neighbors?"

"Sure. We had occasional pizza parties and she'd talk with the other girls who live in the building."

"When was the last time you saw Mandy?" He quirked his eyebrow questioningly.

"She stayed here after the baby was born. I didn't tell the agency."

"What agency?"

"The Forever Home Adoption Agency — F.H.A.A."

"Why would it be their business?"

"They pay our rent until the baby is born, and then we have to find another place to live. Mandy was so alone that I didn't have the heart to ask her to leave. I didn't think she had any place to go."

"Did she say anything about her plans?"

"It worried me when she decided she wanted her baby back." She paused for a second. "I told her I didn't think that was going to happen because she signed some papers. Besides, with all the money the agency spends on rent, food, and prenatal care. It's not likely they'd let her have the baby back."

"Do you know if she talked to anyone at the agency about it?"

"I don't know. I woke up one morning and she was gone. She left her clothes and everything. I've got them boxed in the other room if you want to see them. A new roommate from the agency is moving in soon and I have to get rid of them."

Lane sifted through the few things Mandy Morris owned but found nothing of interest. As he left the apartment, he almost bumped into a pregnant girl with long, blonde hair tied back with a ribbon and about the same age as Mandy Morris. She was carrying a box and looked like she was moving in.

Lane went from apartment to apartment trying to get information about Mandy from her former neighbors.

A brown-haired woman answered the door at the next apartment. She looked like she was eighteen years old if a day. She was tall with a baby bump that barely showed.

Lane pulled out his badge and introduced himself. "I'm Detective Lane Hansen and I'd like to ask you some questions about Mandy Morris."

"Why are you asking questions about Mandy?"

"I'm in charge of her homicide investigation."

"Homicide? Mandy's dead?"

Lane watched her carefully for her reaction. She reached out to grip the door knob as the shock of Mandy's murder hit her full force.

"When did this happen?"

"Six weeks after she gave birth."

"Oh my God. I am so sorry to hear this." She sounded sincere enough.

"Did you know Mandy confided in a nurse at the hospital that she wanted to keep her baby?"

"Oh, no. That wouldn't be permitted."

"Who wouldn't permit it?" Permit it? Since when does a woman need permission to keep her baby?

The girl, wide-eyed from fear, slammed the door in his face leaving him surprised and even more curious than he was before he talked to her.

He took a new tactic with the next girl. "I'd like to ask you some questions about the Forever Home Adoption Agency." She had the same reaction as the first.

Again and again, each girl went from calm and friendly to frightened in seconds. What is it about this adoption agency that is causing such fear? And why won't anyone talk to him about it?

He watched the apartment house from his car until around midnight. During all that time, there was only one person he noticed that wasn't pregnant and that was the guy mowing the lawn. Every single person who entered or left the apartment house was in some stage of pregnancy. It didn't take a rocket scientist to realize the adoption agency housed its pregnant girls here. It was almost like an incubator for adoptive babies. And if the girls got free rent, food, expenses and medical care, what did F.H.A.A. get? He wanted to know more about the adoption agency so he headed back to his hotel and his laptop.

The next day, Lane Hansen sat in his unmarked black SUV with tinted windows less than a block down the street from the adoption agency satellite office in Bloomington. He had a clear view and watched pregnant women go in and out for hours. He'd already checked out there was a clinic on the first floor and the agency offices were on the second.

A gleaming black Mercedes-Benz Roadster slipped into a parking spot near him and he watched a couple get out. The car probably cost more than his annual salary times three.

The couple, who were in their forties, held hands like teenagers on a date. The woman, a statuesque blonde, wore an expensive emerald green designer suit and matching pumps with four inch heels. She seemed happy and excited about something and didn't stop chattering to the man until they disappeared through the entrance of the building. Were they here to adopt a baby? Were they here to buy a baby? Those were the million dollar questions.

He input their license plate into his laptop and watched the loading icon until information danced across the screen. It appeared the happy couple was Mr. and Mrs. Robert Crowne whose home address was in Indianapolis. They'd come a long way to discuss an adoption, he thought. Why not deal with the dozens of agencies in their home town?

He wanted to follow them in, but realized how noticeable a lone, very large male would be in the sea of pregnant women and nurses dressed in scrubs. If his partner wasn't pregnant with triplets and on bed rest, he could wander in with her as part of a couple and snoop all he wanted.

For the remainder of the day, he noted well-heeled couples enter the adoption agency building and he ran the plates for each one. Most of them were from out of town which strengthened his theory that the agency may be involved in illegal adoptions for profit. If he was right and

Mandy Morris had kicked up a fuss about getting her baby back, there was a good motive for her murder.

At nightfall, his growling stomach led him to a nearby mom and pop restaurant. After he ordered dinner, he did some people-watching while he waited for his food. He noticed a couple at a table nearby. They were animatedly discussing their days at work. The woman had blonde hair and looked nothing like Frankie; but she reminded him how much he had screwed up and how determined he was to get Frankie back.

After dinner, he checked into his hotel room and answered emails and phone calls. He called his boss to give him an update. He also looked up the home address of Dr. Eric Caine, who owned the Forever Home Adoption Agency. He waited for nightfall then slipped into a black hooded sweatshirt and running pants along with his black Nikes.

Around ten o'clock, Lane sat in his SUV plugging in Dr. Caine's home address into his GPS. Soon he was on Headley Road going north leaving the city lights behind. He passed the 1200 acre Griffy Lake Nature Preserve with 1.2 miles to go. Soon he rolled to a stop in front of a huge red-brick home set off the road in the midst of a couple of acres of land thick with trees. It matched the photo he'd obtained from the Internet. It seems Dr. Caine bought the house two years ago for 2.5 million dollars. It had six bedrooms, a theatre room, two-story library, billiards room, three fireplaces, exercise room, and a finished basement with a wine cellar. This guy was making serious bucks. He knew some sports pros whose homes weren't this nice.

He did a quick check of the area from the car. A white security gate prevented him from getting closer. The lack of road lights and the dense woods surrounding the house made the area very dark. He drove down the road a bit, made a U-turn then found a dirt road leading into a pasture on the opposite side of the road from the house. He backed his SUV onto a corner of the pasture and turned off the ignition and rolled down a window. He waited until his eyes adjusted to the darkness then pulled out the night-vision goggles head gear he'd bought from a friend on the SWAT team and aimed toward the house.

Though there were lights on in various rooms in the house, but no cars in the driveway. He started to get out of the vehicle but heard the hum of a car motor approaching. He slipped back inside in time to see a red Ferrari Enzo turn into the drive and stop in front the white gate. The car window went down and someone punched in the security code, then the car sped through the open gate toward the house.

Damn. Talk about money. The Ferrari Enzo was one of Lane's dream cars and he knew it didn't sell for under $650,000. The expensive car and the 2.5 million dollar home pissed him off. Medical doctors make good money but not this much. Selling babies must be more profitable than he thought. And Lane wouldn't stop fighting for Mandy until the bastard went down.

Lane considered the thick woods on either side of the house for cover before he decided to get a closer look. He crouched along a line of trees less than a hundred yards from the house. A light flipped on in an upstairs window and he could see that the good doctor had a lady friend in the bedroom with him. Though she wore scrubs, he could tell she was shapely. She pulled the elastic from her ponytail and her golden hair flowed about her shoulders. In no time, the doctor had his arms around her waist and lifted her shirt over her head.

A black Lincoln Town Car pulled in the drive. A tall man with shaggy, blonde hair got out of the car then walked to the front door and slammed his hand on the door bell.

Upstairs, Lane could see the doctor left his lady friend on the bed and rushed out of the room.

The front door flew open and a very angry Dr. Eric Caine came outside. They began shouting.

"What the fuck do you think you're doing?"

"I figured you'd want to know about it as soon as possible."

"Don't you know how to use a cell phone?"

Caine closed the front door and joined the man on the front porch. They lit cigarettes and talked. He couldn't hear what they were saying, but it seemed as if the visitor was doing some back peddling. He kept wiping his brow with his hand and nervously raking his fingers through his hair. His body language indicated he was trying to calm the doctor down. His efforts didn't work because the doctor was still angry, yelling and waving his arms. They ended their conversation and blonde-haired man got back into the Lincoln Town Car and left.

Staying in the wooded areas of the property, Lane moved around the house until he'd covered all sides. He wanted to see if there was a separate entrance to the basement level. There wasn't. As he lowered himself to a more comfortable position, he heard a pop and bark burst from the tree he was beneath, possibly four to five inches from his head. What the hell! He dove and flattened himself to the ground. Someone had just shot at him. A shot that could have blown his head off had missed him by mere inches.

Lane looked carefully in all directions as he pulled out his Glock. Judging from the gouge in the tree, the shot came from an area directly across from him in a section of thick trees. He focused on the area and saw nothing until the moon emerged from a drifting cloud. A figure ran toward the road, crunching leaves and branches under his feet as he ran. Lane flew after him. He reached the road in time to see the dark Lincoln Town Car racing in the direction of town until it blended in with the inky-black of the night.

Two things were clear. Dr. Eric Caine had hired protection, but why? The second thing was Caine would soon know someone was watching him. Caine just didn't know who.

CHAPTER THREE

Lane Hansen headed for his supervisor's office for the tenth time in two weeks. He was on a mission. Lane had debriefed his boss about his interviews with Mandy Morris's friends, his suspicions about Dr. Eric Caine and his Forever Home Adoption Agency. But his boss was still pondering Lane's idea for an undercover op.

Lane had explained to him the case was a heavy hitter that involved a well-known physician who was suspected of running a shady adoption agency. He'd learned that Eric Caine had powerful political ties in the state so there was an element of risk for his boss, who had just been elected to the sheriff position. But it was a risk Lane wanted him to take to put this baby-selling and victimizing, murdering agency out of business and get justice for Mandy Morris.

Lane had suggested that he and a female partner go undercover posing as a couple interested in adopting a baby to get inside Frank's operation to solve Mandy's murder as well as expose a possible baby-trafficking ring.

"Lane, I know you think you're ready to do undercover work, but with this case I need two cops who can pose as a married couple. Unfortunately, we've got three women on the team. One is built like a linebacker and the other two *are* pregnant. So we have no one to play the wife role in your scenario."

"Sir, for this case, why don't we go outside the department? I know a private investigator who can handle herself on a job like this."

Sheriff Tim Brennan's brows drew together. "What's the P.I.'s name?"

"Frankie Douglas. I worked with her last year on the Charles Beatty serial killer case. She's a former sharpshooter for the Army."

"Is this the same Frankie Douglas you shot?"

Lane's face flushed with the guilt he still felt about the shooting. "Yes, sir. It was an accident. We were heading down the stairs of Beatty's cellar to apprehend him when one of the steps gave way. When I fell, my gun went off and the bullet hit Frankie."

"Has Frankie Douglas done police work before?"

"I heard she's a former detective so undoubtedly she's done undercover."

"I think I've heard about her. Isn't she a pretty, tall blonde woman?"

"Oh, she's more than pretty. Think Victoria Secret hot." Lust shot through him as a vision of Frankie appeared in his mind.

"Is that right? Do you have a personal thing going with Ms. Douglas?" The sheriff asked the questions with a raised brow and clenched jaw.

"No, sir. Strictly professional." Of course, if given a chance, he'd make it personal in 2.5 seconds. But did his boss need to know that? Nope.

Brennan glared at Lane then picked up his phone and pushed a number on his speed dial. "Hello, Frankie. This is *Uncle* Tim. I may have a job for you. Would you please drop by my office sometime this week?"

Lane slumped down in his chair and wished for a hole he could crawl in. Damn it. How was he to know his new boss was Frankie's uncle?

Brennan hung up the phone and glared at Lane for what seemed like an eternity. He pushed back in his chair, and said, "I'm Frankie's uncle and I'm also kind of a stand-in dad since her father died when she was fourteen."

"Sir, I meant no disrespect."

"That's good news, Lane. Because if you choose to mess with Frankie in any way, I will personally kick your ass and you can find another place to be detective. Do you understand?"

"I believe so."

"And when I talk to her about the undercover job, if she has any reservations whatsoever about doing this with you, it's off. And if she *does* agree to do it, you damn well better make sure your relationship with her on the job stays professional. Is that understood?"

"Yes, sir."

"There's this saying, 'You don't screw with your partner and your partner won't screw with you.' Understand?"

"I believe so." Lane nodded as he stood, then slowly walked back to his desk. Ideas were swirling in his mind like a mixer in cake batter. There was only one thing he could do. He'd have to convince Frankie that it was a good, if not a great idea, to go undercover with him. He could behave himself and keep things on a professional basis. Couldn't he?

Frankie tapped her long fingernails on the steering wheel. The Monday after a long weekend was never her favorite time for surveillance, but the money was good. Just last night she realized her private investigation company was in the black for the first time in two years. So she wasn't going to whine about being bored and tired.

Finally two hours later, after tracking her for three long weeks, she had "Church Lady" in her sights. The woman approached the Marriott at noon with a tall, dark and handsome man who was definitely *not* her husband, whose photo lay on her dashboard. Church Lady was the nickname her partner, Ted, had given their newest client's wife, Beverly, because her excuses to her husband for being out at all hours of the night and unavailable many times during the day was that she was preparing Sunday school lessons.

Frankie took five photos of the happy, clinging couple entering the hotel. That was an hour ago and Frankie couldn't wait a second more. She flew out of her car and ran into the hotel lobby to use their ladies' room.

Lane Hansen found Frankie's car after threatening her partner, Ted, with a speeding ticket if he didn't give him her location. Unfortunately, Frankie was not in the car. Since it was unlocked with the windows down, he made himself at home in the passenger seat. He had waited ten minutes and had gotten bored, so he snagged her backpack from the back and pulled it into the front seat to have a look. He rummaged inside, pulling out a makeup kit, a stun gun, pepper spray, tape recorder, binoculars, her Glock 21, a plastic bag filled with homemade chocolate chip cookies, and a thermos. He knew Frankie was a huge Starbucks fan and was obviously on a stakeout for a client so he opened the thermos to discover the fragrant, delicious aroma of hot Espresso with a double shot — his favorite. He was in the midst of pouring himself a cup, when in the distance Frankie came out of the Marriott Hotel.

He watched her as she strode toward him. Their gazes locked, causing her face to twist into a distrustful expression. Long flowing hair, whiskey brown eyes, peaches and cream skin, she was gorgeous as ever. He got turned on just looking at her.

"Lane Hansen, what are you doing in my car?" She eyed the thermos in his hand and then shifted her glare to his wide grin. "Besides drinking my Espresso and snagging a chocolate chip cookie from my backpack?" She snatched the backpack out of his lap and tossed it in the back seat.

"Is that any kind of a welcome?" He sipped the Espresso then bit a chunk out of the cookie. "Did you make these cookies? They're pretty good."

"Those were left on my car during the night by a psychotic stalker I've been trying ditch. Last time the fool left food, he left brownies with chunks of laxative baked in." She grinned as she watched his expression as the lie sunk in and he shoved the cookie back in the bag.

"There's something we need to discuss."

"And I'm interested, why?"

"I'm serious, Frankie. Did you hear about that young woman that was murdered and dumped in the woods near Kramer?"

"Actually, I did. I think that's an odd place to dump a body unless you're from the area."

"Yeah, I thought so too. Her murder is my case. Her name was Mandy Morris and she was a nineteen year old student at I.U. When I saw you in Bloomington that day, I was there interviewing her friends. Turns out she gave birth about six weeks before she was killed. I think the adoption agency she was associated with may be trafficking babies and someone at the agency murdered her."

"You're kidding."

"I wish I were."

"So I went to the sheriff and proposed an undercover operation." Okay, here comes the hard part. Talking her into joining the op.

"Good for you. Hope you catch the bastards."

Apparently, she hadn't spoken with her Uncle Tim yet. Lane cleared his throat and chose his words carefully. "Well, you see, the plan includes a couple posing as a husband and wife who are trying to adopt a baby."

"God bless the female deputy or detective who has to set up house with you. May she have nerves of steel and the patience of a saint."

"Actually, that's where I've run into a little problem. Unfortunately, we've got three women on the team. None of them fit the part. So we have no one to play the wife role in our scenario."

"You can't be suggesting…"

Lane noted her icy glare and felt a gut punch to his stomach. Okay, he knew this wasn't going to be easy, and he surged ahead.

"I know how capable, intelligent, and professional you are and that you'd be the first in line to want to catch these perps. I suggested to the Sheriff that you join the operation."

"You did what?! You volunteered me when you hadn't even discussed it with me? Seriously?"

"Frankie, someone has to stop this bastard. I think he's selling babies to the highest bidder whether they are fit parents or not. I also think either he killed Mandy Morris or he had someone else do it. Mandy lost her parents in a car accident. The only family she had left was an aunt who's a fucking nightmare. She thought her boyfriend loved her, but he was just using her and wanted nothing to do with her when he found out she was pregnant.

She had no one and that's why she hooked up with this adoption agency. They paid for everything associated with her pregnancy so she'd hand over her baby. Then when she realized she couldn't give her baby up, I think they killed her. Help me get justice for Mandy. Please, Frankie."

"Lane, I have a company to run." He sounded so sincere he was starting to get to her. She couldn't tolerate any criminal activity that had to do with victimizing or harming women and children.

"Can't your partner handle things until you return?"

"I don't know. Give me some time to think about it." Did she just say she needed time to think about it? Was she completely out of her mind?

Frankie sat in the center of a circle of women on a room-sized mat. Her students joined her every Tuesday for her self-defense class at the Sheriff's Workout Gym.

"Understand that a stranger will attack a woman who appears vulnerable by the way she walks, jogs, socializes, drinks, and shops. Most attackers make a snap judgment by the way you're carrying yourself as to whether or not you will fight back. In short, he'll attack you if he thinks he'll be successful. One of the things we'll practice in today's class is the 'leave-me-the-hell-alone' body language." She stood up and demonstrated the body language. "Everyone pick a partner to practice with. Practice the stance while your partner coaches."

Ted, her partner, entered the room and she walked over to greet him. He was holding his gorilla suit which was full-body protective gear complete with a groin guard. "Are you ready for some punches and kicks?"

"As ready as I'll ever be." Ted turned to the group of women staring at him and looked back at Frankie with

63

uncertainty. "Why do they look like they're going to enjoy this so much?"

Frankie smiled, patted him on the shoulder, and then headed back to her group. "Come back together in our circle. Let's have some Q&A time while Ted gets suited up. What are some of your questions?"

A thin, brunette woman asked, "Is it true that most attacks on women happen outside bars, rock concerts, or parties?"

"It's true that a lot of attacks happen at these places, but in my experiences as a deputy, I found that just as many happen in remote areas such as hiking or jogging paths, parking lots or garages, and empty streets. That is why I advise you to avoid putting yourselves in remote areas where there is no one around to come to your aid if you need it."

Another woman asked, "What if the worst happens and you are the victim of a carjacker?"

"For one thing, you don't consider yourself a victim — *ever*. Right? My best girlfriend was abducted last year and she did what I'd do if it happened to me. She was scared, but she kept her wits about her. She was driving and knew she was protected by a seat belt as well as an airbag. Her attacker was in the backseat pressing a knife against her throat and wasn't protected by either. She rammed her SUV into a large tree. The impact sent her attacker flying over the seat into the dash and knocking him unconscious long enough for her to escape."

Ted stepped over to the group dressed in the gorilla suit ready for the group's next exercise. "Okay, group, last week you learned how to make a fist. Let's see your fists, thumb out." She glanced at the outstretched fists. "Looks good. This week, with Ted's help, you're going to get some practice punching and kicking. Ted is wearing a protective body suit complete with a groin guard so don't be afraid to punch or kick him. There is nothing more valuable than practice."

"What about head butts? Can we practice them too?"

"Since we haven't covered how to do the head butt safely, please don't try to do it in this session." Good Lord. Some of these women were out of control. "Please form a line. I'll time you as each of you practices punching and kicking."

Sixty minutes was over in no time and Frankie dismissed her class. She then cleaned up the room while Ted removed the protective suit.

"Ted, are you up for sparring a bit?"

"Sure."

They circled each other on the mat until Frankie twirled a 360, kicking Ted and knocking him flat on his back.

"Shit, Frankie, where'd you get that move?"

"It's new." Frankie offered her hand to pull him to his feet. She and Ted circled again, each trying to predict the other's move.

Using the same move that Frankie had used on Jerry Richards, Ted grabbed Frankie's thumb bending back her wrist just enough to cause pain but not enough to break it. He then jerked her arm behind her back and dropped her to the ground. Still gripping her arm, he pushed his knee into her back to hold her in place.

Lane was stressed and needed to punch something or someone so he headed for the Sheriff's Workout Gym to lift weights and use the punching bag. He pulled into the parking lot outside and noticed Frankie's car. He trained here at least twice a week and had never seen her around here so he was a little curious. He peered into a couple of rooms but didn't see her.

He got to the next room just in time to see a man straddling Frankie on the mat. He dropped his gym bag and flew into the room, slamming into Ted and throwing him several feet away. He pinned Ted to the mat so fast it knocked the wind out of him and made speaking impossible. Lane was about to give Ted a black eye he'd never forget when he heard Frankie scream.

"Damn it, Lane. What in the hell are you doing to Ted? Are you completely crazy?"

He looked back at the man beneath him and recognized Frankie's partner, Ted. "I don't give a shit who he is. No one's going to hurt you."

"Don't hit him. He wasn't hurting me. We were sparring. We do it all the time. Let him get up!" shouted Frankie. "I'll give you two seconds to get off Ted before you get a demonstration of my martial arts skills up close and personal."

Lane slowly got up and offered a hand to Ted, who jumped to his feet and got in position to take him on.

Frankie placed herself between them. "Ted, please let it go. Take off. I'll see you tomorrow."

Ted turned back as he walked away. "See you tomorrow, Frankie. Fuck you, Hansen."

"Lane, what gave you the idea I needed you or anyone else to protect me? For Christ's sake, I'm a former deputy. I got the same training you did. What the hell were you thinking?"

Shit. This was a hell of a time to tick Frankie off. Not when he wanted her to go undercover with him. It was just when he got to the door and saw Frankie with a man on top of her, he went crazy.

"I'm sorry, Frankie," he said as she grabbed her gym bag and rushed out of the room. Okay, so he was only sorry he'd made her angry again. If he ever witnessed anyone messing with her in the future, he'd do the same thing.

Friday had been a crap day and it wasn't getting any better. Lane thought a beer or two would relax him before he headed home. He had a case that held more questions than answers and was proving to be the hardest jigsaw puzzle ever.

Stopping at the new Club Hoosier bar outside of town had been a mistake. What was he thinking? He sat at the bar straining to hear the rerun of a Pacers game on ESPN playing on the large flat screen TV. In the other room, a deejay was playing loud — make that deafening — dance music that echoed through the bar and made hearing the details of the game impossible. He swore the bass grew louder with each song, matching beat for beat with the pounding in his head. Combine that with the rowdiness of customers and the result was a headache the size of Indianapolis. He checked the other guys at the bar to see if they were annoyed about the volume of the music, but one glance told him they were focused more on hot women in the bar than the game.

He slipped a twenty out of his wallet and was about to hail a bartender when someone tapped him on the back. He turned just as Michael Brandt took the barstool next to him.

"Watching the game?" he asked as he looked for the bartender.

"I gave up. What brings you here?" It was unusual to see Michael out and about by himself. Whenever he saw Michael, Anne was not far away or vice versa. He envied the closeness they had, the way they enjoyed being with each other. He wanted that someday. He wanted that with Frankie — if he could ever win her back.

"Anne's a huge Lady Gaga fan. She and Frankie went to her concert tonight."

"No kidding. Lady Gaga?"

"Oh, yeah. In fact, one of the first times I saw Anne was in a convenience store. She was wearing this glittering Lady Gaga tank top with shorts and we literally bumped into each other, sending her groceries all over the floor."

The bartender appeared and Michael ordered a Coors. Lane decided to stay awhile and nurse his beer.

"Your boss told me about the undercover operation. Are you sure you want to do it with Frankie?"

"Yes, I'm sure. I want to bust the sick freak I think murdered Mandy Morris. In addition, there's a good chance he's selling babies. Who knows what else he's doing. He's going down."

"But are you sure you want to go undercover with *Frankie*?"

"Why not? She's excellent at what she does and she has done undercover before." A better question was why wouldn't he want to go undercover with Frankie?

"I didn't think you and Frankie were on the best of terms."

"Why do you say that?"

"I heard you dumped her after a one-night stand when she was recovering from the bullet wound you gave her."

"Shit. I was so fucking stupid." This was an understatement. It was the worst mistake he'd ever made.

"I'd say. I'd think you'd be afraid to do that to a former Army sharpshooter. I mean you'd already shot her. Wasn't that enough?"

Lane grunted and took a gulp of his beer and seriously thought of ordering another one.

"You're damned lucky she didn't kick your ass or shoot you. She's got a wicked temper."

"I think I'd feel better about it if she did. I made a mistake. A big mistake. And I want her back."

"Good luck with that." Michael chuckled until he glanced at Lane and saw the miserable expression on his face.

"How did you know about it?" Lane asked.

"Frankie is at the house a lot and I overheard her tell Anne. If I were you, I'd steer clear. I know it happened months ago, but she is still pissed about what happened between you two."

"Yeah, I know she is."

"Are you sure you want to do this undercover thing with her? Isn't there anyone else who could do it?"

"No. She hasn't agreed to do it yet. She told Tim she wants to think about it. If she does it, we'll both have to commit to put our past behind us and act like professionals."

"And you think that's possible. Do you believe in the tooth fairy, too?"

Frankie parked the car in the only space available outside the popular bar and joined Anne on the sidewalk, handing her a bag of Lady Gaga concert t-shirts she'd purchased. She glanced at Anne's sequined pink four-inch heels that matched her equally sequined flared pink tank and sighed. Why a pregnant woman would wear those shoes was beyond her and she had hovered over Anne every time she moved an inch all night for fear that she'd fall. When they entered the bar, she was relieved to see Michael. She was passing the baton. He could play helicopter and hover over Anne for the rest of the night.

They'd had an amazing time at the concert and were sorry when it ended. Frankie had played the latest Lady Gaga CD all the way back and was looking forward to relaxing with Anne and Michael before she headed home. Besides, she and Anne had a major craving for non-alcoholic strawberry daiquiris, hot artichoke dip with chips, and then maybe a scrumptious slice of Godiva chocolate cheesecake.

They spotted Michael at the bar talking to someone so they waded through the crowd to get to him. As they approached him, Frankie noticed the "someone" was Lane Hansen and her heart slammed against her chest so hard she nearly stumbled. Her gaze locked with Lane's and a spark of heat flashed between them.

Being within a city block of Lane Hansen was an extremely bad idea. She should turn around and walk right out of this bar and go straight home. But she didn't.

Michael pulled Anne into his arms and kissed her as she gushed about the concert. He then hailed a waitress who found them a booth. Michael took one look at Frankie who was pretending not to gaze at Lane; and one look at Lane who was trying not to stare at Frankie and made a decision. It was a decision that would probably earn him a kick under the table later from his wife, but he ran with it.

"Lane, we've got a booth. Come join us for some junk food and a couple of beers."

As they headed to the booth, Frankie walked in front of Lane so he gave her a once-over. She wore a snug white knit cami under a short black leather jacket, along with black jeggings tucked into black boots with four-inch heels. At five feet ten inches, with big, brown eyes and full sensuous lips, she looked sizzling hot, and every man in the place was fixated on her. A blast of lust hit him so hard it was a wonder he could even walk.

As the evening progressed, Lane watched Frankie drink strawberry daiquiris and shared her hot artichoke dip and chips. When it came time to share the Godiva chocolate cheesecake, he and Michael passed while Frankie and Anne devoured the dessert. They talked non-stop about the concert and Lane began to relax and actually enjoy himself because Frankie was. She animatedly told stories and she laughed. And when she did, it was one of the most delightful things he'd ever heard or seen. Her entire face lit up when she laughed and the sound of it was so contagious, you had to laugh, too. Anne sent Michael to the deejay with requests for Lady Gaga songs a couple of times. When they played, she and Frankie sang along and danced — more like wiggled — in their seats as he and Michael watched with enjoyment. In their line of work finding justice for victims, day in and day out; it felt good to be around happy people for a change.

It was amazing to be sitting this close to Frankie period. The booth was small so she was pressed up against him and he could feel her heat through his jeans. Her scent of fresh flowers and woman was making him a little crazy.

It seemed Michael had a song request of his own. As the deejay played "Lady in Red", he helped Anne slide out of the booth and led her to the dance floor.

Lane immediately saw the opportunity he'd been waiting for, but there was just one thing wrong with the plan. It was the dancing part. It wasn't that he was a bad at dancing, he sucked at it. He was six feet five inches and 230 pounds of solid muscle and putting himself on the dance floor with others was as dangerous as having a rhino in a china shop. Accidentally crushing the delicate bones in his partner's feet was not his idea of a good time.

But he glanced at Frankie and realized he wanted to hold her close to him, more than he'd wanted anything in a long, long time. This slow dance was not an opportunity he was going to pass up — two left feet or not.

He didn't have to be psychic to know that Frankie would refuse to dance with him and that underneath all that laughter; she was still pissed at him. So he slid out of the booth and pulled her with him.

"What are you doing?" He'd yanked her so hard out of the booth that she gasped as she slammed against him.

"It's not what *I'm* doing. It's what *we're* doing."

"What?!"

He led her onto the dance floor and wrapped his arms around her waist. He thought about the toes of her boots and prayed he wouldn't step on them.

74

"This is my favorite song and I really want to dance to it."

"'Lady in Red' is your favorite song? Why don't I believe that?"

He couldn't think of a good response so he tucked her head against his chest and tightened his grip on her waist. He liked the way her four inch heels brought her to his chin and he didn't have to bend much to hold her. Her soft curves molded to the contours of his lean body as he slowly and carefully moved her around the dance floor.

Frankie was feeling the buzz from the second strawberry daiquiri that she shouldn't have drunk, because she didn't drink alcohol. She also shouldn't be dancing with Lane even though she loved the way his hard, muscled arms wrapped perfectly around her body had her pulse racing. He held her hand gently against his chest and she could feel the hard, rapid beating of his heart. Dancing with him shouldn't feel this good. Her internal alarm went off. She remembered how hurt she had been when she'd awakened that morning and found he was gone without a word. He'd hurt her once; he'd hurt her again. She pushed at his chest to put some distance between them and looked up into his eyes.

"Frankie, please don't push me away. I've wanted to hold you all night."

His eyes held a sensuous flame, but they also held a tender plea that made her heart squeeze. Maybe it was the second strawberry daiquiri. Maybe it was his hard body pressing against her that was making her so hot she thought she'd faint. Whatever it was, she went with it. She went onto her toes, entangled her fingers in his short hair, and pulled him down into a kiss. She tenderly explored his lips slowly and thoughtfully as a flame ignited inside her that made her heated and dizzy. She ended the kiss, looked up into his surprised expression, and then pressed her head back against his chest. She felt light-headed and when the music ended, she was grateful she could lean against his hard body for support as he led her back to the booth.

Once they were back in the booth, Lane stared at Frankie, his left eyebrow lifting a fraction. He didn't know where that kiss had come from, but he was up for an instant replay.

Frankie lifted her glass and finished off her drink then started fanning herself with her hand. "Why was it so damn hot in here?"

"Oh, my God. Frankie, is there alcohol in your daiquiri?" Anne's eyes were wide as she asked the question.

"Good possibility," she replied.

Lane heard her giggling just before she laid her head on his shoulder. She tried hard to focus on Anne's face, but the darn room was swirling again.

Michael leaned in close and whispered in Anne's ear. "What's wrong?"

"She can't drink alcohol. One drink and she's drunk. She's had *two* drinks. I was sure I told the waitress to make the drinks without alcohol."

Lane heard this and secured Frankie's glass. One sniff and he was sure the drink had alcohol. He nodded to the other two.

He slid out of the booth and pulled her into his arms steadying her until he was sure she'd stay upright. "Sugar, it's time we get you home." He braced her with his arm around her waist and half-walked, half-carried her out of the bar to his SUV.

Lane pulled his SUV up to Frankie's house and turned off the ignition. She was slumped in the passenger seat like her bones were made of jello. She was giggly, and kept mumbling something about feeling dizzy. He sighed, shook his head, and got out of the vehicle.

When he opened the passenger door, she almost tumbled out. He caught her before she slammed to the ground and held her upright. She kept swaying so he gripped her waist to stabilize her.

She snaked her arms around his neck and whispered, "Lane, you make me so hot."

He held her away and silently wished she was sober and that she meant that last statement. He led her to her house, again half-walking and half-carrying her as she giggled.

They were almost to the porch when she stopped and mumbled something.

"Frankie, what did you say?"

"I feel sick." At that, she projectile vomited looking a little like the possessed girl in *The Exorcist,* only this wasn't pea soup. He stared in shock as it shot down the front of his jeans. He quickly turned her around and held her as she bent down to throw up some more in the bushes.

"I'm so sick." She moaned.

Lane backed her to the SUV so he could open the back to get a towel. There was no way he was going to track in Frankie's house what covered his jeans. He braced her against the vehicle with one hand and wiped his jeans with the other. Deciding he'd done all he could do as far as far as the pants were concerned, he swept her into his arms and ran toward the house before she could get sick again.

He propped her up against the house while he rummaged through her purse for her house keys. Finding them, Lane unlocked the house, carried her in, and slammed the door shut with his foot. He flipped the switch for the lights, then rushed her into the bathroom and placed her sitting in front of the toilet. Watching her to make sure she was going to stay upright, Lane pulled off his boots, his gun and holster, and then stripped off his jeans down to his boxer shorts. Lane placed his gun along with the holster in her bedroom on a dresser. His tie and shirt ended up in a pile atop his jeans in the hallway. He searched through the bathroom drawers looking for a washcloth. Finding a fluffy blue one, he held it in the sink and soaked it with cold water.

Lowering himself so he was sitting behind Frankie, he pulled her gently against him and removed the black leather jacket she was wearing. He tossed it behind him then placed the cold cloth on her forehead.

"Why won't the room stop spinning?" Frankie asked as she leaned against him.

"It'll stop soon. I promise. Do you want a glass of water or anything?" He kissed the top of her head and felt her move her hands to his thighs to steady herself.

"Yes."

He got up, grabbed his clothes from the hallway floor, and made his way to the kitchen. Finding a washer and dryer in an alcove off the kitchen, he popped his clothes in a warm wash and walked back into the kitchen. He washed his hands in the sink, then found a glass, filled it with ice cubes, and cold water from the refrigerator. He trekked back to the bathroom. She wasn't there. He went to her bedroom. Hugging the left side of the bed lay Frankie sound asleep. He tiptoed around the bed and placed the glass of water on her nightstand.

He got as far as the living room when he stopped himself. There was no way he could get his large frame in a comfortable position on her small sofa. The floor wasn't appealing for sleeping either.

What if she got sick again? What if he was in the living room and didn't hear her? He went back to her bedroom and stood at the door. He'd sleep in Frankie's bed tonight but as far away from her on the bed as possible. As much as he wanted to be there, he didn't want to bear the brunt of her temper if she discovered he was in her bed uninvited.

He crept to the right side of her queen-sized bed, grabbed a pillow, and pressed it against the headboard. He sat perfectly still watching her and listening to her soft breathing for the longest time.

The seduction of sleep overcame him and he slipped down under the comforter, careful to hug the right side of the bed. He hadn't been asleep long when movement woke him up. He opened his eyes in time to see Frankie roll over, flinging her arm across his chest, and her leg across his thighs. He froze as she settled her head on his chest. She made a sound like a cat's purr and cuddled closer. Soon he heard her soft, even breathing.

He remembered what Michael had said about Frankie's wicked temper. He thought briefly about her possible reaction in the morning when she realized they'd slept together. Not that they'd done any of the things he'd like to do with her in her bed. He'd just have to risk it.

Streams of morning light slipped through the window blinds and streamed across the bed. Frankie's head throbbed with pain and she shielded her eyes from the light with her arm. Her head hurt, her body ached, and her stomach was doing somersaults. The only thing that felt good was the heat she was near so she inched closer to the source.

Frankie needed an Advil badly. She had to do something about the pain. Pulling herself up in a sitting position, Frankie covered her eyes with her right hand and reached back with her left hand to brace herself. What her left hand touched was not the bed. She gasped and jerked her hand away from her eyes. Oh my God. Lane Hansen slept half-naked in her bed.

"Please tell me this is a dream. I couldn't have been stupid a second time," she said out loud.

"That statement does wonders for a guy's ego."

"What the hell are you doing in my bed? What happened last night?"

"Unfortunately, not what you're thinking. Look down at your clothes, Frankie. Weren't you wearing those last night?"

Frankie looked down, her mind spinning. Lady Gaga. Loud music. Strawberry daiquiris. Being sick. Oh, shit.

"You brought me home last night. I remember. But why are you still here?"

"I couldn't leave you alone when you were that sick."

"Oh, and you couldn't have slept somewhere else?" She eyed him suspiciously.

"I was going to sleep in the living room but was afraid I wouldn't hear you if you got sick again."

Frankie blinked and her heart squeezed. She believed him, damn it. Suddenly, she realized her mouth tasted terrible and her breath undoubtedly smelled as bad. She climbed out of the bed and walked across the room, realizing Lane was watching her. She rushed to the bathroom and turned on the shower then reached for her toothbrush and toothpaste. Peering into the mirror, she noticed she was pale and her makeup was smeared. Her hair looked post-sex messy.

The news had finally arrived. Anne Mason-Brandt was on a mission. She and Frankie had been waiting to hear this news for a couple of months. Harley's girlfriend, Millie, had given birth to four perfect Giant Schnauzer puppies — one of which was earmarked for Frankie. Excited to tell Frankie, she'd jumped in her SUV and rushed to Frankie's house.

Frankie emerged from the shower feeling human again. She smoothed baby oil onto her skin. She then pulled out her hair dryer. The noise of the dryer combined with her still throbbing head was a bad combo and she decided to let her hair air dry. She reached for her robe, but it wasn't hanging on the hook on the back side of the door so she wrapped a fluffy blue towel around herself. Right. Her robe was in her room. She slipped out of the bathroom and peeked into her bedroom. Her bed was empty. Another one of Lane's infamous disappearing acts? She was almost to her closet when she heard the knob turn in her front door. Lane was definitely ghosting again.

Still wrapped in a towel, she walked into her living room at the same time that Anne burst into the room and Lane, in boxer shorts, arrived from the kitchen holding out a steamy cup of coffee.

Anne looked at Frankie in the towel then Lane in boxers and gasped. "Oh, my God! This is so not a good time. I'll come back later. I'll call first." Her face crimson, Anne backed up until she reached the open front door to escape to her car.

Frankie turned to look at Lane who by now had bolted to the kitchen. She rushed to her bedroom, threw on her blue terrycloth bathrobe, and went to the kitchen.

"I thought you'd left."

"Why would you think that?"

"You had no problem shooting out of here like a rocket the last time you stayed over."

"I'm sorry about that, Frankie. I hope someday you'll forgive me."

"Why are you walking around my house half-naked?" Her eyes scanned his body and her temperature shot up. Christ, he was ripped and undoubtedly the most beautiful man she'd ever seen. Her insanely stupid heart was beating out of control.

Lane pointed his thumb to the clothes dryer. "My clothes aren't dry."

She closed her eyes and grimaced as she remembered soaking him the night before with her vomit. Could this get any more embarrassing?

She sat at her breakfast table and he brought her the cup of coffee he'd had in his hand when Anne burst into her living room. He poured a cup for himself then sat across from her.

"I'm not going to be one of those women who drink too much and pretend the next day not to remember anything. I remember it all, including the getting sick part and you taking care of me."

"You remember everything?"

84

"Yes." She eyed him suspiciously.

"So you remember when you told me that I made you hot."

"Okay, that part I don't remember. Are you making that up?" Amusement flickered in the eyes that met hers.

"Nope. Do you want me to turn on some slow music so we can re-enact the moment it happened?"

Visualizing the two of them slow dancing dressed as they were with him in boxer shorts and she in her robe ignited a need deep in her that she fought to douse. Luckily, she was saved her dryer bell announcing the completion of Lane's clothes.

Apparently modesty was not in Lane's skill set because he started pulling pieces from the dryer and dressing right in front of her in her kitchen. Their gazes met and a spark of heat passed between them. She decided she needed to get this man out of her house before she made the monumental mistake of dragging him to her bed. Again.

"Let's talk about your undercover op."

Instantly she had his attention. He stopped buttoning his shirt and moved to the table to sit down again.

"When I talked to Uncle Tim yesterday, he said you promised him you'd treat me as you would any other law enforcement professional. He said you knew better to let things get personal in an undercover operation with a female partner. Is that true?"

"Yes. By the way, it would've been nice to know that my boss, the sheriff, was your uncle."

"I haven't seen you much the past six months." She shot him an icy glare.

Okay, he was moving her away from that discussion. "So have you decided to do the undercover operation?"

"Maybe, as long as we work together to create some rules."

"What kind of rules?"

"We need to have a clear understanding before I agree to do this."

"Okay, I'm open to that. What do you have in mind?"

"Rule number one, things between us are professional *not* personal."

"I agree."

"Rule number two, you stay out of my backpack." She waited for his response, challenging him to disagree.

"Okay, that's a tough one because I know you hide my favorite coffee in there."

"Are you saying you won't agree to number two?" She asked with hands on her hips.

"I didn't say that. I agree, damn it. Are there any more rules?"

"No."

"So you'll agree to go undercover with me?"

She accepted Lane's hand extended to her and shook it. "Yes. I'll tell Uncle Tim tomorrow after I talk to Ted about taking over my self-defense classes while I'm gone. I also need to talk to Anne."

"Why Anne?"

"Ted isn't as computer savvy as Anne. I'm hoping she'll take over that part of the business until I return."

"So why did you decide to help me?"

"You didn't have to help me last night but you did. I'm returning the favor."

CHAPTER FOUR

Sheriff Tim Brennan expected to see Frankie sitting across the desk from him at their 10:00 a.m. meeting. What he didn't expect was to hear the words, "I'll do the undercover op."

"Now you understand the undercover operation is with Lane Hansen?" Tim tilted his brow, looking at her uncertainly.

"I do."

"This is the same Lane Hansen who shot you last year." Tim was having a little difficulty Frankie wanted to participate in an operation with the man that shot her.

"That was an accident."

"And you're sure you want to go undercover with Hansen?"

"Yes, I'm sure."

"If you're sure, so am I." His smile spread ear to ear as he looked at the niece he adored. She had the strong will and determination of his sister, her mother, and conviction of her late father along with his whiskey brown eyes. He felt as protective of Frankie as he did of his only child, Jennifer, who was a student at Indiana University. He didn't know what he would do if anything happened to either of them.

Frankie picked up one of the many framed photos of Jennifer on his credenza. "I miss her. I should have stopped in to see her when I was in Bloomington a couple of weeks ago. Is she coming home for the weekend soon?"

"Not likely. She says she has a lot of tough classes this term and spends all her time in the library, weekends included. Her mom and I haven't seen her in a couple of months."

"Sounds like she's really busy," said Frankie. "So what's the next step for the undercover thing?"

Tim picked up the receiver to his phone. "Let's see if Hansen is in." He touched a button on speed dial. "Hansen, can you meet with us?" He hung up and moved over to a small round conference table near a window and motioned for Frankie to join him. Within seconds, Lane sat across from her.

"Hansen, Frankie has agreed to join you undercover." His tone was even and he made an effort not to frown at Lane. Just because Frankie agreed to do it didn't mean he had to be overjoyed about it.

Lane reached across the table to shake Frankie's hand. "Thank you."

"I have a little lecture that I want you two to take seriously. Keep things between you professional *not* personal. I've seen too many operations go to hell in a hand basket because a cop got emotional. Because he let things become personal. Keep emotions out of it. Do you understand?"

Both Lane and Frankie nodded solemnly.

"For the next seven days, you're in training — starting now. Your first assignment is to be done as a couple. In fact, moving in together immediately is not a bad idea. Adjust to doing things together. Get to know each other better so you can identify each other's strengths and weakness. Learn to balance each other out. Your first assignment is to find out everything you can using all of your resources about Dr. Eric Caine and his adoption agency. You've got until tomorrow at 10:00 a.m. when we will meet in my office. When I see you again, I will have your new identities and the house where you will stay in Bloomington. Now get out of here. You have a lot to do."

Frankie walked with Lane to her car suddenly feeling a little awkward. She hadn't expected to be ordered to move in together so soon.

She tossed her briefcase into the backseat of her car and turned to face Lane, who stood with his hands in his pockets, exposing the very mean- looking gun plastered to his hip. She decided to dive right in. "Let's use my house as base for now. When do you want to move in?"

"I have a couple of things to wrap up in the office then pack at home. I can be there by 8:00 tonight if that's okay."

She nodded and got into her car, her idiot heart flipping over. As she drove away, she thought that moving him into her house was possibly the worst freaking idea she'd ever had.

Jennifer Brennan walked across the I.U. campus preparing mentally for the most important conversation she'd had with anyone in her twenty years of life. For someone who consistently made the Dean's List every term, she felt incredibly stupid. This happened to other women, not to her.

She was early and sat on a bench in front of Paul's dormitory, grateful for the extra time to think of what she had to tell him. Jennifer was convinced that Paul Vance, star football player here on a generous scholarship, was her soul mate. They'd spent every available second with each other since they'd met. She'd noticed him come out of the dorm's front door and her pulse leapt as it did every time she saw him. She loved everything about him from his lean, wide-shouldered build to his unruly, dark hair.

As soon as Paul reached the bench, he pulled her into a kiss sending a warm shiver through her body. "I don't have much time, babe. I've got a psych test tomorrow and an early practice."

"Can we at least go someplace that's more private?"

"Sure. Let's walk."

The campus was beautiful in the spring. At night, it appeared magical. The stars glittered through the tall tree they sat beneath. The cool air swished through her hair and slightly chilled her so she scooted closer to his warmth.

"Do you love me, Paul?"

"Of course I do."

"How much?"

"More than the sun, stars, and the moon." He kissed her on the cheek and thought of the many times he'd said that to her. "So what's going on?"

"I'm pregnant." The words were out and she could feel his body stiffen against her.

He gave her a sidelong glance of utter disbelief. "You can't be. We used protection."

"We did. Except for that time you forgot your jacket with your condoms inside the pocket in the dorm. We couldn't wait."

"Oh, shit." He scrubbed his hands over his face and shook his head. Why in the hell did this have to happen? Shit. Shit. "This can't be happening, Jenny. It just can't. I'll lose everything. I'll lose my scholarship and we both know my folks don't have the money to send me to school. I'm a year away from a degree. Besides that, I'll get kicked off the football team. You know the coach said I have a chance at going pro someday."

"I'm sorry, Paul. It's not like I planned this."

"Are you sure you didn't?"

"What are you talking about?"

"You've been hinting about us getting engaged for six months."

"I didn't get pregnant on purpose. How could you say that? Do you think you're the only one who has something to lose? I'm only a year away from a degree too. Don't you think that means something to me?"

"Maybe we should think about the alternative."

She was stunned by his cool tone. "What are you talking about?"

"Abortion. I could scrape up the money for it."

She halted, shocked. "No. Not an option. I cannot and will not kill my baby."

"Jenny, I don't want a baby now. Not now."

"You've made that pretty clear. Don't worry about it." She got to her feet and walked away forcing him to run to catch up with her.

"What's that mean?" He pulled at her arm and she jerked it out of his hand.

"Fuck you, Paul. Oh, I forgot, I already did. And what a monumental mistake that was."

"Jennifer, stop."

"Stop what? Breaking up with your sorry ass?"

"You're breaking up with me?"

"Absolutely. Stay completely away from me. You are such a disappointment. You actually just asked me to kill your baby. You are not even close to the man I thought you were."

Lane arrived at Frankie's house promptly at eight o'clock, dragging in two large suitcases. Trying to appear perfectly calm, even though she was shaking inside, she directed him to the guest room that was located right next to her bedroom. She left him to unpack and went into the kitchen to finish loading her dishwasher. After about ten minutes, the front door opened and closed. Then it opened again and Lane popped into the kitchen holding a big white wrapped box with an equally big red bow on top.

"It's for you." He unloaded the box on the breakfast table. "Come here and open it."

"Lane, why would you get me a gift?" She felt a little uncomfortable. This kind of behavior from Lane was so unexpected she didn't know how to react.

"Actually, it's for both of us."

Now she was curious. What in the world was he up to? Joining him at the table, she pulled off the red bow then dug her long nails into the white wrapping paper until she could read the black lettering on the box that read Cappuccino and Espresso Machine. She didn't know if it was her nervousness or that she remembered the rule she'd made him agree to — stay out of her backpack. Frankie started laughing. She laughed until tears filled her eyes. She started to hug him, then remembered the professional part of the deal, and stiffly put her arms to her side and backed away.

"Good one, Lane. Do you know how to use that thing?"

"I'm great in the kitchen. I'll have this set up and brewing in no time."

"Since we have a lot of research to do yet tonight, I'll leave you to it while I get my laptop. Meet me in the living room when you're ready. Let's start with a debriefing on what you learned during your interviews in Bloomington."

"Someone shot at you near the doctor's house?!" The thought of Lane being shot tore at her.

"Yeah, the bullet hit the tree I was under."

"You act like it was nothing. You could've been killed. Why would someone shoot at you because you were in a wooded area near someone's house?"

"I think Dr. Caine has hired protection. I saw the shooter drive away in a Lincoln Town Car, the same car I saw earlier at the doctor's house. He and the doctor had a heated discussion about something. He must've seen my SUV when he left and double-backed and searched the woods for me."

"So we add this hired protection to our research list. Once we start surveillance, we'll get a photo to run."

Spread out on Frankie's sofa, Lane peered over his laptop and looked at Frankie who sat with her own laptop in a chair near him. "I can't find any criminal records for Eric Caine in NCIC."

"That's the National Crime Information Center, right?"

"Yeah, I want to look a couple more places until I give up. Do you have anything yet?" He grinned when he noticed a line of dried whipped cream froth from her cappuccino on Frankie's upper lip and decided not to tell her. He had the urge to pull her to him and lick it off. Definitely not a good idea and would qualify as a violation of Rule #1: Keeping things professional not personal.

"Yes, but I'm still looking. Did you know he has six adoption satellite offices with clinics in this state? It looks like the location in Indianapolis is the largest one. I wonder why he chooses to live in Bloomington instead of Indy?"

"No clue."

"Apparently, Dr. Caine is quite the social butterfly. I've got five articles with photographs from several Indiana newspapers. In each one, Caine is hosting or attending a charity event with women who look like models on his arm."

"No kidding." He drained his mug of the last drops of espresso.

"Nope. Evidently, the good doc is into blondes big time. This guy looks like a material-boy. He wears a lot of designer suits. My guess he's into money, fast cars, and image. I bet that's why he wants to be photographed at these charity events."

"I can attest to the fast car part. He drives a red Ferrari Enzo."

"No way! That used to be my dream car. Those things cost over six figures."

Lane just stared at her. She had the same dream car? What the hell were the chances of that? He shook his head and went back to his laptop. Soon he announced, "There's nothing in ViCAP on the bastard either. He's squeaky clean so far."

"He's just flying under the radar. We'll get him, Lane."

She spent a couple more hours doing one Internet search after the other. Her back started to cramp so she stretched and checked to see what Lane was doing. He was lying on her sofa fast asleep with his laptop balanced on his chest. She watched him for a long time then quietly put her laptop on the ottoman and went to a closet for a soft blanket. She slowly removed the laptop from his chest and covered him with the blanket. He looked so peaceful with every muscle in his face relaxed. As tempted as she was to ruffle his hair and wake him with a kiss, she resisted. She wasn't going to be the one to break Rule #1. She turned off the lights and headed for her bedroom.

Frankie lay in her bed for the longest time unable to sleep because she was thinking about Mandy Morris. The poor girl was only nineteen and had already had to mourn the loss of both her parents, loved a man who didn't love her back, and bore his rejection of her pregnancy with his child. It was a lot of sorrow for someone so young to have had to experience. And that someone had snuffed out her life and dumped her young body like garbage made her furious. She agreed with Lane. They had to get justice for Mandy Morris.

Hours later Lane tossed and turned on the couch in the living room. Was he dreaming or was he really hearing a shrill screech outside the window? He put a pillow over his head, but he could still hear it. The sound was escalating and now added to it was a bumping sound that grew louder. He cursed and threw the pillow across the room before sitting up, at first wondering where he was. His gaze traveled over the living room that didn't belong to him. Then he remembered being at Frankie's house working on his laptop which now sat on the coffee table. He yawned and stretched. He must have fallen asleep.

Something bumped against the front door again. Lane got up to check it out. He opened the door and a huge, bruiser of an orange cat raced inside and bolted into the kitchen. Frankie hadn't told him she had a cat. The thing must be hungry. He sleepily headed to the kitchen to find the cat food.

Once he flipped on the kitchen lights, he scanned the room for the cat but didn't see it. From the corner of his eye, something caught his attention. In an orange blur, the cat streaked from one end of the kitchen counter to the other propelling itself toward Lane like a missile. Suddenly, the cat was airborne, a hissing, spitting, and scratching demon that landed on his chest and clawed its way to the top of his head that it used as a springboard to escape to the living room. Lane stumbled, hitting his head on the kitchen cabinet. What the hell was that?

Rubbing his head, he stepped into the living room to look for the cat. Without warning, the cat launched himself from behind the sofa. This time he latched onto the zipper of Lane's jeans and hung on as Lane did a frantic dance to get him off. Finally, he was able to remove the cat then made a beeline for Frankie's bedroom.

Knocking wildly on her door, he shouted, "Frankie! Let me in!" He saw the cat crouched and ready to spring from the end of the hallway. Lane twisted the doorknob to her door and jumped in, slamming the door behind him.

"Oh my God, Lane. Can't you get through the first night without trying to break Rule #1?" She slid up to a sitting position, and then turned on the lamp on her small bedside table. "What's going on? Why are you pressed against the door like that? Do we have a burglar?"

"Frankie, something's very wrong with your cat. I think he may have flipped out or something if cats do that. He may be completely insane. He was throwing himself against your front door so I let him in. He raced to the kitchen so I thought he was hungry so I went in there to get him some food. That's when it happened."

"Lane, there's something I need to tell..."

"Not now. You've got to hear this," he interrupted. "I was in the kitchen when suddenly he launched himself at me like an orange fur ball missile! I think he was aiming for my eyes. I could've been blinded!"

"Lane..." She got out of bed and moved toward him. His eyes were wild. She watched him as he turned and locked the door.

"No, it gets worse. I tried to find him in the living room. Like a flying ninja, he shot out from behind the couch and nailed himself onto my crotch. Once I fought him off, I ran to your door and started knocking. I looked down the hall. There he was, in a crouched position, ready to launch at me again. That's when I came in here. Like I said, something is very wrong with your cat."

Standing directly in front of him, Frankie gently rested her hands on his arms and said, "Lane, I don't have a cat."

"Then whose maniac did I let in?"

"I don't know." She examined his face. "Your face is really scratched up and bleeding. Sit down on my bed while I find my first aid kit."

"I don't need first aid. I need your Glock."

"No way. You are not shooting a cat in my house." She found a small first aid kit in a dresser drawer and opened it on the bed. She took out a couple of foil wrapped alcohol swabs."

"Frankie, I don't need you to do this."

"You don't want to get cat scratch fever, do you?"

"What's cat scratch fever?"

"I'm not sure, but every time I got scratched as a kid, my mom would talk about cat scratch fever as if it were the plague." As gently as she could, she swabbed the scratches on his face. "Are there any more scratches?"

"Check my chest. He landed there first," Lane said as he unbuttoned his shirt.

"Damn. He really scratched you." She opened up another alcohol swab and dotted each scratch. "Any more?"

He started to unzip his pants and she slapped his hand. "Seriously? You're hell-bent on breaking Rule #1, aren't you?"

A mischievous grin sliced across his face as he pulled her into his arms and kissed the top of her head. "Just kidding, sweetheart."

Her brain told her to break away, but her body refused. She loved the feel of his strong arms holding her against the warmth of his body and a brief shiver rippled through her. She ran her hands up his back loving the feel of his hard muscles and the indentation of his spine. His closeness was so male and the scent of him, musk and man drove her crazy with need. She looked up into his eyes to see a flicker of desire as he bent to claim her lips in a kiss that was so hot and driving it took her breath away. He pulled way far too soon.

"I just had an ugly thought," Lane said.

"What?"

"Rabies." Yes, that was a word that could dampen the libido. "We've got to trap that cat."

With a blanket in hand, Frankie crept softly out of her bedroom with Lane close behind, moving toward the living room. They heard movement under the chair, and then the cat bounded toward the kitchen.

"I think that might be Miss Francis' cat. She lives down the street." She went into the kitchen to get a better look with Lane right at her side with the blanket. "It is. That's Fluffy."

"I can think of a better name for it like, cat-from-hell or Chuckie."

"I don't think Fluffy has ever been outside before. He's an inside cat. I bet Miss Francis doesn't even know he got out. I'm going to call her." Frankie ran back to her bedroom and returned with her cell phone.

"It's three o'clock in the morning. Aren't you afraid you'll give her a heart attack by calling this early?"

"I think she'll have the heart attack if she discovers Fluffy missing before we tell her." She punched her neighbor's number in her cell phone.

"Frankie, about that kiss. Do you think we need to worry about that as a violation of Rule #1?"

"No. It was kind of an emergency situation and our adrenalin was spiking. It meant nothing to either of us." It was such a lie she almost choked getting it out.

The next day they sat in the sheriff's office at his conference table. They had briefed him on what they'd discovered about Dr. Caine. Tim had been staring at Lane and finally asked, "What in the hell happened to your face?"

When Lane hesitated, Frankie jumped in. "It's my fault, Uncle Tim. Near the front yard, I'm making a combination rock and flower garden. I'm not finished and I left a couple of large rocks out and last night Lane fell over them into my bushes." She glanced at Lane who wore a grateful grin.

"Well, I hope your face heals before you meet with the doctor. I have your identities," said Tim. He shoved two envelopes across the table; one to Lane, the other to Frankie. "In these envelopes are fake driver's licenses, social security cards, and a couple of credit cards. Your new names are Lane and Frankie Henderson. You're a married couple who just moved to Bloomington from Chicago. You've got money, but you don't have what you both want and that's a baby."

"What kind of work are we in?" asked Lane.

"Lane, you're a successful investor who buys and sells foreclosed properties. You moved to Bloomington because your wife, Frankie, is an I.U. grad who loves the area. You two can live anywhere you want because most of your business is done over the Internet."

"Frankie, you are a housewife who participates in a variety of charities. This is to appeal to the social side of Dr. Caine. Sometimes he holds charity events in his home. It's your job to get you and Lane invited to them." Tim pulled a thick manila envelope out of the stack of papers in front of him.

"Inside the envelope is a set of car keys to a new black Cadillac Escalade with tinted windows and a red Mazda Miata convertible courtesy of a drug dealer raid last month. You'll also find a pair of wedding rings. Frankie, the diamond in yours is real. It's borrowed from a local jeweler so please don't lose it." Tim smiled at her and continued.

"I've saved the best for last. My best friend in high school, Sam Webster, is selling his home in Bloomington. He and his wife, Bonnie, have already moved to Atlanta, where he got transferred two months ago. I had dinner with Sam and Bonnie last weekend and told them about this case. They insist we use their house as your base as long as we need it for this op."

"You're kidding?" Frankie looked down at the realtor flyer of the house. It was the most incredible house she'd ever seen. A brick and stone dream home.

"Nope. Sam and Bonnie know how to build a house. Fifteen rooms including a gourmet kitchen, two master suites, wine cellar, theatre room, and huge backyard with a lake at the far end of the property."

"That's amazing. And they're willing to loan it to us?"

"Yes, but there is one small catch. They have a nosy realtor. So tomorrow afternoon, Mr. and Mrs. Lane Henderson, have an appointment to go through the house. Later we will submit a lease-to-buy offer that Sam and Bonnie have already approved. You can move in as soon as the realtor calls you about the signed deal."

Jennifer Brennan removed the paper gown she was wearing in one of the examination rooms at the clinic owned by the Forever Home Adoption Agency. She looked down at her a small baby bump. She picked up her clothes and redressed. She gulped hard, hot tears slipping down her cheek.

She'd made the toughest decision of her life and decided to give the baby growing inside her away. She hadn't seen the baby's father, Paul, in weeks and had successfully avoided his calls. He'd had his say loud and clear. How could she have been so blind? She thought they would marry after they graduated from college. She believed with all her heart he was her soul mate. Now he was a star in an ugly scene she wished she could forget. A flash of grief ripped through her.

Jennifer missed her parents. They'd always been her shield, protecting her against the ugliness of life. Being their only child, they had high expectations for her. She needed them, but the last thing she could cope with was the disappointment in their eyes if they learned about her pregnancy. How could she tell them she'd gotten pregnant and the father wanted nothing to do with the baby? Jennifer couldn't. She'd continue to call them each week with excuses why she couldn't come home for the weekend or holiday. Having the baby and giving it away was her only answer. They'd never know.

The doctor had told her she was beginning her fourth month of pregnancy. Soon the loose tops she wore with jeans wouldn't hide her condition. The agency made arrangements for her to move out of her dormitory on campus to an apartment that she'd share with another pregnant girl until the birth of her baby. She'd start packing as soon as she completed enrollment for the online courses she'd take during summer school.

"Frankie, are you ready yet? We need to leave soon or we'll be late," Lane called down the hallway as he did a quick check of his watch. Frankie had disappeared to her bedroom thirty minutes ago. He wondered if she was a little nervous about the trip. It was the first time they'd use their undercover roles. He heard a door squeak open so he grabbed his navy suit jacket from the chair and slipped it on over his gray pants.

Frankie walked into the room making his breath catch in his throat. She was looking down as she fiddled with a silver hoop earring so he scanned her body. She wore a blue and white floral sundress that accentuated her creamy skin, long neck, and ample cleavage. The dress cinched at her tiny waist and clipped off at her knees. She wore matching blue sandals with tiny pearls and crystal beads on the straps. She tossed a navy sweater on the chair near him.

"God, Frankie, you're beautiful." As he whispered the words, he realized it was an understatement. She was exquisite with soft layered hair framing her face. Her whiskey brown eyes glittered with intelligence, and her full lips were made for kissing. She was smokin' hot in every way. Being so attracted to a woman like Frankie was foreign to him. His preference in women was usually the big-breasted cheerleader types. That all changed when he met Frankie. She was a woman who could take his breath away by her beauty and kick his ass in 2.5 seconds. Yes, it was definitely a first and was, surprisingly, a big turn-on.

He cursed Rule #1. If he could, he'd throw caution to the wind, pick her up, and take her back to his bed. He'd start by kissing those full lips and work from there until he got her naked and beneath him. But there was good reason for Rule #1. They both needed to stay focused on the case or they'd put justice for Mandy Morris at risk. Neither of them would do that.

She looked up at him, blushed and lowered her thick, black lashes over her eyes. She was still fiddling with the earring when he stepped forward. He reached out to brush the hair out of her eyes. And what he noticed next stopped him in his tracks. He extended a finger and rubbed a circular scar of raised pink skin on her shoulder.

"This is where I shot you, isn't it?" Even though he knew it had been an accident, Lane didn't think his feelings of guilt would ever leave. He couldn't get past the fact that he was the one who had physically hurt her.

"It was an accident."

"Frankie, if you ever want to get plastic surgery to remove it, I'll pay for it."

"No way. I'm one of those people who like scars. Each scar tells a story of a life event. This one reminds me that the woman, who was to become my best friend, was found alive that day and the serial killer, who wanted to snuff out her life, did not succeed."

Lane smiled as he handed the navy sweater to her. "It's a good thing you're wearing this. I don't think your scar story is something you'd want to share today in your starring role as Mrs. Lane Henderson."

Lane and Frankie arrived at the home viewing in Bloomington and immediately realized that Tim's friends were right about one thing. Their realtor, Sally Nelson, was nosy and she had an expertise in gossip. They immediately got the lowdown on each neighbor. In addition, the short, round woman with beady eyes amplified by thick glasses didn't seem to believe any questions were off limits.

The house was tastefully decorated and furnished. According to Sally, the Websters had moved into a fully furnished condo in Atlanta and had left their furniture behind. Although the house had been built ten years prior, it looked brand-new with gleaming stainless steel appliances in the huge kitchen. The family room had warm oak plank hardwood floors and a built in entertainment center that housed a sixty-one inch flat screen television that Lane admired. The living room was cozy with a long overstuffed sofa and two matching chairs embracing the red brick fireplace on a far wall. A red oriental rug adorned the wooden floors.

The many windows throughout the house gave it a bright and warm feeling. From the foyer, a grand curved stairway led the way upstairs to the two master suites and three smaller guest rooms.

"How did you two meet?" Her glasses slid down her nose and over the rims her eyes. She did a quick, lustful assessment of Lane's body.

Frankie's eyes widened. They hadn't practiced the answer to that question, so she demonstrated how well she could think on her feet with Lane nodding in agreement throughout the short story. "We met in a Starbucks. He ordered Espresso and I ordered Latte and they mixed up the orders. We started talking and one thing led to another."

"That's a cute meet. Come upstairs and I'll show you one of the master suites. From the looks of you two, I'll just bet you'll spend a lot of time in there." She cackled wildly and led them up the stairs. Frankie caught Lane grinning and shot him an icy glare.

In the master bedroom, Sally asked, "When are you going to have your first baby?"

"As soon as we can," Lane responded.

In one of the guest bedrooms, she asked Frankie, "Is Lane as hot as he looks?"

"Hotter," Frankie said with a grin as she looked out the window.

For the rest of the home tour, Sally popped an intrusive question in each room like clockwork, which gave them a workout on their background stories. Lane set up a time to call Sally the next day after she'd reviewed their offer with the sellers. While they were still in Bloomington, Lane gave Frankie a tour that included the adoption agency building, the apartment house where the pregnant women lived, as well as Dr. Eric Caine's sprawling mansion. Frankie took photos at each stop.

When they arrived back at Frankie's house, they ordered pizza, which gave them more time to get on their laptops to search for more information about the adoption agency or Dr. Eric Caine.

"Yeah, baby!" She called out. Suddenly, there it was — the opportunity Frankie had been praying for. "Here's an ad asking for volunteers to work phones for a charity Dr. Caine is sponsoring. They need people to collect donations for college scholarships for disadvantaged kids. There's also a dinner and dance planned at the doctor's home at the end of the fund drive to reward volunteers and supporters. If I'm chosen as a volunteer, and I will be, I'll be able to work myself into his charity but also have an opportunity to get inside his home."

"Seriously?"

"Very serious. Watch me as I complete this online form. I'm there."

Someone was pounding on Frankie's front door. Lane grabbed his cell phone to check the time. Christ, it was three in the morning. What the hell? He pulled on his jeans, jerked his revolver out of its holster, and hid it in the back of his pants.

He flung open the guest room door and moved into the hall almost slamming into Frankie, who half-asleep, just stared at him.

Wide-eyed, he stared back. Frankie stood in front of him dressed in a tight white tank and sleep pants decorated with tiny pink hearts. He couldn't take his eyes off her beautiful, round, perfect breasts with nipples jutting through the thin white cloth. He imagined his mouth sucking on those perfect breasts with Frankie writhing beneath him. It took all the self-control he had not to pick her up and throw her on her bed and take her. He gritted his teeth and prayed his arousal wasn't as obvious to her as it was to him.

The pounding on the front started up again, getting more forceful and frantic. Frankie moved first and raced to the front door to look through the peep hole. Crap, it was Missy Kent from her self-defense class.

She opened the door and Missy flew past her.

"Please, Frankie, lock the door. He may have followed me." Missy was screaming and crying at the same time. Her lip was split, and her right eye had swollen shut. There were ugly bruises on her arms and throat.

Frankie slammed the door closed and slid the deadbolt into place. She then gently took Missy's hand and led her to the kitchen. Lane peered out the front window then went to his room to get his shirt.

In the kitchen, Frankie pulled out a chair for Missy and looked her over for injuries but found nothing other than what she'd already noticed.

"Missy, you need to call the police."

"No, that's the last thing I should do. They won't do anything then he'll really let me have it when he gets home!"

"I'm going to make some coffee and then we're going to talk about why you should reconsider calling the police." Frankie slipped a coffee filter into her coffeemaker then poured the coffee grounds. Once it was filled with water, she tapped the "on" button.

"I'm sorry, but I already called the police. A deputy is on his way." Lane said as he sat at the table with Missy. He held up his badge. "Besides, I am the police."

"Oh my God. Who the hell are you?!" Missy sobbed uncontrollably into her hands. Through her hands, she asked, "You called the police?"

Frankie motioned for Lane to leave the room. He went to the living room window and watched for a deputy to arrive. Suddenly a truck whipped into Frankie's driveway, brakes squealed as the driver stopped the vehicle. A man leapt out of the truck and ran to the front porch. Lane met him at the door.

"Is Missy here?" The man looked around Lane into the house. The guy was a couple feet away, yet Lane could smell the beer on his breath.

Lane moved onto the porch and closed the door behind him. "Let's calm down and talk about what's going on."

"Who the hell are you? Where's Missy? I know damn well she's here 'cause that's her car."

Lane pulled out his badge which made the man take a step back. He motioned to one of Frankie's wicker chairs and the man sat down just as a county sheriff car parked in front of the house.

In the kitchen, Frankie set a mug of hot coffee in front of Missy along with a box of tissues.

"I did the de-escalation steps you showed us. He was so angry that I'd burned his dinner he left the house for the tavern. By the time he got back, he'd had too much to drink and was still furious about the meal. But I did what you taught us. I angled my body so that it was about forty-five degrees from him to make myself a smaller target just like you told us. Then I held my hands up at chest level with my palms forward."

Frankie reached across the table to hold Missy's hand. "What happened next?"

"I was really scared, but I tried to appear as calm as I could. I started talking to him slowly and calmly. I kept softly saying his name, without anger. But when I asked him to please leave, he belted me. Then he grabbed me by the arms and I stomped on his instep as hard as I could. It gave me time to grab my purse and drive here."

"Missy, you did a good job. But you have to talk to the police. You have to let them help you."

"Do you really think this is my first rodeo? Do you think I haven't called them before? They talk to him and he turns into Mr. Congeniality who has a totally different story than the one I gave them. They always take his side."

"This time is different. You have dark bruising on your neck and arms. This is evidence, Missy."

Lane entered the kitchen with a deputy in tow.

"Missy, this is Deputy Jerry Thomason. Please talk with him and tell him what happened tonight."

Frankie immediately moved toward Jerry and shook his hand. He was one of the best deputies they could have sent for a domestic call. He cared about victims and did all he could for them. Too many deputies were burned out about domestic calls. They'd been attacked by too many victims as they hauled the abuser away.

Lane touched Frankie's elbow and nodded toward the living room.

"The husband's here. He's on the porch with Jerry's partner," he whispered.

"You're kidding. He followed her here?" she asked, clearly surprised.

"Yes. He's drunk and he's limping. He claims Missy did something to injure his foot."

"She defended herself."

She started to walk into the kitchen, but Lane grabbed her arm. "Frankie, do you think you could throw on a robe or something before these deputies get as turned on as I am?" He stared at her breasts.

Frankie looked down to see her emerging nipples jutting out of her thin tank top and ran to her bedroom.

Frankie, wearing a thick, terrycloth robe, re-entered the kitchen. Jerry was now sat next to Missy who was showing him her injuries as he jotted notes on a small pad. Frankie poured him a mug of hot coffee and placed it on the table.

She then poured another and joined Lane in the living room, handing him the mug. She sat with him until Jerry emerged from the kitchen. "I'm going to talk to my partner, and then we'll arrest the husband. He's going to jail tonight for assault. She needs to go to the emergency room, so her injuries are documented. She's calling her sister now to come here to follow her to the hospital."

Jerry went outside. Soon there was a loud commotion so Lane followed. He stepped onto the porch as Jerry and his partner wrestled with Missy's husband to get the handcuffs on. He kicked and screamed in the back of the deputies' car.

Later, Lane and Frankie sat in the wicker chairs on her front porch and watched as the upper edge of the sun appeared on the horizon. Missy and her sister had left for the hospital only an hour before. They both knew trying to sleep was a useless endeavor.

"She'll go back to him. I'll give her forty-eight hours," said Frankie. Most cops had the sickening knowledge it was likely the abuse victim went back to her abuser during that time frame.

"I know. When I was a deputy, I once jailed a guy that had beat his wife so badly her face look like a pizza by the time he was through. I'd never seen anyone beaten like she had been. She checked herself out of the hospital and appeared at his court hearing to bail him out of jail."

"And then the cycle continues until he kills her or she gets out." Her words were laced with her frustration.

"Unfortunately."

"Once they make up, Missy will blame me for interfering in their relationship. He'll make sure she stays angry with me. He'll probably tell her that I'm trying to break them up. She'll quit my self-defense class which is the worst thing she could do." She shook her head with disappointment.

"She got in her car and drove over here because she knew you would help her, Frankie."

"That won't matter," said Frankie as she sighed. "She said she'd get counseling, but I doubt if she will. Most of them don't. "

"The only person who has control of this situation is Missy. It's her life and her decisions. We can only hope she starts making better ones." Lane stood up and took Frankie's hand. "I'm making us the best breakfast you've ever had. Make the coffee while I do the rest."

"Coffee? Oh, hell no. I want some of Lane Hansen's coffee made with the new cappuccino maker. Whipped cream on top, please."

"You're on."

CHAPTER FIVE

Dr. Eric Caine looked across his glass desk at the couple sitting in front of him. The husband was big as a barn and could've been a pro football player instead of a mortgage investor. He obviously wasn't batting a home run in the fertility department either or he wouldn't be here.

The wife looked like she walked off a Victoria Secret runway. His eyes were transfixed. She was everything he lusted for in a woman. For one thing, she was blonde and natural blonde at that. She sat in front of him in a white linen sundress that accentuated her smooth, lightly tanned skin as well as the rise of her firm high-perched breasts. Her facial structure was delicately formed with high cheek bones, and full lips. As she talked, her eyes glittered under long dark lashes. He was grateful he was wearing his starched, white lab coat because right now he had a boner hard enough to hammer nails. Damned inconvenient, considering if the husband noticed, he could probably wipe the floor with him.

"We've been married three years," Frankie began, fully aware that the doctor was undressing her with his eyes. Sex appeal was one of her go-to weapons in her P.I. arsenal. Inwardly she smiled a little as she thought of how she'd like to use it to bring this murdering, baby trafficking bastard to his knees.

She sat up a little straighter, pulled her shoulders back, and continued, "We have all we want at this point in our lives — the house, the cars, the vacations. But what we really want is a bundle of joy that would make our lives complete." Fully entrenched in her role as the loving wife, she ran her index finger down Lane's arm as she looked adoringly at him.

"According to your application, you've been trying to get pregnant since your honeymoon?"

"That's right. According to our doctor, Lane, here, is shooting blanks."

Lane shifted in his seat and stared at Frankie.

"Oh, I see," said Dr. Caine.

"Your adoption agency has a wonderful reputation as I'm sure you know. Do you think you have a baby for us?"

"I'm certain we can work something out, Mrs. Henderson."

"One of the things we need to discuss is money. I'm not sure if you're aware, but our agency provides medical care, food, and lodging for young women throughout their pregnancy. In today's economy, you must realize that those expenses are not cheap. Therefore, we ask for a deposit of $50,000. Another $50,000 is due when your baby is born."

"*Our* baby. Lane, honey, isn't the sound of that just wonderful?" Frankie cooed as she patted Lane's hard thigh.

Lane grabbed her hand and squeezed as he faked a smile. He was still annoyed about the "shooting blanks" remark. This acting stuff was harder than he thought it would be. He looked at the doctor, who was checking Frankie out again. That was the part that bothered Lane the most. The good doctor couldn't keep his eyes off of Frankie, whether it was her cleavage or her long legs, and it pissed him off. Lane wanted to fly across the desk and deck him. He clenched his jaw and spoke, "The money is not a problem. When can we expect our baby?"

"I cannot give you a definite date, but it should be soon. Let me walk you to my assistant's office who will take your check. I hope to be contacting you very soon."

Outside, the early summer sun toasting their skin, Lane led Frankie with his large hand planted firmly on her backside, to the SUV. Once they reached the vehicle, he unlocked and opened the passenger door. Then, just as she was getting in the car, he bopped her soundly on her butt.

"Oww!" She waited for Lane to circle the car to get in the driver's side. "What was that for?"

"Shooting blanks? Where in the hell did that come from? Where was I when we practiced that dialog?" He shot her a glare and slipped the key in the ignition to turn on the air conditioning.

"I guess I ad-libbed a bit."

"Here's an idea — no more improvising. We're supposed to be partners. How about keeping me clued in?" He shot her his best intimidating glare and she shot one right back. That was the thing about Frankie. She was fierce. She didn't back down. He didn't understand why he liked that about her. But he did.

"Yeah, well here's a clue. You smack my butt again and you're going down."

He inhaled deeply and clenched his jaw. Then he did what he positively, absolutely shouldn't have done. He grabbed the lever beside his seat and pushed his seat back, and then he lifted her across the console until she plopped in his lap, the skirt of her dress flying upward.

"Lane, what are you..."

He kissed her hard, right there in broad daylight, in the SUV parked in front of the adoption agency clinic in a parking lot filled with people getting in and out of their cars. He didn't care who saw them. Right then, the only thing he could think about was this relentless lust and the sexual frustration that had been building up like a log jam in a raging river. It was short circuiting his brain. And in that moment of time, he didn't give a damn about personal versus professional. He wasn't waiting another freaking second. Her mouth felt hot and soft. He parted her lips so he could taste her — that sweet woman taste laced with the rich cappuccino he'd made her that morning.

"Lane, you have to stop."

"You were kissing me back. It didn't feel like you wanted me to stop." He was so aroused there were beads of moisture dotting his brow. But, there was no way he'd let her get away with painting the picture that he was the only one getting excited here.

"Right, then *we* have to stop. Like you said, we're partners. We can't let things get personal. We can't let our emotions get in the way and risk making a mistake that would help that bastard get away with killing Mandy."

Her words were like a splash of ice water to his libido so he helped her get back into the passenger seat. She was right. They were here on a job. The unbridled lust was way too inappropriate for the current circumstances. They needed their full attention on how to bring down Dr. Caine and his agency. He put the vehicle in reverse and pulled out of the parking space. They headed toward the house several miles away.

They were quiet during the ride; each at a loss for words.

"Did you know that when this job is over, I'm going to be a new mom?"

"What did you say?" He nearly ran off the road. Did she just say she was pregnant?

"I'm going to be the mom of a black Giant Schnauzer puppy whose daddy just happens to be Anne's Harley."

"Really? That puppy is going to grow up to be one big dog. Harley is the size of a pony."

"You thought I was saying I was pregnant, didn't you?"

"No, of course not."

"Bullshit. Your face drained of color and you looked like you were going to have a stroke. Don't worry, Lane. If I had gotten pregnant as a result of your one-night stand, I wouldn't have told you."

He pulled the SUV into a public park and parked in front of a small lake. "Oh, is that right?" Now he was angry. What the hell? Yes, he was a bastard for leaving that morning, but irresponsible? Hell no.

"Yeah, that's right. I don't need a man's help to raise a baby."

"When did you become a man-hater, Frankie? Before or after? Do you really think I don't regret leaving that morning?" She wouldn't look at him, which infuriated him even more.

"Then why did you?"

"You wouldn't understand. Besides you're still so pissed about it, you wouldn't listen to what I had to say anyway."

"Who said I was pissed about it? Who said I even cared?" She challenged, and then looked away when he just stared at her.

He pulled out of the park and back onto the road. Damn it. Was she ever going to forgive him for the one-night stand? She was so wrong about that. To Lane, a one-night stand was something a man did then forgets about the woman because the pairing didn't have meaning. The night he spent making love to Frankie was one he'd never forget. Their encounter was etched in his mind and haunted his dreams.

When they arrived at the house, he bounded up the stairs for his bedroom. He pulled some running shorts, socks, and a shirt out of a drawer, and then fished his Nikes out of the closet. He had to do something to burn this damn anger and lust out of his system and he hoped going on a run would do the trick. After he changed and came out of his room, Frankie was nowhere in sight which was just as well. He bounded out the front door and down the road that ran in front of the house.

Dressed in a red tank with white shorts, Frankie poured sweet tea over ice in the kitchen. Grabbing her laptop, she headed for the rocking chairs on the front veranda. She'd heard the slam of the front door earlier. Frankie didn't know where Lane went and she didn't care. The Escalade was parked in the driveway, so he couldn't have gone far.

On the veranda, she sat on a wicker chair and opened her laptop, and logged on to read her email. Anne had sent a briefing about some computer work she'd completed for Frankie's lucrative insurance company client. She and Ted were going to Indianapolis to do surveillance on a guy who thought he was going to get away with cheating his insurance company out of thousands in disability claims. Frankie had mixed feelings about the trip. Yes, she knew Anne would enjoy it because surveillance was something new to her. Anne didn't realize the dangers like Frankie did. Luckily, Ted would be with her.

On the other hand, she didn't think Michael would think too much of the idea. He'd become even more protective of Anne since she'd gotten pregnant. Michael Brandt was another lucrative client and Frankie didn't want him annoyed enough to pull his business, not that Anne would let him.

She saw another email waiting in her inbox with a name that was unfamiliar. Vanessa Wainwright? She opened it and got a pleasant surprise. She was asked to join a group of volunteers to answer phones for the telethon benefiting Dr. Eric Caine's charity. She smiled to herself. Excellent. Here was her opportunity to get inside the good doctor's organization and she was looking forward to it. In fact, it might be a good idea to ignore the invitation and set up an appointment with Dr. Caine to discuss volunteer opportunities. It was definitely something to consider.

She got on the Internet and went to Facebook to search for Eric Caine. She discovered that he had a page and clicked on the link to visit. Most of his page was public so she didn't have to be a friend to view the content. In the photo section, she discovered a multitude of photos of Caine in various activities. There was a photo of Caine standing in front of his red Ferrari Enzo, another one of him sunbathing with a bikini-wearing blonde near his pool, and still another standing in front of his luxurious home. Each photo told a story about a man with expensive tastes living the lifestyle of the rich and famous. The guy was narcissistic if nothing else. It was obvious he thought quite highly of himself.

The sound of running water toward the side of the house caught Frankie's attention. Then Lane came into view wearing athletic shorts and shoes. His shirt, if he'd been wearing one, had been discarded. He held the hose over his head. The water ran rivulets down his perfectly sculpted body. She knew it would be smart for her to look away. But who said she was smart? It took only a second to take in every gorgeous detail about him — his lean, wide shouldered-build, his sandy hair, his gray eyes that darkened when he was angry or aroused. The same gray eyes that were staring right back at her right now. Their gazes locked and a spark of heat flashed between them.

"Are you checking me out, Frankie?"

"No, of course not. I heard the water. That's all."

He turned off the water, headed toward the porch, and plopped down in the rocking chair next to her.

"What are you doing?"

"I'm checking out our favorite doctor's Facebook page."

Lane leaned over to see her screen. "Find anything interesting?"

"Not really. Everything I found just affirmed what I already suspected, that Caine is a materialistic, narcissistic sociopath."

Lane grinned and nodded his head. "It's nice out here. Someday I want a house with a porch. My apartment is more or less a base for changing clothes, gulping down meals, and sleeping since I got promoted to detective. It doesn't really feel like a home like your house."

She eyed him curiously. That was certainly an unexpected remark from a Type A detective constantly on the run chasing a case. Where were these nesting urges coming from?

Jennifer cursed her luck that the new apartment she'd share with another pregnant girl was on the second floor. She'd already made three trips to her car for boxes and was breathless from the exertion. She laid the boxes down in the living room and sat on the sofa to rest before getting the final load from her car. Although she was sure the apartment wasn't new, it had freshly painted walls in sky blue with thick ivory carpeting. The tufted sofa and chair was modern in design in a dark blue, with dark wood end tables and tall glass lamps. The living room and kitchen area blended together with a ceramic countered bar to separate the two rooms. The two bedrooms were large for an apartment with spacious walk-in closets. It seemed the Forever Home Adoption Agency had spared no expense in the quality of her new home.

The only thing missing was her roommate who had left a note saying she'd be doing errands until later. Jennifer pushed herself up from the chair to go to her car for the rest of her things.

While Lane was meeting in the next county with his boss about a case that was being assigned to another detective, Frankie had a meeting planned of her own.

Dressed in a tight, black ribbed tank top with a black linen skirt hugging her curves, she bent down to pull on her four inch heeled leopard pumps. She checked her outfit in the mirror and slipped the glittering diamond bangle bracelet she'd treated herself to after she received an especially large check from a client. She slipped her favorite silver hoop earrings on and she was good to go.

Surprised that Dr. Caine's receptionist didn't give her a hard time for not having an appointment; Frankie entered his office and found him standing behind his glass desk, wide-eyed and obviously curious about her impromptu visit.

"You are so kind to meet with me today."

"Please sit down and tell me why you needed to see me." He scanned her body with lustful eyes, much like before, as she sat in the visitor chair across from him.

"I thought you might have some ideas on where I could do some volunteering." She paused and fanned herself with her hand. "Did you know it's nearly ninety degrees out there today? And it's only June." A wave of apprehension swept through her. What if he gave her no opportunity to do what she came to do?

"Hold that thought. I'll go get us a bottle of water."

"That sounds wonderful." A powerful relief filled her.

The second his office door closed, Frankie slapped a listening device to a chrome desk leg, then leapt to her feet, and moved to his side of the desk, bending down to the PC hard drive on the floor. She took the lipstick case she was holding in her hand and removed the top to reveal a flash drive that she inserted into the USB port. She started counting the seconds until the computer monitoring software loaded onto Dr. Caine's computer. One second, two seconds... The software would enable her to receive data from his computer like recorded keystrokes, email, and chat correspondence as well as the websites he visited on her laptop. She was up to twenty seconds when the program ended with a beep. She heard a sound at the door and looked up to see the doctor entering the room with two bottles of water.

She ripped the flash drive out of his hard-drive and shoved it into the rest of the lipstick case and tossed it on the floor. She threw herself on her hands and knees and patted the carpet as if looking for something.

"What are you doing?" He stared at her suspiciously as she continued to pat the carpet in the area behind his desk.

"I was going to re-apply my lipstick and I dropped it. I think it rolled back here. Do you see it?"

"Here it is." He bent to pick up the gold lipstick case then handed it to her.

"Thanks. I can be so clumsy." She moved back to her chair, tossed it into her purse, and accepted the cold bottle of water he handed her across his desk.

"I believe we were discussing volunteer opportunities. I have a scholarship program for underprivileged young people. We are planning an upcoming telethon and we need volunteers to answer phones. Does that sound like something you'd be interested in?"

"That's exactly what I'd like to do. How do I get started?"

Jennifer Brennan was layering slices of bread with mayonnaise then covering each with ham when her new roommate, Ally Black, entered the apartment. Ally was maybe five foot three inches and was so pregnant she waddled like a duck. With long dark hair that framed a delicate heart-shaped face, she looked much younger than Jennifer had imagined. Ally looked like she should be giggling with her teenaged-girlfriends rather than planning the birth of a baby.

"Hi, you must be Ally. I'm Jennifer and I hope you're hungry because I made sandwiches and have some soup on the stove."

"Sounds great. Sorry I wasn't around when you got here to help you move in."

"No worries. You shouldn't be carrying boxes up those stairs anyway. Come sit down."

Ally perched on a bar stool, watched Jennifer pour cream of tomato soup into two bowls, and set one in front of her along with a ham sandwich. "So how far along are you? You're barely showing."

"Almost five months. How about you? *You're* definitely showing."

"I'm eight and a half months along thanks to the son-of-a-bitch who got me pregnant." Ally spoke in a low voice, taut with anger.

"You sound angry."

"Wouldn't you be if you woke up in the middle of the night and found your new foster mom's son on top of you?"

Jennifer took a quick sharp breath. "He raped you?"

"Not according to my foster mom, who blamed me before throwing me out."

"I'm so sorry. What happened then?"

"I was only sixteen so I was put into another foster home. When it was discovered I was pregnant, they contacted Forever Home Adoptions and here I am."

"So you agreed to give your baby up for adoption?" She was still a kid herself and Jennifer's heart ached for her.

"What choice did I have? I'm seventeen and haven't finished high school. My mother died, and she didn't even know who my dad was, which put me in the foster care system. I got bounced from one foster home to another. What kind of home could I provide for a kid?"

Lane spooned a rich dollop of macaroni and cheese onto Frankie's plate along with some steamed broccoli. He filled his own plate then carried both to the table.

Setting Frankie's plate in front of her, he said, "I don't want to hear a word about counting calories. You've got to try my Mom's recipe for mac and cheese."

She scooped some of the cheesy casserole on her fork and tasted it. "Oh my God, your mom is a genius. This is incredible." She looked at the gorgeous man who sat across from her and smiled. How could a man that hot be so good in the kitchen? Okay, he was good in another room of the house too, but she tried not to think about that.

After they finished dinner, Lane stood, stretched, and then looked down at her. "When it gets dark, let's do some surveillance of Eric Caine's house. Are you game?"

"Bring it."

Close to midnight, Lane parked the SUV at a vacant house he'd located near Dr. Frank's residence. It was a good mile away, but he didn't want to chance parking in the woods across from the house because he was sure he got made last time and nearly got a bullet in his head as a souvenir.

A full moon made visibility excellent and since it was a weeknight, the area was very quiet as they walked alongside the road. Frankie, wearing dark-green, lightweight sweats, had her backpack perched on her back and her hair tucked inside a dark baseball cap. Lane, dressed in black sweats, had his binoculars hanging around his neck, his revolver in its holster at his hip, and a black baseball cap on his head. He swatted at mosquitoes as they walked.

They soon entered the wooded area alongside Caine's property, crept around the trees and waded through the thick undergrowth. They picked a spot that gave them a view of the front of the house as well as the side then crouched down. Mosquitoes flew in dark clouds around them so Lane pulled a small can of bug repellent out of his pocket and sprayed Frankie then himself. They sat together under a huge oak tree and watched the house which bore no lights inside. Only the outside lights were on.

Around one o'clock, Lane heard vehicles approaching, tapped Frankie and they both got into prone positions. The white security gate hummed as it opened, and the doctor's red Ferrari Enzo pulled into the driveway then the garage. Close behind was the black Lincoln Town Car Lane had seen before.

He was eager to get a better look at the hired gun. Lane watched as a tall man with dark, blonde hair nearly reaching his shoulders got out of the Town Car. He carried a six-pack of beer and waited on the front porch until Dr. Caine opened the front door. The two men went inside and lights in a front room came on.

Frankie slowly got to her feet and started walking in the opposite direction. Lane whispered, "Where are you going?"

"I'll be right back," she said as she headed deeper into the woods.

Nature must be calling; Lane thought. He pulled out his binoculars. The blinds were open in the windows of the front room and Lane could see the two men drinking beer and having a conversation. Thirty minutes went by without Frankie's return and Lane was getting a little antsy. She was a trained professional and could take care of herself — so why he was feeling protective?

In the distance, he noticed movement near the Town Car. He aimed his binoculars in that direction and saw Frankie nearing the car, removing what looked like a small digital camera from her pocket. At the same time, the front door opened. Crap. The driver of the Town Car emerged from the house and walked toward the car. Frankie was now crouched at the back of the car taking a picture of the license tag. Did she know the driver was heading straight for her?

Lane slipped his revolver out of his holster and aimed toward the driver, not even sure he could even make the shot to help her, if needed, at this distance. As the driver rounded the front of the car, Frankie, still in the crouched position, slid around to the passenger side staying beneath the car window level. When the driver slammed his car door, she dropped and rolled over some ornamental bushes lining the driveway then lay still, flattening herself to the ground. The Town Car's motor roared to life and the driver quickly backed down the driveway. His heart racing, Lane watched as the security gate opened and the Town Car raced down the road toward town.

Angry, he slammed his revolver back into his holster and gritted his teeth as he waited for Frankie to return.

Minutes later, she arrived, her face split into a wide grin. She patted Lane on the back, and then said, "I got it. I got his license tag. We can look it up and find out who he is."

Lane was so furious he could hardly whisper. "Are you freaking serious, Frankie? You nearly gave me a heart attack. What the hell were you thinking just taking off like that? What part of being a partner don't you understand?"

"What? Why are you so mad? What did I do? I got his license tag. We needed it to ID him."

"I'm your partner, Frankie. And if you want the specifics, *I'm* the lead on this operation. You don't take an action like that without telling me. I shouldn't have to guess what the hell you're doing. You're not the fucking Lone Ranger." His accusing voice stabbed the air. He got to his feet and moved through the foliage toward the road as she trailed several feet behind.

"Screw you, Lane Hansen," she hissed.

"Give me the date and time and I'll check my calendar," he called over his shoulder.

Frankie marched on, silently called him every name in the book including ungrateful asshole. Then she realized he was right. They were only as strong as their partnership. He did need to know what she planned as she needed to know his strategies, so they could support and protect each other. Damn. She had been on her own too long. She ran her private investigation company as she pleased and the majority of her jobs she did alone.

By the time she got to the SUV, he was inside and had started the car. She barely had time to get in when he drove off. She glanced at his profile. His jaw was clenched and his eyes blazed. There was no mistake he was still angry and she didn't blame him.

"Lane, I'm sorry," she whispered.

"What? I couldn't hear you?"

"I said I'm sorry I played Lone Ranger." Apologizing was not her strong suit and hot tears filled her eyes.

He pulled off the road, his voice cold as he said, "Don't do it again, Frankie."

She stared out the window and knew if she did the Lone Ranger thing again, he'd ask for her removal from the case. It was then she decided not to tell Lane she'd installed the computer monitoring device on Frank's office computer.

Jennifer and Ally were settled in front of the television watching an episode of "GCB" when Jennifer's cell phone rang. She looked at the display. It was her dad.

Crap. She moved to the back patio to take the call in private.

"Hi, Dad. How are you?"

"I'm fine, but I'm missing my girl."

Her heart sank. She missed her dad and mom so much it hurt. "I miss you too, Dad. But I've been so busy with my classes that I've barely had time to breathe."

"I know, honey. Can't blame a dad for missing his girl, can you?"

"I love you, Dad. Don't forget that."

"Right back at you. Listen, I'm going to be in Bloomington on Tuesday. Can we meet up for lunch or something?"

"No, I'm so sorry, but my geology class has a field trip that day." She bit her lip. She'd never lied to her father, but she couldn't let him see her and guess that she was pregnant. She knew him. She'd be in his car headed for home before she could blink.

"I understand. Just thought I'd try."

"Why are you going to be in Bloomington?"

"I need to talk to your cousin, Frankie. She's doing a job for the department and we have a meeting."

"Frankie's in Bloomington?" Crap. That was all she needed. If Frankie was in Bloomington, why hadn't she contacted her? Frankie was a private investigator. What if she found out she was no longer living at the dormitory? Jennifer had no doubt if Frankie made that discovery she would look for her and quite possibly find out where Jennifer had moved. A shiver ran down her spine.

When the call ended, Jennifer went back into the house to join Ally in the living room. Moans floated down the hall from the bathroom, so she tapped on the door. "Ally, are you okay?" She got no answer so she opened the door.

"Jennifer, I think my water just broke and the labor pains are getting worse and worse." Ally cried.

"How long have you been having labor pains?"

"All day. I didn't want to say anything in case they passed. But they're not. They're getting worse and worse. Oh my God! It hurts."

"Here's my cell phone. Call your doctor."

Hours later a frightened Jennifer stood in front of the nurse's station for the third time in an hour asking about Ally's condition.

A young nurse wearing her hair in a tight bun finally noticed her. "Aren't you Ally Black's friend?"

"Yes, I am. Do you have any word on how she is doing?"

"Honey, she just delivered the prettiest little girl you've ever seen. Come with me and I'll show her to you."

The nurse led Jennifer down a long hallway then stopped in front of a large window that revealed ten or more tiny babies swaddled in either pink or blue blankets on the other side. She pointed out Ally's baby girl. The little munchkin had a shock of black hair the same shade as her mom's.

"She was only six pounds and five ounces, but she's fully developed so she'll be fine."

"She is so beautiful." Jennifer's heart squeezed as she watched the tiny baby lift her arms and squeeze her fingers into fists. For the first time, she wondered what her own baby would look like. Would he or she look like her or the man had who let her down? A lone tear ran down her cheek and she quickly brushed it aside. "Where is Ally? When can I see her?"

"She did fine during the delivery and should be in her room by now. She's in 323C if you want to see her."

Jennifer rushed down the hall until she reached Ally's room. The new mother sat in her bed eating an ice cream sandwich.

"So you get a new baby and ice cream too?" Ally smiled and glanced to her right. It was then that Jennifer realized Ally was not alone. A tall man with longish blonde hair stood in the corner near the only window. His hair, which looked overdue for a shampoo, fell in pieces about his face.

"Jennifer, this is David from Forever Home Adoptions." The man nodded in response but said nothing as she moved closer to Ally's bed.

"Have you seen your baby, Ally? She's beautiful," Jennifer gushed.

"No." She noticeably glanced at David then back at Jennifer. "It's best I don't see the baby since I'm giving her away."

"Okay, I understand." Jennifer sat on Ally's bed and patted her hand.

David took that as his cue to leave. Still saying nothing, he nodded at Ally then left.

"He's a little creepy," Jennifer said once she was she heard his steps retreating down the hall.

"No kidding. I woke up and he was staring at me. I had no idea who he was, so he introduced himself as David from the adoption agency. He said he was visiting to remind me of the papers I signed to give my baby away. He told me it was best if I didn't see my baby before I give him or her up. Well, he's not the boss of me," Ally said as she buzzed for a nurse to request to see her baby.

Soon a nurse wheeled her baby into Ally's room and placed the tiny infant in her arms.

"Isn't she the most beautiful thing you've ever seen?" Ally whispered as she gently touched her little cheek. "She's so tiny and fragile."

"She's beautiful, Ally." Jennifer squeezed back a tear as she watched Ally hold the squirming little angel.

Suddenly Ally placed the baby back in the protective plastic of the cart and started crying so hard she launched into hiccups. Jennifer didn't have to ask her what was wrong, she knew. She stretched her arms around Ally and held her until the sobbing and hiccupping stopped.

"Now that I've held her, I don't know if I can go through with giving her up. I want to keep her. I want to be the kind of mother to her that I never had. What am I going to do?"

"Ally, that's your decision and yours alone. I don't care what papers you signed, if you want to keep your baby then you keep her."

"I'm keeping her. That's what I decided. I'm not giving her up and I'm going to call the agency and tell them. I'll get a job and work out a payment plan to pay them back all the money they spent on my room and board. I'm keeping her." Her mouth curved into an unconscious smile as she watched her baby.

The next day, Jennifer entered the hospital with a large gift wrapped in pink under her arm. She rode the elevator to the third floor and headed to Ally's room. When she reached the room, a woman in scrubs was changing Ally's sheets. "Good morning. I'm here to see Ally. Can you tell me where she is?"

"Ally's not here. She left with her dad not even an hour ago. He got her checked out and away she went."

"She left with her dad?" How was that possible? Ally had told her that she never knew her father. "Are you sure she left with her father?" Jennifer glanced at the woman's name tag — Carole.

"Yes, I was in here and he introduced himself to me before they took off. He seemed in an awful hurry."

"Carole, where's the baby? Where is Ally's baby?" Her heart sank. Something was very wrong.

"I think the baby went home with her adoptive parents. About thirty minutes before Ally left with her dad, I saw him with a couple in the waiting room. The woman was holding the baby and the man was filling out some paperwork."

Numb, Jennifer left the room and headed toward the nursery. She was right. The baby was gone. And so was Ally.

CHAPTER SIX

Frankie sat at one end of the long dining room table beneath the crystal chandelier and Lane sat at the other. They were facing each other, laptop to laptop, as they searched for the identity of the driver of the Lincoln Town Car. Frankie pressed the Enter button on her keyboard and nearly jumped out of her chair.

"I've got him, Lane! David Edward Chambers."

"Okay, let me input that name into IAFIS and see if Mr. Chambers has a record."

"Think he'll be in there?"

"It's the largest database in the world with the fingerprints and criminal histories for more than seventy million subjects, so there's a good chance he'll be in there if he has a record or has been in the military."

A computer email alert beeped from Frankie's laptop prompting her to quickly close the email account she'd forgotten was open. After she'd installed the computer surveillance software on Dr. Caine's computer, she'd created a separate email account devoted to information the software gleaned. She didn't want the reminder to go off again and draw Lane's attention to the special email account. Not that he could find it, unless he was looking for it, and knew what he was looking for. She should tell him that she planted the recording device in Dr. Caine's office and installed the computer surveillance software, but she couldn't. He'd kick her off the case, and even scarier was the thought that he'd tell her Uncle Tim.

Lane, whether he realized it or not, needed her help. So what if she occasionally went outside the box? Okay, more than occasionally. But he needed the information the two surveillance tools would provide to solve the case and put Mandy's killer away. She'd just have to figure out a way to give him the information without telling him how she got it, since she'd undoubtedly broken a couple of laws by planting the bug and installing the software. They'd just have to find a way to confirm the information so it could be used as evidence in court.

"Got it!" Lane called from over his laptop. "David Chambers served in the military spending time on the front lines in Iraq as well as Afghanistan. In both cases, he served on the sniper team."

"You're so lucky he missed you the night he shot at you in the woods. Does he have a record?"

"Two instances of domestic violence, once while in the military and once after he came home. The second time he put his wife in the hospital. She must've dropped the charges because there's no record of a trial or that he served time."

"Nice guy," Frankie said, her voice laced with sarcasm. She got out her cell phone and called the Forever Home Adoption Clinic. "Hello, I'm from the Henderson Mortgage Company and I need some information about an employee by the name of David Edward Chambers. Yes, I'll hold on to speak to someone in Human Resources."

"What are you doing?" Lane whispered.

"Listen and learn."

"Hello, this is Jane Sell from the Henderson Mortgage Company, and I need a little information about your employee, David Edward Chambers so that we can complete his application. Is Mr. Chambers employed by you? He is. In what capacity? So he is a personal assistant and driver for Dr. Caine? How long has he been employed by Dr. Caine? Ten years? That's a long time. One last question, how much did Mr. Chambers earn last year? $210,000? Well, I think that is all the information we need. Thank you very much. You have a good day."

"Personal assistant? He makes $210,000? Give me a freaking break. The guy's a hired gun."

Frankie rolled her eyes and shook her head in disgust. "Yeah, and you just have to wonder how far this guy will go to protect Caine's interests. He doesn't seem the kind of guy afraid to get his hands dirty. But would he kill for him?"

Jennifer cleared her throat at the nurses' station to get the attention of one of the two nurses glued to their computer screens. The nurse in the stork print scrubs moved to the counter.

"I'm looking for the young woman who was in Room 323C. Her name is Ally Black. She had a baby girl last night."

"Sure, let me look it up." She moved back to her computer and pushed a couple of keys on her keyboard. Soon, she looked back at Jennifer. "It looks like she checked out this morning." This confirmed the information she'd already gotten from the nurse's aide changing the sheets in Ally's room.

"What about her baby girl? Where is she?"

After she clicked through a couple of screens, the nurse said, "I'm sorry. I can't give you any information about the baby due to the patient privacy laws."

Jennifer nodded and walked to the waiting room to sit down and think. She'd had a sleepless night waiting for Ally to show up at the apartment. Why didn't she come back for her things? Where was she? How was she going to find her? She pulled her cell phone from her purse and dialed the number for the Forever Home Clinic and asked to talk to a nurse.

"I'm looking for one of your patients, Ally Black. She checked out of the hospital last night and I can't find her."

"What did you say your name was?"

She hadn't given her name, but offered it now, "Jennifer Brennan. I'm a patient too."

"Jennifer, I cannot release patient information to you. I'm sorry."

Moving toward the elevator, Jennifer slammed the cell phone back into her purse and pushed the button for the parking garage. Just as she slid in to the driver's seat of her car, her phone rang.

"This is David Chambers from Forever Home Adoption Agency. I'm the personal assistant to Dr. Caine. Do you remember me? We met yesterday in Ally Black's room."

She remembered him all right. He was the man who gave her the creeps. "Hello, Mr. Chambers."

"Call me David. I just learned from our head nurse that you have some questions about Ally Black. Maybe I can help you."

"I'm looking for Ally. She's checked out of the hospital, and she didn't come back to the apartment last night. All her things are here."

"Well, don't worry about Ally. She's just fine. In fact, I just talked to her. She's staying with her father at his condo at Flagler Beach in Florida."

"Really?" He was lying. Ally's own mother didn't even know who her father was. There was no way Ally was with him.

"Yes. They're having a great time. She said she'd be staying in Florida for at least a couple of months, maybe permanently. I'm sure she'll pick up her things from the apartment when she returns."

"Where's her baby?"

"Ally's baby was adopted by a couple who will give her the best home a child could want."

"I'm surprised to hear that. Ally had changed her mind. She'd decided to keep her baby."

There was a long pause, and then David said, "Once she had time to think about it, Ally realized she couldn't support a baby at this point in her life. She did the best thing for the child. She gave her to a loving home."

Frankie had gone to bed early, but after an hour of tossing and turning, she flipped on the bedside lamp, grabbed her laptop and started reviewing the emails sent to and from Dr. Caine. A message of interest popped up on her screen. An email from a realtor revealed the doctor was buying a house in the Cayman Islands. She clicked on a link and a photo of the home appeared. It was a gray with white trim, two story, ocean view home with its own private beach. With water views from all rooms, a French balcony graced the second level. A patio with a hot tub jutted out from the first floor. All for 2.6 million dollars. The baby-trafficking business must be very, very profitable.

Another email revealed a Cayman Islands bank account. Frankie jotted down the account number. She'd come up with a way of getting the information to Lane without revealing her source.

A beep announced the arrival of a new message that Frankie immediately opened. It was to the doctor from David Chambers.

We have a problem. Need to talk to you. Meet you at your house at midnight.

Crap! Why couldn't they meet for this little chat in the doctor's office where she'd planted the listening device? One thing was for certain, she needed to get some listening devices into Dr. Eric Caine's home — the sooner the better.

She looked at the clock on her bedside table. It was eleven o'clock. There was still time to do surveillance out at Dr. Caine's house. She could enter through the woods then move to the window of the front room where the two usually met. She'd be able to hear the conversation. There was one big reason why she couldn't do this — Lane. What if he heard her leave and followed her? She'd be kicked off the case before she could say, "I can explain."

Frustrated, she shoved the laptop from her lap and headed downstairs to the kitchen. With any luck, there were still a few of Lane's chocolate chunk cookies left. The man should enter the Pillsbury Bake Off with those mouth-watering morsels. She thought of Jill, a classmate at the police academy. She was sure Jill would describe Lane's cookies as being so delicious, that eating them was almost an orgasmic experience. She chuckled as she entered the kitchen. Excellent! There were about six cookies left in the clear glass cookie jar.

Frankie went to the cabinet and pulled out a dessert plate and a glass. She plopped a couple of cookies on the plate then grabbed the milk carton from the refrigerator and poured a full glass of milk. As she closed the refrigerator door, a pair of strong arms encircled her waist then lifted her off the floor. She screamed, and then heard Lane laughing behind her as he set her back on the floor.

"Damn it, Lane. You scared me."

"You like my cookies, don't you?" Lane asked.

"They're okay." Frankie backed against the counter, taking a bite out of one of her cookies. He was watching her intently and she thought she detected a flicker in his intense eyes.

He trapped her against the counter with his hands braced on either side of her waist. He was so close she could feel his heat. The intensity in his eyes made it hard to breathe. His gaze lingered on her mouth as he slowly lowered his head to lick melted chocolate from her lower lip. A hot jolt of lust surged through her veins as he raised his head. Dropping the cookie, she snaked her arms around his neck, entangled her fingers in his hair, pulled him to her, and fully pressed her lips to his.

He groaned and pushed his hard length against her, molding her body to his until the blood pounded down to his sex. The taste of chocolate and pure Frankie was intoxicating and he kissed her with the hunger he'd had for months. He was starving for her, and the way she kissed him back let him know she was hungry for him too.

He lifted her slightly and felt her wrap her legs tightly around his waist, pressing against the rock-hard evidence of his arousal. His body screamed with need. If he didn't get inside her soon, he'd explode. He started to lower her to the kitchen floor, but stopped himself. He wanted her badly. But not on the kitchen floor. Not this time. He wanted this time, which really wasn't the first, to be special and be something she wouldn't easily forget. He wanted to spend the night, and the next morning too, slowly making love to her. So he headed for the stairs to get to one of the bedrooms. Only she pulled him into another passionate kiss so he gently laid her on the steps and crushed her to him. His body was on fire, a heady combination of lust and need.

He felt her hips rock against him. He knew if he didn't get her upstairs soon, they'd never make it there.

"Lane." Her voice was breathless.

"Hmm."

"It's your cell."

He opened his eyes and looked down at her. "Baby, what did you say?"

She slid her hand down to the back pocket of his jeans. "Your cell phone."

"God damn it. Who calls at this hour?" He braced himself on an elbow, angrily jerked the cell phone out of his pocket, and looked at the display — Sheriff Brennan. He glanced back at Frankie, still beneath him. "It's the sheriff." He rolled over on his side. She rolled with him and stayed pressed against him.

"Hansen."

"Where in the hell were you and why do you sound out of breath?"

"Sorry, sir, I left my cell phone in other room and ran when I heard it." He didn't like to lie to his boss, but he also didn't want his boss to know how close he was to breaking Rule #1 with his favorite niece.

"Another body's been found. A farmer found it in the woods near Kramer. It was dumped very close to where Mandy Morris was left. It's a young girl, Lane."

148

"Leaving now." He ended the call and shoved the phone back in his pocket. He got to his feet, pulling Frankie up with him.

"I heard," she said, her eyes wide and dark.

"We have to go." He was already bounding up the stairs to change his clothes and get his gun and badge.

By the time he reached the SUV, Frankie was already sitting in the passenger seat.

Lane slammed the vehicle into reverse to turn around, and then raced down the road toward the Interstate.

The doorbell was so freaking loud, he thought his skull would explode at the sound. Dr. Eric Caine had had a hell of a day and a migraine raged in his head. Now David Chambers had some sort of a problem. This meant *he* had a problem, and he was in no mood for one. He jerked the door open and motioned for Chambers to come in.

Chambers walked into the living room, flipped on a table lamp and sat on the sofa. "This may be nothing. Or it may be a problem."

Dr. Caine sat on a nearby chair. "Just spit it out." Sometimes Chambers was such an idiot he didn't know why he put up with him. If Chambers didn't know so much about his operation, he'd fire his ass. And then there were the things Chambers had done for him that could send them both to prison for a long, long time.

"I took care of..."

"Shut the hell up. I told you, I don't want to know. You already told me it was taken care of. That's all I care about."

"Something related to that happened today."

"What?" The doctor rubbed his throbbing head. The dim light from the table lamp was making the pain worse.

"Ally's roommate at the apartment, Jennifer Brennan, is asking a lot of questions."

He remembered Jennifer Brennan with her big, brown eyes and long, blonde hair. If she were only a couple of years older. Yeah, right. Like age ever stopped him before. "What is she asking about?"

"She wants to know where Ally is and why she didn't return to the apartment after checking out of the hospital."

"Who's she asking?"

"She called the clinic head nurse who told me. I called her back and told her Ally was in Florida with her father and that she may not be coming back."

"Did she believe you?"

"I don't know. She's suspicious. Ally told her she'd changed her mind about giving the baby away."

"Shit! Is she asking about the baby too?" Christ! He hated complications and this could be one that could land him in prison for life.

"Yes. Do you want me to take care of her?"

"No, not yet. But keep an eye on her."

Lane and Frankie arrived at the crime scene within an hour. Having slapped an old police dome light from his suitcase on the dashboard, he'd flown up the Interstate with speeds as high as 95 to 100 mph. The medical examiner and the crime scene technician vans were still parked with half a dozen sheriff cars alongside the road. Flood lights in the distance illuminated the crime scene. They were already out of their vehicle when they noticed a deputy headed toward them.

Lane pulled out his badge and the deputy let them pass, telling them to steer clear of the dirt path where technicians were collecting evidence. They entered the woods, wading through scrub and underbrush as they followed the yellow plastic crime scene tape, careful not to add their footprints to the dirt path. They passed a crime scene tech who was making a cast of a shoeprint on the path. Soon they could see a group of men in a huddle focusing on a small body on the ground. As they approached, Sheriff Brennan raised his head, noticed Lane and Frankie, and then moved away from the group to walk toward them.

"You got here just in time. The medical examiner is getting ready to take her back for the autopsy once the techs complete the shoe and tire print casting. He wants to do it as soon as possible. He thinks she's only been here a day or so. She looks young, younger than Mandy Morris. Can't be more than sixteen. The doc's got a daughter about her age and he's taking it bad. So keep that in mind if you ask him any questions. He's in a nasty mood."

"What do you think happened?" Lane asked as he brushed an insect out of his hair. He heard the buzzing of flies and knew there must be a thicket of them covering the body by now.

"The kill wasn't clean like with Mandy Morris. It looks like her clothes are ripped by the undergrowth so she must've run from her killer. We won't know for sure until the doc finishes the autopsy. I saw the entry wound, and it was surrounded by soot, so I think the kill shot to her back was in close range and most likely went clear through her heart." He paused as two men with a stretcher passed them tramping through the brush. "Now that you're here, I'm heading back to my office. Call me when you get the autopsy results. The prosecutor will want a briefing."

Frankie joined the huddle of men to see the body lying face down, her arms stretched above her head. The victim's loose top was ripped in places, probably the result of a pursuit by the perp. She was small and didn't look much over five feet tall. There was a tattoo of a tiny heart on her ankle. A couple of her fingers were bloody with the fingernails missing indicating she put up a fight. There was a ring of dark abrasions with dark bruising circling each wrist suggesting the killer had tied her up to subdue her.

Frankie joined Lane as he talked with a crime scene technician.

"What did you find?" she asked.

"The killer left tire tracks on that dirt lane we've got cordoned off on the other side of those trees. There were some pretty clear shoeprints that we're casting too. Already got the farmer's shoe impressions for comparison." He pulled a plastic bag out of his kit. "Oh, and she had a cell phone." He held up a zip-locked bag containing the phone. "I'll get it to you later after we've processed it for fingerprints."

"Let me know when you've run her fingerprints through AFIS for identification."

"No problem."

Frankie turned to see the men lifting the girl's body, now in a black body bag, strapped onto a stretcher. She watched them as they headed toward the road trudging in the thicket of weeds and undergrowth next to the dirt path that was still cordoned off. The medical examiner trailed behind. She felt Lane's presence behind her instead of turning in his direction.

"I'm going to the autopsy. Do you want me to drop you off at your house?"

"Oh, hell no. Do you think I haven't attended an autopsy before? This isn't my first time off the ranch!"

It was one in the morning, but one wouldn't guess the time by the lighting and bustle of activity in the autopsy room, Frankie thought as she peered through the large glass window. Dr. Meade was scrubbing up next to a stainless steel sink. His assistant, Joan, was arranging surgical instruments on a white cloth lined tray.

"The x-rays are done," called a male assistant who wheeled in the body covered with a white sheet from Radiology where they'd taken extensive x-rays. Frankie knew this was protocol in gunshot wound cases. Bullets were unpredictable and often moved in unusual paths through the body, especially if they should strike bone.

The x-rays would help the doctor identify the exact location of the bullet if it was still lodged within the body.

Per protocol, the girl's clothing had been stripped from her body, carefully placed in brown paper bags and handed to a crime scene technician along with the body bag and the sheet that was wrapped around her body. Once in the lab, the items would be searched for trace evidence such as hairs, fibers, dirt, and any other materials.

The paper bags had been removed from her hands which meant her nails had been scraped for trace evidence and her fingerprints had been taken.

Frankie looked at the tiny body lying under a clean white sheet, her dark hair spilling over the stainless steel table. She looked so very pale and innocent that Frankie's heart squeezed. What kind of a monster would kill this girl? What threat could she possibly have offered?

Lane joined her holding two paper cups filled with hot coffee. He handed one to her. She sipped the brew as they both moved into the autopsy room. Dr. Meade was ready to begin. He adjusted the tiny microphone clipped to his lab coat and began.

"The deceased is a white female with a weight of one hundred pounds and height of sixty-three inches..."

Three hours later, Frankie and Lane ran three blocks in the pouring rain to Michael Brandt's office. By the time they reached the building, their clothes were soaked through and the air conditioning chilled them. They dodged into the restrooms and soaked up what moisture they could with paper towels. Then they met in the hallway and took the stairs up to the meeting they'd been summoned to in the prosecutor's office.

Joining Michael, the sheriff, and Dr. Meade, they sat at a round conference table.

"Doc, what was the cause of death?" Michael asked as he watched the sheriff bring a full pot of coffee to the table along with some pastries.

"A gunshot wound through the back. The bullet sliced through the aorta of her heart then it exited through her chest," said Dr. Meade.

"The lab called me," said Lane. "They found the bullet lodged in the victim's loose blouse. They think it is a .38 hollow point like the one used to kill Mandy Morris. They're sending the bullets to ATF in Indianapolis for definitive identification. In addition, they're running her fingerprints for identification."

"Another thing you need to know is that this girl had given birth within days of her murder," offered Dr. Meade.

"Do you think this murder is connected to Mandy Morris's?" Michael asked the question of the sheriff who gave Lane the nod to respond.

"Yes, I do," said Lane. "Her body is dumped in the same place as Mandy Morris's and she was killed with a .38 hollow point bullet. She'd recently given birth, just like Mandy."

"What about a motive?" Michael looked to Frankie for her input.

"Once we get identification, we'll see if she's associated with the Forever Home Adoption Agency. If she is, my bet is that she decided to keep her baby. If the baby had already been sold, as we suspect, that creates a big problem for Dr. Caine who owns the agency. We had to pay $50,000 up front and are expected to pay another $50,000 once the baby arrives. I imagine the dollar amount for this baby is the same. That's a lot of money. Like I said, this is a big problem for Caine and getting rid of the mother is one solution."

"How close are you to getting into Dr. Caine's inner circle?"

"We've identified a person who appears to be Dr. Caine's hired gun. His name is David Chambers, and he's a former Army Sniper. He's registered a Wesson Smith & Wesson Model 438 Bodyguard which can shoot .38 hollow point bullets. He drives a Lincoln Town Car that is registered under Caine's name. We're looking forward to getting the results of the tire print analysis to see if we have a match." Frankie looked at Lane then continued. "I'm a volunteer for one of his charities, and he's having a dinner at his house this weekend for the volunteers. Lane and I hope to get more information then."

The sheriff's cell phone sounded and he moved into the hallway to take the call. When he returned, a worried expression creased his face. "If you two are going back to Bloomington today, you better take off. The weather report predicts severe storms in this area."

They were less than twenty minutes into their two-hour drive when the sky darkened. Moments later rain pelted the SUV windows and glossed the highway surface. Around them, vehicles slowed down. The ones that didn't learned first-hand how slippery the surface of the road had become.

Frankie felt a wave of anxiety sweep over her and she bit her lower lip. She'd never been a big fan of thunderstorms. As a child, she'd typically hid under her bed. She was even less of a fan of driving through these kinds of conditions. Hail began beating against the vehicle as the thunder rumbled overhead.

"Lane, do you think we should pull over?"

"Not yet." He glanced at her. "Hey, are you okay?"

"Sure." Her response was a lie because icy fear now gripped her heart as the thunder boomed louder and the hail pelted the car harder.

Frankie glanced at Lane whose focus was on the road. He gripped the steering wheel tightly and increased the speed of the windshield wipers.

Frankie turned the radio on and searched for a channel with a weather report. Each station was filled with more static than the last. Finally, she gave up and turned it off. They were in farmland now and the rain was so heavy she could barely see a couple of feet beyond her car window.

She looked down to see Lane was now holding her hand with his fingers laced through hers in her lap.

"Honey, at the next town we'll pull over at a restaurant or something."

She met his gaze and nodded in agreement. Then she looked out the window. The wind seemed to have picked up because the raindrops assaulting the vehicle popped against the glass.

Something pulled at her to look behind them. She turned in her seat so she could look out the wide window at the back of the SUV. She saw her worst nightmare — a turning, twisting, spinning top of a dark monster spewing rain, dirt, and debris as it headed right for them. Tornado! She didn't know she had screamed until Lane grabbed her arm and jerked her around in her seat.

Lane adjusted the rearview mirror to see the twister cutting a swath through the farmland behind them, leveling the farmhouse they'd passed just minutes ago. It was following the highway and was now directly in back of them pounding the miles between. He couldn't out drive it and there was nowhere to turn. He saw a farmhouse in the distance. If they could make it there, the house may have a basement or storm cellar.

He looked in the rearview mirror again. The twister was closer. Its black funnel dangled crazily from a thick storm cloud, the narrow end whipping back and forth like a tail. It was getting too close. He had to do something.

A sheet of metal came out of nowhere, slamming against the windshield, and holding on like it was super-glued to the glass. He slammed on the brakes too hard, making the car hydroplane until it hit a ditch and flipped on its side. The airbags deployed and Frankie was screaming. He yanked off his seat belt, slid toward the middle console, and pushed on the driver's side door with his feet as hard as he could but it wouldn't budge. He frantically searched the floor and found his large Maglite flashlight and struck the driver's side window again and again until it shattered. He used his coat to remove the most deadly of the glass still stuck to the frame then turned to Frankie. He unlocked her seatbelt. She looked dazed, maybe in shock, but he had no time to examine her. He dragged her out from under the airbag and out of her seat. He pulled her to him and hugged her hard, calling her name.

"I need your help, Frankie. Focus. We have to climb out that window and find shelter. Do you hear me?"

He shook her slightly and she moved, focusing her eyes on his face. He took that as a good sign and pushed her butt to help her climb through the window. Once she was through, he followed, landing on his arms on the hard pavement. He grabbed Frankie's arm and started running as quickly as the strong wind and hail would allow. Once they were a safe distance from car, he looked toward the farmhouse again. It was too far away. They wouldn't make it there in time. He looked back as a stretch of wire fencing, complete with the heavy wooden posts, swept across the highway just feet away from them.

He thrust Frankie into a deep ditch at the side of the road and threw himself on top of her to protect her from the flying debris. She struggled beneath him until he shouted at her to hold still. Instead, she squirmed until she moved in a position to wrap her arms around his head to shield him from the flying projectiles that assailed them from every direction.

A blinding bolt of lightning sliced the oak tree across the road from them as expertly as a surgeon. The amputated section of tree slammed to the ground, its upper branches atop Lane, ripping his shirt and raking deep scratches across his back. He gritted his teeth to keep from crying out and gripped Frankie. He feared she would disappear in the swift wave of dirt and debris sandblasting their bodies.

Lane heard the rush of water and realized the drainage ditch was filling, and if he didn't find another place for shelter, Frankie could drown. They had to reach the farmhouse. There was no other place to go. He pulled Frankie up and ran as he half-dragged her down the road. The savage wind and golf ball size-hail assaulted them as they ran. Power poles were snapped in two like match sticks, but they dared not stop to watch.

They were on the gravel lane leading to the house when Frankie twisted her ankle and fell. He yanked her to her feet then scooped her up in his arms and kept running until he reached the back door. It was locked, so he kicked it in. He heard glass shattering inside and realized the powerful winds had blown out the front windows of the house. He set Frankie down.

"Is your ankle broken?"

"No, I can walk on it."

It was dark, but a bolt of lightning lit the room enough so he knew they were in a kitchen. There was a closed door at the end of the room and he prayed it led to a basement. He jerked the door open as another flash of lightning revealed a staircase. He pulled Frankie to him and held her arm as they both felt their way down the steps to a dim basement illuminated only by a row of small windows that faced the backyard.

He waited for his eyes to adjust to the dimness of the room and soon he could make out an old washing machine, dryer, and an ancient sofa. The rest of the basement was filled with boxes.

"Is anyone here?" he called out, wondering where the people who lived here were.

"Frankie, help me look for a lantern, candles, or a flashlight."

They searched every inch of the basement, many places by touch because it was so dark. There was nothing. They'd have to rely on the small windows that lined the far wall for light. Frankie found a couple of blankets near the dryer.

Another rumble of thunder let them know another storm was moving in. Lane raced to the area beneath the staircase and moved the boxes stored there. Frankie brought the blankets she'd found and laid them inside. She bent down and got inside, lining her body up against a cement blocked wall. Lane followed her and sat pressed against her. He felt the top of her head, looking for injuries.

"What are you doing?"

"You have a bump on your head the size of an egg." He ran his thumb lightly over the area then moved on until he covered her entire head.

"It's okay. I hit my head when the SUV turned over. No biggie."

"How many fingers am I holding up?"

"Are you crazy, Lane? It's dark in here. How am I supposed to see your fingers?"

Lane smiled and hugged her against him, feeling her body stiffen as a deafening clap of thunder roared through the house. The wind picked up and something hard hit the basement windows. His ears started popping so he yawned for some relief.

Suddenly what sounded like a freight train roared toward the house. Another tornado! It had to be. Lane grabbed one of the blankets and threw it over the two of them. He hugged Frankie to his chest.

Simultaneously, the three basement windows blew out, launching tiny fragments of glass like missiles. The blanket whipped about them as the wind tore through the basement and propelled objects about the room. A stuffed storage box slammed against Lane's back. The rest of the boxes tumbled like dominos, sending their contents airborne and deadly.

The basement door at the top of the steps crashed down to the landing. A deafening explosion pierced their ears as the house collapsed above them sending splintered pieces of wood, glass, and metal hurtling down the stairs.

An unholy pressure pulled at Lane and Frankie as if trying to separate them. Lane threw his arm over an exposed staircase beam and held on tight, at the same time crushing Frankie to his chest as flying pieces of debris peppered them. He refused to let her go.

As suddenly as it arrived, the storm left, leaving behind a clear, sunlit sky exposed through the gaping window frames. Lane let go of the wooden beam to cradle Frankie on the floor.

"Frankie, are you okay?"

When she didn't answer him, he panicked and began rocking her back and forth. "You've got to be okay, honey," he whispered. "I can't lose you. I love you too much. Please be okay."

Lane carried Frankie over to the sunlit section of the basement, stepping over debris as he went. Laying her on the floor, he lifted her wrist to check her pulse. Blood tricked down her forehead from a cut near her hairline and bruises were forming on her cheekbones and neck. He then checked for broken bones and found none. Putting his ear to her mouth, he could hear her soft breathing. He pulled her up to a sitting position and shook her slightly.

He held her until she opened her eyes to look at him. "This is a good example of why I'm not a big fan of storms."

Later, a State Trooper picked them up as they walked alongside the highway and gave them a ride home. They entered their house in Bloomington.

"Take off your jacket. I want to see your injuries." Lane was already pulling at her jacket when she stopped him.

"I'm okay."

"Take it off, Frankie. I'm not kidding." She pulled the jacket off as he turned her around. There was a scattering of bruises, cuts, and scratches on her back trailing down her spine. "Damn it. You should've let that trooper take you to the hospital."

"I don't need a hospital. I need a bath."

Without saying a word, he scooped her up in his arms and took her up the stairs to her room. He set her down on the bed as he ran hot water in the garden tub in her bathroom.

She was too exhausted to protest. When she heard him turn the water off, she crept to the bathroom, her muscles so sore it was hard to walk. When she entered the bathroom, he pulled at her tank top.

"Lane, I can take my own clothes off. Now get out of here."

When he quietly left the room, she turned off the lighting and lit two rose-scented candles that were on the far end of the tub. She quickly shed her clothes and got into the tub. The water was steamy hot and just right. She gritted her teeth so she wouldn't cry out as the water stung her cuts and scratches. She laid her head back against a towel Lane had rolled for a soft pillow and sighed with pleasure.

She must have fallen asleep, because the sound of running water and the sweet rose scent of her shower gel awoke her. Lane hovered over her and was squeezing shower gel onto a washcloth. She started to cover herself with her hands but he would have none of it.

"I've already seen you naked, so stop being embarrassed. Let me take care of you."

She slowly dropped her hands away and closed her eyes as he gently made circular motions with the gel until it turned into frothy suds he smoothed over her body. He washed each of her long legs, and then pressed her forward to do her back. She nearly moaned with both pain and pleasure as he washed her back. He shampooed and rinsed her hair. When he finished, she pulled at the shirt that he still wore.

"Take these off and get in." She ran more hot water and as he tossed his open shirt to the floor then unzipped his jeans and pushed them down. Next his boxer shorts came off. She couldn't help staring at him. Christ, the man was ripped and truly gorgeous. How had she managed to keep her hands off of him?

He slipped into the water and sat between her legs with his back to her. She pulled a wash cloth from a basket nearby.

"You're not going to make me smell girly, are you?"

She laughed and grabbed a bottle of a musky scented shower gel that she squeezed onto the cloth. She gently washed his back, working carefully around the cuts and deep scratches he'd gotten while protecting her from the storm. She then slipped her arms around his waist, holding him close as she washed his chest and neck. She gave the cloth to him to wash the rest as she squeezed shampoo into the palm of her hand to lather in his hair. She used a cup to rinse.

Frankie got out of the tub first and wrapped a thick, large white towel around her then tossed one to Lane. She grabbed another towel to wrap around her head then walked into her bedroom and slipped into a gauzy light blue nightgown. She sat on the end of the bed as she rubbed her hair with the towel.

Lane appeared in the frame of the door, wearing only the towel as he leaned against the doorframe. A vague sensual light passed between them.

"You're really beautiful, Frankie." Slowly and seductively, his gaze slid over her, making her pulse race.

"So I'm guessing now is not the time to discuss Rule #1?"

"Rule #1 can go to hell."

"I agree. Protection?"

"Be right back."

She heard him walk to his bedroom and laid her head on a pillow. Within seconds she drifted into a deep sleep.

In her dream, she was running as fast as she could to escape the tornado barreling toward her. Where was Lane? She couldn't stop running to look for him. "Lane!" She screamed until her voice was hoarse. She saw him ahead lying in a ditch. She threw herself next to him and he pulled her into an embrace. She kissed him, her tongue exploring the recesses of his mouth, tasting him.

Suddenly, a violent gust of wind hit them and he was gone. "Nooooooo." She jerked upright in bed, nearly panting with fear. She patted the area around her as if expecting him in bed with her. When she realized he was not there, she climbed out of her bed, turned on the hall light, and headed toward Lane's room.

CHAPTER SEVEN

When she reached his door, she could see Lane lying beneath a white sheet that was carelessly tossed across his naked midsection on his bed. Moonlight bathed his lean, muscular body, while the cool night air streaming through open windows ruffled his hair as he slept. She could hear him breathing. He slowly opened his eyes as if he sensed her presence.

"Frankie?" He blinked a couple of times as if she was an apparition.

"I'm cold," whispered Frankie as she wrapped her arms around herself to stifle a shiver.

"Do you want me to get you some blankets?"

She moved a step toward him. "No, I want *you* to be my blanket."

She watched as Lane sat motionless for a second, but then he moved over so he could peel back a section of the blanket and sheet on his bed for her. She slowly moved to him, desire's heat rushing through her body.

The breeze caught her hair and whipped it about her face. Her thin blue nightgown fluttered. She made no effort to cover herself. Vaguely aware of breathing in and out, she found it wondrous she could breathe at all. She'd never wanted a man like she wanted Lane. Never.

She reached the edge of the bed and crawled in next to him, positioning herself so her head lay on his shoulder. His musky and very male scent intoxicated her. He pulled her near and she sighed with pleasure as she tried to press even closer against him.

"Are you getting warm?" he asked as he lightly rubbed her arm.

In response, she licked and nibbled on his ear lobe and snaked a long leg across his thighs. She whispered, "Oh, I think you can get me much warmer than this."

Braced on his elbows, he looked down at her. "Baby, I think I can." The warmth of his smile echoed in his voice.

He possessively claimed her lips crushing her to him sending shivers of desire racing through her body. His kiss felt so good, she wanted to drink him in so it never ended. A hot jolt of lust surged like molten lava through her veins. It was a heady combination of desire and need that burned out of control.

Her body was on fire, as he trailed hot kisses down her throat to her breast, tracing her sensitive, swollen nipple through the gauzy nightgown with his tantalizing tongue until she nearly screamed with pleasure. He pulled down the top of her nightgown and she knotted her fingers in his hair as he moved his attention to the rosy peak of her other breast.

His body temperature seemed to spike, and the heat coming off him set her already hot blood to boiling. He seemed focused on taking her slowly, exploring her body with sensual care. He pulled at her nightgown until it bunched around her ankles and pushed it off the bed. He kissed his way up her body, his hands slowly moving upward, skimming either side of her body to her thighs. Then he cupped her and she cried out loud as a bolt of desire shot through her body. Passion pounded the blood through her heart, chest and head. Her body was on fire as his magic fingers stroked her until she cried out for release as she shattered into a million glowing stars.

She'd imagined him making love to her many times over the past seven months. But the fantasy didn't come close to this. This was a trillion times better. He claimed her lips again, his tongue plunging as another part of his body would soon do — in then out until she was frantic with need. She arched against him.

"Lane, please," she begged. She needed him inside her. She needed her body melted against his in a timeless dance of lust. God, she wanted *this* man.

He bent slightly above her, staring down into the heat of her eyes, as he stroked her tortured body. She was aflame with his touch as he reached over her to open the drawer in the bedside table. She heard the ripping of foil then he covered himself. She arched her hips up to meet him as he pushed inside her. Her breath caught at the force of it. He pulled out, and then pushed in again, making a low groan in his chest.

Their bodies grew slick with sweat as she moved her hips against him and he picked up the perfect pace. She clutched at him, careful of the injuries on his back as he pushed and pushed into her in a hot, slick dance she wished would never end.

She felt a white hot fire in her core. It was building and building until she exploded with pleasure, screaming his name. Moments later, he made a violent thrust and shuddered against her as he found his own release.

His was the hard breathing of one who'd just run a marathon. Christ, he'd never felt like this — like a sexual bomb had just exploded in his body and he may never recover. He rolled over pulling her atop him stroking the length of her hips and thighs as he came back to earth.

Finally, he opened his eyes and found Frankie staring at him. He used his thumb to gently brush her hair out of her eyes.

"Just so you know, if you're thinking of ghosting or disappearing like you did seven months ago, I intend to shoot you. And we both know I won't miss."

"Baby, you're going to have to shoot me to keep me *away* from you." He looked into her eyes and in a husky whisper said, "You're not questioning my *staying* power, are you?"

He pushed her hand down to his arousal and pulled her into a deep kiss. Then proceeded to demonstrate he was around to stay in the most sensual way he could.

She awoke the next morning to the muffled sounds of Lane talking on his cell phone in the hallway. He disconnected the call and walked back to the room, leaning against the doorframe wearing only boxer shorts and looking like a model in a fragrance ad with his dark looks and amazing body. The man radiated testosterone.

"That call didn't wake you, did it?"

She pulled the sheet up to cover herself, yawned, and stretched. Her sore muscles reminded her of the night before and she blushed. "Was that about the case?"

"They identified the dead girl. Her name is Ally Black. She was seventeen years old. She ran away from her foster home a couple of times so Children Services had her fingerprinted."

"Did you find out anything else?"

"No. After a shower, I thought I'd make my famous country breakfast with blueberry pancakes." He raked his fingers through his hair and placed his cell phone on his dresser. "Then we can talk about the case."

"Sounds like a plan." She got out of bed, wrapped the sheet tightly around her body and was heading toward her bathroom when Lane scooped her up off the floor. He carried her fireman-style to his bathroom and deposited her on the floor then he turned on the water in his shower.

"Did I say I wanted to shower alone?" He pulled her into a deep kiss and Frankie decided Lane showering alone wasn't going to happen on her watch.

David Chambers was a man who did not like surprises. He wandered through every room of his ranch-style home looking for his wife and two daughters.

Finding no one home, he searched his mind for a reminder of a missed appointment or something. But it was mid-day in June and his wife and kids should be home waiting to have lunch with him.

In the kitchen, he opened the refrigerator door to see if his wife left him anything for his lunch. There was nothing. As he closed the door, a slip of paper drifted to the floor. He picked it up and read it. In a rage, he crumbled it into a tight ball. Leaving him? Was she serious? She knew better than to take his kids and leave him. Hadn't he warned her a dozen times what would happen if she ever left him? Did her last trip to the hospital not convince her he meant what he said?

He kicked a wooden chair near the kitchen table and sent it flying until it slammed into the back door. She'd pay for this. He'd find her just like he did the last time she had left. Only this time, there'd be any hospital visit for her. She'd pay just like the two bitches he snuffed out for Dr. Caine.

David turned on the computer in his home office and watched as it came to life. He surfed to their bank's website then logged into their joint bank account and found it was empty. He doubled his fists and pounded them on the desk, then clicked his mouse to view recent transactions. She'd used their VISA card to reserve a hotel room in Nashville, Tennessee.

He sent a quick email to Dr. Caine.

I'll be out of town for a week or more for a personal emergency. You have my cell phone. Use it if you need me. —D.C.

He snatched his car keys out of his pocket and raced to the Lincoln Town Car.

After a late breakfast, Frankie and Lane sat in the formal dining room at either end of the long table starting up their laptops. They had a name for their victim, Ally Black. Their task this morning was to use technology to discover her identity. Frankie was going to look into Ally Black's bank records while Lane searched for any relatives to notify of her death.

"So far, I'm hitting a brick wall with relatives. I found a death certificate for her mother. There is no father listed on Ally Black's birth certificate. The girl had been in and out of foster homes. Her life seems as depressing as Mandy Morris's," said Lane.

"What about the foster parents? Should you notify them?" She asked the question while at the same time wondering why they hadn't reported the girl as missing.

"Her last foster home is on High Street. I'll go there this afternoon. Have you found anything interesting in her bank records?"

Frankie scrolled through the girl's bank records. "Well, there are direct transfers of $500 from a company with these initials — F.H.A.A."

"Christ, did you just say F.H.A.A.?" He jumped out of his chair and leaned against the back of hers, eyeing her laptop screen. "Those initials stand for Forever Home Adoption Agency. Mandy Morris received the same deposits from them."

"I knew it! She *was* mixed up with Dr. Caine's adoption agency."

"Frankie, please pull up any bank transactions with pizza delivery or anything like that. Let's find out where she was living. I'm willing to bet she lived at the same apartment complex where Mandy Morris lived. The one owned by Caine."

"Here's one — Family Pizza and here's the phone number."

He punched the number on his cell phone and walked into the kitchen for more coffee. When he returned, he said, "Bingo. Got her address. Ally lived in the same apartment complex as Mandy Morris. Want to go with me to interview her roommate and neighbors?"

"I wish I could, but I have a telethon volunteer meeting that I can't miss. I'm anticipating the day when Dr. Eric Caine is sitting in a jail cell instead of planning a fundraiser. By the way, don't forget that he's having a dinner party on Saturday. It's a black tie event."

Jennifer spent the morning looking through Ally's things. She had so little. There were four maternity tops in her closet along with some maternity jeans and a pair of worn Reeboks. She pulled out a small box from her closet floor that contained folded notes from friends, some woven bracelets, and a few photos of Ally standing with a couple of other teenaged girls. She was smiling in the picture. The last time Jennifer saw her smiling was the night she was holding her baby for the first time. She wiped at a tear that rolled down her cheek.

Maybe it was the curiosity she inherited from her father that made her question Ally's disappearance from the hospital. Whatever it was, she couldn't let it go. She didn't believe Ally left the hospital with her father. How could she when she didn't even know who her father was?

She should go to the police with her suspicions. But what evidence did she really have to inspire them to investigate David Chambers? Besides, her father was a county sheriff who knew practically every cop in the state. She refused to let her family know about her pregnancy, so going to the police wasn't an option.

She put Ally's things back in the box and pushed it in the closet where she found it. Then she went into her bedroom and pulled a sketch pad out of a drawer. Grabbing a pencil, she sat on the bed. She couldn't remember the last time she'd sketched. The creative outlet had always relaxed her. But this time, she wasn't sketching to relax. She had an idea and she was going to follow it through.

Jennifer worked the drawing until she was satisfied, and then sprayed it with hair spray to set it. She reapplied her lipstick, grabbed her purse, and flew out her door. On the landing, she slammed into a huge man in a suit. The impact sent the contents of her purse flying.

"I'm so sorry," the man muttered and he dropped to his knees and began picking up her items on the stairs.

"No worries. I'm in a hurry." She snatched her wallet and keys out of his hand, finished off the rest of the stairs, and raced to her car.

Lane dusted himself off and continued up the stairs. Once he got to Ally Black's apartment, he pounded on her door. If he was lucky, she'd had a roommate he could interview. At any rate, he wanted inside her apartment to see if she left anything behind that might be incriminating evidence to nail Dr. Eric Caine and anyone associated to him to the wall.

"There's no one home. I haven't seen Ally in a long while and her roommate just left." A young pregnant woman appeared at his right.

"Her roommate?"

"Yeah, the woman you just bumped into on the stairs. She just left in the blue Honda Civic."

By the time Jennifer reached the hospital, her clothes clung to her and she felt wilted as a result of the unseasonably warm June day. Her broken car air conditioner didn't help the situation. She wiped perspiration from her brow and hurried into the building.

Once she reached the third floor, she went to the nurse's station.

"Hi," she said to the first nurse who noticed her. "I'm looking for Carole. Her name is spelled with an 'e' on the end of it. She works here."

"Sure, I know Carole. The last time I saw her, she was in the C-wing. I'll page her to meet you here."

Moments later, Carole arrived at the nurses' station.

"Hi, Carole. Do you remember me? I talked to you the other day when I was looking for Ally Black."

"Sure, honey, I remember you."

Jennifer pulled the sketch she'd done of David Chambers out of her purse, unfolded the picture and showed it to Carole. "Does this look like the man with Ally the day she left the hospital?"

"Aren't you the talented one? Yes, that's Ally's father."

Lane looked around him to make sure no one was watching, and then pulled a credit card from his wallet. He slid the card in the vertical crack between the door and the frame near the lock. Within a second, he was in Ally Black's apartment. He looked around the living room and found it tidy with no mail or personal papers lying about. He walked into the kitchen and found it just as clean. Apparently, her roommate was a clean freak.

He entered a hallway that led to the bedrooms. He peeked in the first one. There was a pink paisley comforter on the twin bed along with at least a dozen frilly pillows. He noticed a journalism college textbook lying on a desk. This couldn't be Ally's room. She hadn't finished high school.

Lane left the room and entered the second bedroom. There was a matching comforter in blue on the bed but no pillows. There were no personal objects on the white dresser or the desk. Really odd. In the other crimes involving young women he'd investigated before, there were always an abundance of personal items on furniture like photos, framed or not, jewelry boxes, and journals. The fact there was nothing personal in this room piqued his curiosity.

He slid back the closet doors. There were a couple of women's tops hanging on hangers. He noticed a box on the floor and pulled it open. With the exception of a photograph of Ally with some friends, there was nothing in the box that would help him. He heard voices and looked out Ally's window to see a couple of women carrying bags past the apartment. Then he heard a door open then slam shut in the distance. It was time for him to leave before the roommate returned.

Jennifer sat in her stifling hot car outside the Forever Home Adoption Agency building. It was David Chambers who took Ally Black from the hospital, not her father. So what did that mean? Did he do something to her? Could this be something as innocent as David giving Ally a ride to the airport? Were her imagination and suspicions in overdrive? What in the hell was wrong with her? Why couldn't she let this go?

She thought of Dr. Caine. He was such a nice man. The day she met him, he seemed to know how hard it was for her to sign the papers to give up her baby. She remembered how he came around his desk and consoled her as she cried.

Besides owning the adoption agency and clinic, he was a respected physician. The nurses in the clinic adored and respected him. He had a right to know if a member of his staff behaved in a way that was questionable. She had to tell him.

Dr. Caine's secretary ushered Jennifer into his reception area after reporting the doctor was on a conference call that would end soon. She tried to look at a magazine but couldn't concentrate so she set it down. She wondered how Dr. Caine would react when he heard her story about his employee. She heard his footsteps then the door of his office opened.

"Hello, Jennifer. It's good to see you again. Why don't you come in and tell me why you needed to see me today." He stood back as she walked past him then pulled out one of the guest chairs in front of his desk for her. He slid around his desk and sat down.

"I've come across some information about one of your employees," she began. Anxiety made a giant knot in her stomach. She bit her lower lip and willed herself to continue talking.

"Is that right? What is it you think I should know?"

"Ally Black, one of your patients, disappeared recently after giving birth."

"Go on," he urged

"I visited with her the night she gave birth. She'd changed her mind, Dr. Caine. She'd held her baby and decided she couldn't give her up. She was going to tell you the next day. But the next day she was gone." Jennifer took a deep breath and tried to relax.

"What do you mean, she was gone?" A flicker of apprehension coursed through him.

"I went to the hospital to visit her and the staff told me her father had taken her home."

"That seems reasonable."

"The thing is, even Ally's mother didn't know who Ally's father was. The man was an enigma. David Chambers took Ally from the hospital was not her father."

"How do you know David took Ally from the hospital?"

Jennifer pulled the folded sketch from her purse and handed it to him. He visibly paled as he looked down at the sketch on his desk. "One of Ally's nurses identified him today as the man who took her from the hospital. He told the nurse he was Ally's father."

"David may have simply been giving the girl a ride and the nurse misunderstood his role."

"No, she and the other nurses told me that David presented himself as Ally's father. And now she's disappeared. She hasn't come back to the apartment for her things. That's not logical. If she were going someplace, she'd want to take her things with her. I think David had something to do with her disappearance."

"Why are you telling me this? Why haven't you gone to the police with your story?"

Jennifer looked down at her hands. "I'm not sure the police would take me seriously. But you are David's employer. Besides that, you're a respected physician in the community." Despite her best efforts, tears streamed down her face. "They'd listen to you. Please help me find out what happened to her. I just want to know if she is okay."

"Jennifer, I don't want you to worry another second. I'll find out what happened to Ally if it's the last thing I do. Can you give me a couple of days? I want to talk to David to make sure this is not a misunderstanding before I go to the police. Can you do that for me?"

"Of course. I'm sorry to unload this on you. Would you call me to let me know what you've found out?"

"Yes. I will. I promise you." He stood, prompting Jennifer to stand too. He walked around his desk and led her to the door. "Please don't worry, Jennifer. I'll find out what's going on."

Panic was rioting inside Dr. Caine, but he willed himself to appear calm. Christ, this was the last thing he needed. This girl could ruin everything he'd worked for. The quick and disturbing thought raced through his mind and try as he might he couldn't erase it.

Damn him. That freaking idiot, David. Ally Black was the problem David Chambers had assured him had been taken care of. The liar told him he took care of everything and that he needn't worry. What the hell was he going to do? David was God-knows-where. Coming up with the solution to this problem was now up to him. It was painfully obvious Jennifer Brennan wasn't going to let this go. It was sheer luck she hadn't already alerted the police. It was clear he had to handle this on his own.

Lane held up his wrist to check his watch again. Damn. If Frankie didn't hurry up, they were going to be a hell of a lot more than fashionably late to Dr. Caine's dinner party.

"Frankie!" he called up the stairs. "Are you almost ready?"

He heard her as she closed her bedroom door upstairs. Frankie stood at the top of the stairs and he lost his breath. He merely stared, tongue-tied. On an average day, Frankie was beautiful. Tonight she was stunning, wearing an apple-red sheath dress that hugged her curves and exposed her long, long legs. On her feet were her favorite leopard pumps with three inch heels. The dress's square neckline accentuated the rise of her firm breasts and Lane felt his arousal instantly stand at attention. This woman was drop-dead gorgeous and he wanted her flat on her back beneath him in his bed just as soon as he could arrange it. But for now, and throughout the evening, he needed to exhibit some control and keep his hands to himself.

"You're looking very hot, Mrs. Henderson."

"Not so bad yourself, Mr. Henderson." She neared him to adjust his silk tie. Her closeness sent tiny sparks of fire to his sexual center. She finished with the tie and said, "We need to talk about something before we go."

"Like what? It better be fast. In case you haven't noticed, we're running late, sweetheart."

"I intend to flirt with the evil doctor tonight to get some information. Just want to remind you to watch your temper."

His jaw clenched, his eyes slightly narrowed as he imagined a couple of scenarios. None of which he liked. "What kind of flirting are we talking about?"

"My goal is to keep it verbal, a little eyelash fluttering, and maybe some innocent touching of his arm. That kind of thing."

"Exactly how far are you willing to go to get information from him?"

"If the situation was reversed and the doctor was female, how far would you go?"

"I asked you first."

"I'll go as far as I need to prevent another woman from being murdered or another baby being sold to the highest bidder."

There it was — yet another glaring reason not to let things get personal with your partner. Lane knew himself well enough to know that if Eric Caine tried to get busy with Frankie he'd kick Dr. Caine's ass. And if she was asking him to stand by and passively watch, that was a personal hell he'd rather not experience.

He yanked her to him, encircled her waist with his arms, and crushed her against him. He possessively took her lips and delivered a mind-blowing kiss. He eased back. Her eyes still held surprise from the kiss.

"That's to remind you who you're coming home with tonight."

They pulled up to Dr. Caine's home in the Mazda Miata that the sheriff loaned Frankie for the operation. Thanks to the tornado, the Escalade was still in the repair shop. A wide-eyed teenaged valet took the car keys from Lane and acted like he was at a dealership taking a test drive. Lane groaned as the kid squealed the wheels as he turned the car into a makeshift parking lot across the road.

Lane tried to put himself in a better mood, but it was difficult to do because he couldn't stop thinking of a certain sociopathic, slime-ball doctor putting his filthy hands on the woman he was crazy about. In the car, Frankie kept trying to tell him she wouldn't let it come to that, but he wasn't convinced.

As they walked through the double doors of his mini-mansion, Dr. Caine took the opportunity to ignore Lane's presence while he blatantly undressed Frankie with his eyes. He embraced her like they were old friends. A muscle flicked angrily at Lane's jaw as he watched the scene.

Finally, the doctor noticed Lane's outstretched hand and gave him a decidedly unenthusiastic handshake.

Speaking directly to Frankie, Dr. Caine said, "I'm so glad you were able to be here tonight. I'm looking forward to getting to know you better." He pressed a kiss to the top of her hand before she could withdraw it. He made her skin crawl but she attempted a smile. She leaned against Lane, placing her hand in his. She squeezed and made a silent prayer that he rein in his temper.

"Please mingle with the other guests in the living room. Dinner will be served in about thirty minutes," Caine said.

The living room was massive with a white brick fireplace, with built-in bookshelves lining one wall. The other was lined with glass panels that opened to a terrace that ran the length of the house. A wrought iron fence laced with tiny white lights graced the red brick terrace.

There were at least thirty people in the living room and even more out on the terrace.

"I'll get us something to drink," suggested Lane. But before he could go to the bar, Frankie grabbed his arm.

"Aren't you going to ask what I want?"

"Nope. You're having ice water or soda. I'm well aware of your drinking capabilities." The beginning of a smile tipped the corners of his mouth.

"Very funny. Ice water is fine."

He returned some time later with her ice water in a wine glass. He held a bottle of dark German beer for himself. They watched the crowd together for a moment.

"It looks like the guests are a mixture of volunteers and possibly some adoptive parents," she whispered.

"I don't see David Chambers. Do you?"

"Oh, he won't be here tonight." The second the words slipped out of her mouth, she realized her mistake.

"How do you know he won't be here?"

A long, uncomfortable moment passed. She didn't want to lie to Lane, but confessing that her knowledge came from the computer surveillance she'd installed on Dr. Caine's computer would earn her Lane's wrath as well as a swift boot off the case. "I overheard one of the volunteers talking the other day."

His gaze lingered on her eyes, and she knew he realized she either lied or had a case of jittery nerves.

"Time to mingle," she called over her shoulder as she pressed through a group of guests near them and settled by a couple close to the fireplace. She needed to get away from Lane before he asked more questions.

From across the room, Dr. Eric Caine stared longingly at Frankie. She was the sexiest woman he'd seen in a long, long time. Heaven knew he liked his blondes. If he had his way, and of course he would, he'd be spending some up close and personal time with her very soon. He got what he wanted and had since childhood. No exception. He'd have Frankie Henderson and once he worked his considerable charm, there'd be nothing her husband could do about it.

He watched her as she talked with Harry and Tara French, a couple he considered quite lucrative. They were adopting their third baby from him. He glanced at his date, Candace, and thought of how tiring she'd become. He'd plucked her off a runway in New York and they'd been together for a month. She was model beautiful but needy and spent money a little too freely for his taste. "Candace, would you please get me a glass of chardonnay?"

He nodded toward the bar, and then watched as she moved away. He made a beeline for Frankie and tore her away from her conversation with Harry and Tara French with the pretense of showing her the house. He placed his hand at the small of her back as he led her out onto the terrace.

Frankie had been watching Eric Caine eying her from across the room and was not surprised to see him heading toward her.

"This is one of my favorite places, Frankie," he said as he ran his index finger along her arm. "I like to be outside when the weather permits. I like to have breakfast out here when possible or lounging over there to read."

"I like your terrace very much. It looks like you put a lot of thought into the landscaping." He was standing so close she could feel the warmth of his breath. Her instincts told her to run while the investigator part of her told her to stay put and keep him talking. "So, where do you like to vacation? Do you have a favorite place?"

"Actually, I do. I love the Cayman Islands. Have you ever been there?"

"No. What is it like?"

"With a clear blue ocean and miles of white sandy beaches, it is truly a paradise."

"Really? Do you go there often?"

"As a matter of fact, I am purchasing a vacation home there. I'd love to have you as a guest, Frankie."

"How nice of you to offer," Frankie said as she shot him a sexy smile. He'd just confirmed the information she received via computer surveillance. It was information she'd share with Lane who would undoubtedly discover the Cayman bank accounts online.

"*Your* baby is on its way."

"What did you say?" Now he had her attention.

"I met with a young woman the other day that has a striking resemblance to you — natural blonde hair and eyes the color of whiskey. Her baby is due in a few months. She's an I.U. student, intelligent and beautiful. It's uncanny how much she looks like you."

"They say we all have a twin somewhere." Frankie said with deceptive calm.

"The baby has a good chance of resembling you. I'll contact you as soon as it is born."

"May I meet the mother?"

"No, I'm sorry. We discourage meetings between the mother and the adoptive parents. Any meetings like this we've tried in the past have not worked out."

"I'm disappointed."

He slipped an arm around her and leaned in to whisper. "Maybe we can work something out, Frankie." His tone left her no doubt how he'd like to work out this little favor of a meeting and her stomach turned. The thought of him laying his hands on her was disgusting.

"Frankie, I thought you'd like a refill on your drink."

It was Lane's voice she heard and she spun around so fast she almost lost her balance. He was holding out a glass of ice water for her. She noticed a muscle flicked angrily at his jaw as he glared at Dr. Caine, who hastily removed his arm from her shoulders.

"Lane, I wondered where you were. We were just talking about your baby," said Dr. Caine.

"Is that so?"

"Yes, but I'll let your wife fill you in. I see some guests who look hungry. I better check on dinner."

Dr. Caine couldn't get off the terrace fast enough, and bumped into a waiter holding appetizers as he raced toward the kitchen.

"May I have the drink?" Frankie asked.

When he handed it to her, she placed it on the nearest table and walked back to him. She used his tie to pull him to her, then went up on her toes and kissed him, moving her lips over his in a sexy tease until lust quaked through his system. He deepened the kiss, crushing her against him. After a long moment, she pressed against his chest, so he opened his eyes and eased back.

"I just wanted to remind you who you were taking home tonight," she whispered.

After dinner, with a beer in his hand, Lane leaned against the wall watching and listening. A man and woman nearby were talking to another couple about their impending adoption. Dr. Caine had promised them a baby boy with blue eyes and dark hair like the husband. Two women near the couple were talking about the doctor's wealth and availability in the dating arena.

Lane searched the room for a stunning woman in a red dress, but Frankie was nowhere to be seen. He moved slightly so that he could see the foyer and noticed Frankie sneaking up the spiral staircase to the upper level of the house. She kept glancing toward the crowded room as if to see if anyone noticed her, which made him suspicious. Why was she going upstairs?

He took a swig of beer, and then wandered toward the foyer pretending to admire one of the doctor's expensive paintings. Scanning the room for the doctor, Lane noted he was on the terrace talking with a tall man who was clinging to his date.

Lane headed up the stairs, periodically checking the crowd. He reached a long hallway and noticed Frankie entering the third room on the right.

As luck would have it, Dr. Caine's home office was behind the third door Frankie tried. She slipped inside and quietly closed the door behind her. She crept to his desk, turned on a small lamp, and fired up his computer. She withdrew a lipstick case from her purse and removed the cap revealing the flash drive inside.

Frankie froze when she heard a sound in the hallway and looked at the crack of light beneath the office door for shadows. None appeared. After a moment, she went back to work and inserted the flash drive into the USB port of doctor's hard drive. She nervously glanced at her watch. She'd been away from the party maybe two minutes, three minutes tops. She counted to ten to calm herself. By the time she got to number seven, the surveillance software was installed and she'd now be able to review Caine's emails sent from this computer as well as chats through the special email account she'd set up on her laptop. Just as she reached down to pull the flash drive out of the hard drive, she heard voices just outside the door.

Lane's hand was on the door of the room he saw Frankie enter when he heard the footsteps of someone climbing the stairs. He leaned against the wall in a lazy stance that defied the anxiety that ran up his spine. Eric

Caine was heading toward him and the suspicion in his eyes was unmistakable.

"Mr. Henderson, is everything all right?"

"Yes, everything's fine. I saw my wife slip up here to use the ladies' room and I'm waiting for her."

"Oh, you're waiting in front of the wrong room. That's my office. The bathroom is down here." He waved for Lane to follow him down several doors to the left. "I forgot something in my bedroom. You can wait here for her."

Lane stifled a sigh of relief and leaned against the wall. In seconds, he heard the doorknob of the office door twist and Frankie emerged. He raced down the hall to her and nearly slammed her against the wall.

"What the hell were you doing in there?"

Before she could respond, Eric Caine stepped into the hallway from his bedroom. Lane pushed her against the wall with his body and kissed her so hard she bumped her head. The doctor walked past them without saying a word.

Lane wouldn't let her go until he heard the doctor's footsteps on the stairs. He ended the kiss and glared at her. "So what were you doing in there?"

"I was looking around. What's the big deal? Isn't that why we're here — to look around?"

"Do you realize how close you came to getting caught?" He was incredulous. Her risk taking was unnerving. First, she was nearly discovered by David Chambers while photographing his license plate and now this. Lane's mind took a turn and he remembered Sheriff

Brennan's warning about how letting things get personal between partners changes things. He hated to admit it but the sheriff was right. One thing the tornado experience had taught him was he was terrified that something would happen to her. Whether he'd told her or not, he was deeply in love with her and didn't know what he'd do if anything happened to her. The risks taken by a partner were one thing, but the risks taken by Frankie were quite another.

"But I didn't get caught, did I?"

He just stared at her for a moment, and then led her by the arm down the hall to the stairs and back to the party.

Frankie tried to make small talk during the drive home, but Lane seemed distracted. Once they got inside the house, he stood at the door with the car keys in his hand just staring at her. Though she was desperate to, she couldn't read his expression. Did he realize she'd bugged the doctor's home office without telling him? Was he angry? Was it something else?

She gambled. She stepped toward him, went up on her toes, grabbed his tie, and kissed him roughly, as she pulled his shirt out of his pants. Lane tensed for only a second until lust took over and he pulled her off her feet, spun her around, and pressed her against the front door.

He was breathing hard. She could feel his chest rising and falling against her breasts. There was no mistake he was turned on — hot and hard —pinning her to the door and kissing her until she thought her body would burst into flames.

He reached around her, found the dress zipper, pulled it down and pushed her dress to the floor, spilling around her ankles.

"Red lace bra *and* panties? You're killing me, Frankie."

He took her lips again hard and pressed against her, running his hands against the silk of her body, driving a sense of urgency through her. She pressed her breasts against him, her nipples hard and aching.

He unhooked her bra and dangled it by his thumb. "This I like."

He bent and blazed a trail of kisses down to her breasts and licked each one as he looked up at her. "But these, I love." Then his mouth was on her breasts sucking each of her tender nipples. She gasped in sweet agony and knotted her fingers in his hair.

Licking and kissing, his mouth slid down her flat tummy teasing her belly button then down further until he placed a soft kiss on her mound. His voice was husky as he whispered, "This I love, too."

He cupped her sex, gently massaging until the tension building inside her became unbearable. Heat pooled between her legs. If she got any hotter she was sure she'd melt. Waves of ecstasy throbbed through her, hotter and hotter, until she gasped in sweet agony.

"Oh, my God. Lane, I need you inside me."

"Baby, let me kiss you all over until you scream your pleasure. Don't make me stop."

"I need you NOW. Please," she begged.

"Where?"

"Upstairs."

"I hope you're not tired, sweetheart, because we are going to have a long and very active night."

With that, he scooped her into his arms and climbed the stairs to his room. "Oh, and you can leave on those hot leopard heels."

CHAPTER EIGHT

"I thought a cheese omelet, whole wheat toast, and coffee was your favorite breakfast? You're hardly touched your food, Dr. Caine." asked Miriam, the housekeeper, as she approached him on the terrace. "Dr. Caine, would you like more coffee?"

"Yes, please bring the entire pot as well as some aspirin. I think I'm getting a migraine from all the pounding in the basement."

He closed his eyes and rubbed his temples. Actually, the pain had started last night when he'd broken up with Candace. The sobbing, screaming, and the rest of the drama had gotten so bad he'd called a cab to take her to the airport. He would've done anything at that point just to get her out of his house. The things women believe. She actually believed him when in a fit of passion he had said he wanted to marry her. Seriously? Candace was gullible and stupid and he was glad to be rid of her. There was only one woman in his fantasies now and that was Frankie

Henderson. It was only a matter of time until she replaced Candace in his bed.

Miriam quickened her steps to get to the kitchen and back with his coffee and aspirin. She'd experienced early on how his mood darkened when he had a headache. She remembered too well the time she used the wrong sheets on his bed and he'd thrown a vase at her barely missing her head. Her husband had wanted her to quit after that, but the money was too good.

His head hammered with pain, throbbing as each nail was pounded in the basement as the workers completed the room he was building for Jennifer Brennan. Yesterday morning, before his dinner party, the plumber installed a sink and toilet. The furniture company delivered the twin-sized bed that he'd bolted to the floor. Once the workers finished today, the room would be finished and ready for its occupant. Jennifer had become an expensive annoyance.

He was amazed at his luck, that she'd come to him about David Chambers and Ally Black instead of going directly to the police. Stupid, nosy little bitch. Once he had her locked up in *her* room downstairs, he wouldn't have to worry about her running her mouth to the wrong people. Christ, how long could she have known Ally Black? Five minutes? According to her records, she'd moved into the apartment with Ally the day the girl gave birth. All this carrying on about a woman she barely knew was ridiculous.

He congratulated himself on what he considered the brilliant plan of locking Jennifer Brennan up until she gave birth. What he'd told Frankie Douglas the night before was true. There was an amazing resemblance between Jennifer and Frankie. He thought it might please Frankie that her new baby looked like her. Perhaps, the Hendersons would be so pleased that they'd cough up more money. Not that $100,000 was anything to sneeze at. Still one could only hope. Maybe Frankie would be so pleased she'd want to grant him a sexual favor or two. Yes, one could hope.

The morning sun had shifted so he put on his designer sunglasses. He unrolled the local newspaper and read the front page. He'd opened the second page when Miriam arrived with the coffee pot and aspirin. Taking the pot from her, he was pouring hot coffee into his cup when he noticed Ally Black's photo in the middle of page two. He dropped the glass pot which shattered into a million pieces, splashing coffee that scorched him through his pant legs. Miriam came running with a kitchen towel and wiped up the hot liquid from the table. She tried to dab the liquid from Dr. Caine's legs but he pushed her away.

"Why the hell did you hand me the pot like that? You made me drop it and now I'll be damn lucky if I don't have third degree burns. Go get my medical bag, you fool!" he screamed. She dashed out of the room and returned with his bag. "Get out of my sight!"

He threw the bag in a chair and went back to the paper to read the article. Jesus Christ! They'd found Ally Black's body. His heart raced and he held his breath as he read.

The body of a sixteen-year-old girl found in a wooded area near Kramer has been identified as Ally Black. The medical examiner reports her death as a homicide. The Sheriff's Department will not release additional information about the homicide at this time. Area residents are becoming more and more fearful that a serial killer may be at work. The body of another young girl, Mandy Morris, was found in the exact location not even a month ago.

What in God's name was David Chambers thinking dumping both bodies in the same place? The man was a moron. Damn it. And now *he* was in so deep with Chambers he'd undoubtedly go down with him if he didn't do something. He needed to have a strategy but how could he plan when he was so freaked out. He inhaled a deep cleansing breath and exhaled in an attempt to calm himself.

Maybe the situation was not as bad as he imagined. If the sheriff had anything substantial, they'd have it in the paper. At the very worst, the police would've already pounded on his door. The thought sent a chill down his spine.

Suddenly, he knew what he'd have to do. He had to eliminate the link between David and himself. He'd have to eliminate David Chambers. But not before Chambers killed Jennifer Brennan for him.

He threw his napkin on the table and headed for the basement to see how far along the workers were. He needed to make sure Jennifer Brennan kept her mouth closed and the only way to do that was to lock her in that room just as soon as he could manage it.

Frankie Douglas woke up in heavenly bliss with Lane's long, hard body spooning her, his arm possessively thrown across her, holding her in place. She listened to his even breathing and smiled. She'd never had a lover like Lane. Sex with him was an athletic event.

She hoped the house was insulated well, because Lane, true to his promise, had kissed each part of her body, and did some other equally erotic things until she gripped the sheets in both hands, arched her back, and screamed.

His arm tightened around her, letting her know he was awake. Then she felt him plant soft kisses on her neck and shoulders as his warm hand flattened on her tummy. She felt like purring like a cat as she snuggled closer feeling his erection. Let the athletics begin.

David Chambers pounded the hood of the Lincoln Town Car in a fit of rage. His wife and kids had not checked into the Nashville hotel. They'd cancelled their reservations. Now, he had no freaking idea where she was headed. Added to his anger was the fact that he was quickly running out of money since his wife had drained their joint bank account. He got in the car and punched Eric Caine's phone number into his cell.

"Hello."

David knew the doctor always checked his display to see who was calling him so why was he answering the phone like that?

"It's David. My wife took my kids and left me. I followed her to a hotel in Nashville, but the bitch cancelled her reservation. I have no idea where she went and I'm out of money."

"And that's my problem, why?"

"I'll tell you why. I need money and you're going to wire it to me." What was with the attitude?

"What if I don't?"

"If you don't wire $5,000 to me within the next hour, you're going to wish you'd never met me."

"I already do."

"What are you talking about?"

"A little article in the paper caught my attention this morning, David. It seems the body of a young woman was found in a wooded area near Kramer."

"Shit."

"Oh, and that's not all. It seems the body was found in the exact place another young woman's body was found. Does the name Mandy Morris ring a bell?"

"You're kidding. I didn't think either one of them would be found for years."

"You were wrong, you freaking idiot! What the fuck have you done?! I only wish that were the only thing going wrong. Jennifer Brennan came to see me about her theory that you did something to Ally Black. If she runs her mouth to the police, it's over — the adoption agency, the clinic, the money, cars, and houses. I'll lose it all."

"I'll head right back and take care of Jennifer Brennan."

"No you won't. I have plans for her that don't include you at the moment. Stay away until I call you to come back."

"But what am I going to do about money?"

"Figure something out. I'm not giving you squat."

Paul Vance stood outside Jennifer's dormitory and just stared at the building while he cursed himself. It was his fault things were such a mess.

He should've proposed to her the minute he found out she was pregnant with his child. Hell, he should have asked her to elope. God knew how much he loved her. He'd come close to proposing to Jennifer at least a dozen times the past two years. He knew by the third date that he wanted to spend his life with her. So what did he do when she needed him most?

He turned his back on her. First he accused her of getting pregnant on purpose. That was a laugh. *He* was the one who forgot the condoms that night. *He* was the one who was so turned on he couldn't stop.

But even worse than the accusation, he'd suggested she have an abortion. He actually told her to kill his baby that was growing inside her. What kind of monster was he?

When was he ever this miserable and filled with self-pity? Never. Of course, he'd never made a mistake of this magnitude before. His parents would disown him if they knew what he'd done. He'd deserve it. If Jennifer never forgave him, he'd deserve that too.

Paul leaned against a tree. He knew he looked like crap with dark circles hovering beneath his eyes and he'd lost weight. Even his coach had made a comment about his appearance and had asked if he was sick. Paul couldn't sleep because every time he did he dreamed of Jennifer and that last night together. He was having trouble with his grades because he couldn't concentrate on his studies. Paul could do nothing but think of Jennifer and how he might never see her again.

Then there was his baby. Suddenly the world was filled with happy parents pushing their babies in strollers. Paul saw them everywhere. He wanted that kind of happiness for Jennifer and himself no matter what price he had to pay. Even if it meant quitting school and getting a job. He could finish his degree online or in the evenings. Other people did it, so could he.

But could he really do it? Could he give up his chance at pro football? His coach had told him he had an excellent chance of getting drafted. It was something Paul had dreamed of since childhood. Maybe he could work it out so he could marry Jennifer, stay in school and stay on the football team. Then he'd still have a chance for the pros. Perhaps Jennifer could drop out of school and get a job until the baby arrived.

Paul didn't blame Jennifer for ignoring his voice mail and email messages. He'd called her or had written several times per day for weeks and he received no response. Yesterday, he'd made the decision. He was going to see her no matter what. He couldn't take it any longer. If he had to wait outside her dorm night and day, he'd do it. She had to listen to him. She had to forgive him. He'd gotten dressed in a white shirt and patterned tie with black pants. She'd always liked it when he got dressed up.

He noticed her friend, Carrie, come out of the dorm and he approached her.

"Hey, Carrie. I'm looking for Jennifer. Have you seen her?"

"No, I haven't. But you can go upstairs and ask her roommate. She might know where she is."

He took her advice, entered the building and took the elevator up to the fifth floor. In a moment, he was knocking on Jennifer's door. The door whipped open and her roommate, Tobi, invited him in and motioned for him to sit down.

"I'm looking for Jennifer." He looked around the room, half expecting to see her at her desk.

"That makes two of us."

"What do you mean?"

"It means I haven't seen her for weeks. In fact, none of us on this floor have. None of my friends have seen her on campus attending classes either. I've asked."

"Weeks?" Suddenly he was filled with apprehension.

He watched as Tobi moved toward Jennifer's closet and slid back the door. "This is all I know." She moved aside so he could see that the closet was empty. All of Jennifer's belongings were gone.

He left the building and walked around for an hour trying to think of where Jennifer might have gone. At one point, he pulled out his cell and called her. Still no answer. He left a message. "Jennifer, damn it, call me back. I'm worried sick. Where are you?"

It turned out to be a mid-afternoon teleconference debriefing with Sheriff Brennan that didn't brief anyone of much of anything.

"There's no word from forensics regarding any DNA found on Ally Black's clothing," Lane reported. "The lab is so backed up I don't expect to hear anything about DNA in the cases for six to eight months. Nothing to report on the shoe and tire prints found at Ally's crime scene either."

Lane paused before giving his boss the last bit of bad news. "In addition, ATF hasn't sent the ballistics report about the bullet found in Mandy's body and the one found in Ally's clothing. We still have no clue what kind of gun the killer used."

Frankie reported, "Dr. Caine recently purchased a house in the Cayman Islands."

"No kidding," said the sheriff. "Check to see if he has bank accounts there too."

"There's something else," she began. "At the party, Dr. Caine told me he'd have a baby for us soon."

"That means he'll want the additional fifty thousand. I'll get the marked bills ready."

"He made an odd remark that the child's mother had an uncanny resemblance to me."

"Frankie, it's obvious the guy has it bad for you. He said that to impress you," said Lane.

"I wish I could agree with you but I can't shake the feeling that the remark means something."

Sheriff Brennan didn't have much to add except the media was driving him crazy with their serial killer theories. He said he'd talked to half the residents of the entire county over the past week. The sheriff had done his best to calm them down, but didn't feel he'd made much progress. People were locking their doors and arming themselves. The murders were all people were talking about. The gossip only accelerated the fear that ran rampant throughout the county.

Sheriff Brennan ended the call with, "We need an arrest and fucking soon. Do you both understand me?"

Jennifer was bored. There was only so much cleaning she could do in such a tiny apartment. Nothing on the television was even remotely interesting and she'd finished all her online course assignments. It was turning out to be the longest day ever.

She decided to make tuna salad for her dinner and removed a couple of cans of tuna from a cabinet and two boiled eggs, an onion, sweet pickles, and mayo from the refrigerator. She was chopping the onion when she looked across the room and saw the local paper on an end table. She'd forgotten she'd retrieved it earlier from the front porch. She'd read it while she ate her sandwich.

She spread the salad on two slices of whole wheat bread then set the plate on the bar beside her glass of milk. She grabbed the newspaper and set it next to her food.

She'd finished page one and her sandwich, when her cell phone rang. She reached across the bar for her purse and withdrew her cell.

"Jennifer, this is Dr. Caine. I apologize for disturbing you this evening."

"That's ok. Have you learned anything about Ally Black or David Chambers?"

"Actually, that's why I called. I need to talk to you right away about David Chambers before I go to the police."

"What did you find out?" Her heart skipped a beat. If Dr. Caine was going to the police, he must've discovered David Chambers did something bad to Ally.

"I can't talk over the phone. I need to see you in person at my house tonight."

"Your house? You want me to come to your home?"

"I'm so sorry to ask it, but I'm in the middle of a very important meeting with two adoptive parents. The meeting should end by 8:00 p.m. Can you be here by then?"

A moment of silence passed as Jennifer thought it over. She wasn't comfortable going to his house. But if he had information that would lead to Ally, what choice did she have?

"Hold on for a second so I can get a pen and paper to write down the directions." She slipped an ink pen out of her purse and ripped a section of newspaper to write on. "Go ahead."

The next morning, Paul Vance combed his fingers through his dark hair and thought about taking off his jacket but adjusted his tie instead. It felt like it was ninety degrees in the room. He wiped the sweat from his brow with the back of his hand. Paul was so nervous, he gritted his teeth like he used to when he was a kid in trouble with his mom.

The situation couldn't be more intimidating, especially when his girl's dad was a powerful county sheriff. Here he was sweating it out in the reception area outside the sheriff's office. What if Tim Brennan refused to see him? What if Jennifer had already told him about the pregnancy? What if he was angry? Paul decided he didn't care. He just needed to talk to her. If that meant bearing the wrath of her father, then so be it.

He walked up to the receptionist's desk again.

"Listen, it's been an hour. When will Sheriff Brennan be free to meet with me?" Christ, if he had to spend another hour in this sauna he may have a heat stroke.

"Honey, I told you last time you asked. Sheriff Brennan is on an important conference call."

"Did you tell him my name? Did you tell him Paul Vance was waiting to see him and that I have something important to discuss with him about his daughter?"

"Yes, I did. But if you want me to, I'll slip a note to him to tell him you're still here."

"Yes, please do that."

As he placed the telephone receiver in its cradle, Sheriff Tim Brennan looked up to see his receptionist slide a small white piece of paper across his desk then leave. He read the name Paul Vance and smiled. There was only one reason why his daughter's boyfriend would be here to see him. He was going to ask him for Jennifer's hand in marriage. He was sure of it. It was an old fashioned, traditional thing to do, but he was impressed that the kid would show him this kind of respect. It wasn't that he didn't expect Paul Vance to propose to his daughter. Paul and Jennifer had been together for two years. It was obvious they were crazy in love. He and his wife, just the other night over dinner, had discussed how right they were for each other.

He glanced at his favorite photo of Jennifer on his desk. It was taken the day he'd taught her to drive. She had been sixteen years old and still wearing braces on her teeth. His eyes filled with tears for a second. Where did time go? It seemed like only yesterday, Jennifer was his little girl. Now there was a man in the next room who wanted to marry her. He dialed his receptionist's number.

"Send him in."

Tim met Paul at the door and shook his hand enthusiastically.

"Good to see you, Paul. Have a seat." He motioned for Paul to sit down then he returned to his chair behind his desk.

"Thanks for seeing me, sir," he began. "I know you're a busy man."

"I always have time for you. What's on your mind, son?" A smile threatened to appear at the corners of Tim's mouth.

"I need to see Jennifer."

"What do you mean you need to see Jennifer? I'm confused. You attend the same college with her. Aren't you two still in a relationship?" Tim's investigative antenna went on alert.

"I need to talk to her, sir. If she's here and she's told you she doesn't want to see me, I understand. But I'm not leaving this town until I see her."

"Why do you think Jennifer is here?"

"She has to be here. I've looked for her everywhere. I went to her dorm last night. Her roommate hasn't seen her in weeks. Her closet is empty too." Paul paused and wiped the sweat beading on his brow again. "Christ, I know I fucked up big time. When she told me, I was so shocked I couldn't think. She's got to forgive me for what I said. We can work this out."

"Told you what? Work what out? What did Jennifer tell you?"

"That she's pregnant."

Tim lost it. He rounded his desk knocking files and books from that end onto the floor. He jerked Paul out of his chair, grabbed him by the throat, and slammed him against the wall. He had never experienced such fear and anger. It was combustible mix.

"You son-of-a-bitch. Jennifer is pregnant?!"

"Yes, sir," Paul managed to say.

"What did you do when she told you? Just how did you fuck up?"

"Oh, God. I can't believe what I said to her. Please let me talk to her. I love her more than my life. Please."

Then it hit Tim. Paul said he and the roommate hadn't seen Jennifer for weeks. That made no sense. She lived on campus and so did Paul. She called home every weekend. He loosened his grip on Paul's neck, pulled back, and stared at him. Yes, she called every weekend. Jennifer's pregnant? If that was true, why hadn't she told her mom and dad? He'd talked to her last Saturday. The call came as he and his wife was sitting down for dinner.

"Jennifer isn't here. We haven't seen her in months. She told us she couldn't come home because she was so busy with her classes. But she calls home every weekend."

"I'm telling you, she's gone. Her roommate hasn't seen her in weeks. Her closet is empty. If she's not here then where is she?"

Tim already had his cell phone out, punching Jennifer's number. He listened until finally her voice mail sounded. "Jennifer, this is Dad. Honey, I need for you to call me right away. It's urgent."

Outside on the patio, Lane was turning burgers on the grill when his cell phone rang. He put down the spatula, held the cell phone to his ear, and while listening to the caller went inside. In the kitchen, he disconnected the call.

"Frankie, that was ATF. They've emailed the ballistics report for Mandy Morris. I'm going upstairs for my laptop."

He was already bounding up the stairs, when Frankie called out, "Hey, bring my laptop downstairs with you too. It's on my bed."

Lane retrieved his laptop from his bedroom then he went to Frankie's room where her laptop was open on her bed. He was reaching for it when he heard a ding and an email sprang to life on her screen. He reached out to close the laptop so he could carry it, but a name on the email caught his attention — Dr. Eric Caine. Why was Dr. Caine sending emails to Frankie? Why hadn't she mentioned it? They'd just had a briefing with the sheriff and she hadn't said a word about receiving emails from him.

He took a closer look at the email message. It was from David Chambers to Dr. Caine.

Send me money NOW or you'll regret it.

He read the message again. Then he closed the email and reviewed the received list of emails in the account. Each one was sent to Dr. Eric Caine. A click of the mouse took him to the sent folder where he reviewed a list of emails sent *by* Dr. Caine. He couldn't believe it. Frankie had installed some kind of surveillance on the doctor's computer without telling him. They didn't have a warrant to do this. Furious, he slammed the screen down and carried both laptops to the kitchen where Frankie stood slicing tomatoes.

Tim Brennan had lied to his wife, Megan, and that was something he never did. There were things he didn't tell her, like some of the horrors he'd witnessed as a cop. But he'd never lied to her. He loved her too much.

Megan had walked in their bedroom as he was packing his clothes. He told her he had some emergency police business, he'd be out of town for a few days, and that he'd call her soon. They'd been married for thirty years, so she was used to calls in the middle of the night that took him to crime scenes he'd never tell her about. So, his leaving suddenly for police business was no big deal to her.

He hated the lie, but he told it to protect her. She'd had a heart attack the year before and telling her that their only child was missing might be something her heart couldn't withstand. At any rate, one part of him still had hope this was nothing to worry about and that he'd find Jennifer in Bloomington. When he did, she'd be in the front seat of his car heading for home.

The other part of him, the cop part, knew that time and again when they didn't find the missing person within forty-eight hours, it was likely the person was dead. Jennifer had been missing for weeks from Paul and her college friends. But he had just talked to her five days before. He shook his head in disbelief. She couldn't be dead. That was not an option.

He changed from his sheriff uniform to a gray suit, white starched shirt and navy tie. He didn't want to call attention to himself as he conducted his own search for his daughter.

He heard Megan rattling around in the kitchen. He pulled his suitcase through the hallway into the living room where the photo he'd taken of Jennifer last Christmas was in a frame on the fireplace mantel. It was the most recent picture he had of her. He shoved it, frame and all, under his jacket and headed for his car.

Jennifer pulled her car into Dr. Caine's driveway after he buzzed her in at the security gate. She stopped the car for a moment and looked at his home in awe. It was huge and she'd never seen a more beautiful home all lit up in the night like it was Christmas. She collected her purse, shoved the driving directions in her pocket then got out of her car and headed for the front door.

She'd barely removed her finger from the doorbell button when the doctor opened the door to welcome her. Obviously, he'd been waiting for her arrival. She walked past him into the foyer and scanned her surroundings. Directly in front of her was an elegant spiral staircase leading to the rooms upstairs. To her right was a living room with a white brick fireplace and built-in bookcases filled with classics.

"Your home is amazing," she said, clearly impressed. She looked at the doctor who was smiling now and reaching for her arm.

"Thank you, Jennifer. I'm very proud of my home. Why don't I give you a tour before we talk? I've done some new renovations in the lower level that I'm most excited to have you see."

If her father thought kicking him out of his office was going to stop him from looking for Jennifer, he was wrong.

After waiting in the parking lot for close to an hour, Paul finally spotted Sheriff Brennan heading toward his car in quite a hurry. Staying a couple of cars behind him, Paul followed him to the Brennan home where he'd been a guest many times. He scanned the area looking for Jennifer's car but it wasn't there.

It wasn't long before he saw Tim Brennan dragging a suitcase to a white Honda Accord, where he opened the trunk and threw it inside. He fired up the vehicle and headed down the road, eventually reaching Interstate 65 where he headed south. Paul followed, realizing the man was going to Bloomington. Had he talked to Jennifer? Did he know where she was? If her father did know Jennifer's location, Paul would know it soon, too.

Frankie was finishing a lettuce salad in the kitchen when Lane carried in both laptops. He put his down on one end of the small kitchen table and put hers down at the other. He went outside to check on the burgers on the grill, flipped them over before returning.

Too angry to talk, he clenched his jaw and turned on his laptop then read the email with the ATF report. Mandy Morris was shot with a .38 hollow point bullet with a Ruger, Taurus, or Smith & Wesson.

"Frankie, what kind of guns did you say were registered to either Dr. Caine or David Chambers?"

She wiped her hands on a dishcloth and came to the table to sit down in front of her laptop. "I don't remember, but I'll look it up."

Watching her open the laptop, Lane asked, "Is there anything you want to tell me, Frankie?"

"About what?"

He just glared at her as she looked at her screen and saw the email from David Chambers to Dr. Caine. He knew the exact moment when she realized that he now knew what she'd done. She blinked, her cheeks burned with color, and she cleared her throat.

"I can explain," she began.

"I'm all ears. I want to hear it, every last detail, especially the part about why I knew nothing about any of it."

"Give me a break, Lane. You had to know that I sometimes do things out of the box. Why do you think my private investigation company is doing so well? Sometimes you have to break the rules to get the job done."

"Have you forgotten you're a sworn deputy for this op?"

She didn't answer for a long moment, and then said, "I saw an opportunity to get some information we couldn't have gotten any other way and I went for it."

"Why don't you start your explanation from the beginning? Don't leave anything out." His face colored with anger.

Lane's cell phone rang and he whipped it out of his jeans pocket. He had only said a couple of words when he ended the call and grabbed the keys from the kitchen counter.

"We'll continue this conversation later. The sheriff wants to see us right away. He says it's an emergency."

"Why does he want us to drive all that way back home? Can't he do a conference call?"

"He's at the Courtyard Marriott on College Avenue. He's here."

Frankie knew as soon as they entered her uncle's hotel room that something was very wrong. His face was pale; his muscles looked tense and ready to snap. He also looked like he could drop from exhaustion any second. He motioned for them to sit at a small table in the room then sat down himself. He pressed both hands over his eyes as if they burned with weariness. She looked at the stack of papers on the table and noticed her cousin, Jennifer's photo.

"I need your help," he began. "Jennifer is missing and I need you to find her."

"Missing? What do you mean she's missing?" Frankie struggled to stay calm. Surely she had misheard him.

"Just what I said, she's missing and has been missing for maybe five days or so. Her bastard boyfriend told me earlier today and I didn't want to believe him. So I drove down here. I talked to her roommate and some of her friends. No one's seen her for weeks. "

"How could that happen? Hasn't she been calling home?" she asked wanting to put all the pieces together. She glanced at Lane who was staring at Jennifer's photo lying on the table with an odd look on his face. Surely, he'd seen Jennifer's photos in frames all over her uncle's office.

"We got a call from her every weekend. The last call was five days ago."

A knock at the door startled them. As her uncle moved to answer it, Frankie made a wish it was Jennifer she would see when he opened the door. Instead a tall young man with dark, unruly hair appeared. She recognized him as the man Jennifer often brought to family dinners.

"What in the hell are you doing here? Get out!"

"No, I'm not leaving." Paul Vance met Tim Brennan's glare head-on. "I've been following you all day. Did you find out anything?"

"I said, get out. Do you want me to throw you out?" he seethed with mounting anger.

"No, I'm not leaving. You need me. I know this campus and town much better than you do. I know where Jennifer goes and where she doesn't. I'm staying. I want to find her as much as you do. Let me help."

Frankie went to her uncle and squeezed his arm. "Uncle Tim, let him stay. Maybe he *can* help."

Tim was incredulous. "Help? Do you want to know how much he's helped so far? Jennifer is pregnant with his child. So what does he do when he finds out? He dumps her."

"That's not true. I didn't dump her. I said some things I wish I could take back, but I never stopped loving her. I need to find her as much as you do."

"Get out!"

Paul looked at Tim Brennan then Frankie, and backed toward the open door and into the hallway. "Please call me when you find her. Please."

Tim slammed the door then returned to the table where he sat down in the chair opposite Lane. Frankie watched him gulp the rest of his coffee. She knew how emotions could get in the way of an investigation. Her uncle had to calm down, because this was the most important investigation of their lives.

Jennifer awoke in a strange room. Her mind was fuzzy. She sat up and looked around. The walls of the room were covered by a royal blue foam material that looked like egg cartons. There was a small white sink and toilet in the corner. A white, wooden dresser with four drawers was on the other wall. Other than the twin bed where she sat, those were the only objects in the room. The only light came from a horizontal strip of small basement windows located near the top of the opposite wall.

She remembered now. She was with Dr. Caine. He'd offered a tour of his home but she had asked for a glass of water. He'd returned from the kitchen with a glass of ice water and when she drank it. She remembered an odd bitter taste but she was so thirsty she ignored it. He'd led her through the house and by the time they'd reached the lower level she'd felt so sleepy she could barely stand.

That's when he'd helped her lie down on the twin bed and fled the room, slamming the door behind him.

She looked at the door. It looked thicker than the average bedroom door and had a glass peep hole which she thought was odd. She moved to the door to open it so she could find Dr. Caine, but it wouldn't budge. That's when the terrifying realization hit her. She was locked in.

Dr. Eric Caine pulled his sports car into his garage and pressed the button on his visor to move the garage door down to its closed position. He'd spent the morning making the rounds at the clinic. He yawned and thought a nap sounded like a good idea. It had been a long night — a productive one, but long just the same. He twisted his key in the locked door and entered his house.

He noticed the coffee pot was still on and realized Miriam must have cleaned earlier. He hoped she'd stayed out of the basement but then thought again. Even if she'd cleaned the basement, she wouldn't have heard a sound from Jennifer's room. He'd gone to a lot of trouble and expense to have it sound-proofed.

He poured a mug of black coffee, and then headed for his room upstairs to change clothes. In the hallway, he noticed a light on in his office. That idiot maid was always leaving lights on, even after he'd lectured her.

He entered the room. Startled, he nearly panicked and fled the room. David Chambers was sitting behind his desk.

"What the fuck are you doing here?"

"It was hard to stay away with no money," answered David.

The doctor glared at him and asked, "How did you get into my house? What are you doing in my office?"

"It was easy to get into your house, and you're damn lucky I chose to wait for you in your office."

"What are you talking about?"

David held up a gold lipstick case between his index finger and thumb. "Do you know what this is?"

"Yes, stupid, that's lipstick." The man was a moron, and the quicker he could get him out of his house the better.

David pulled off the top to reveal the flash drive beneath. "Oh, it's more than a lipstick, smart-guy. It's a flash drive that someone used to install surveillance on your computer."

Dr. Caine eased up closer to the desk to look at it. "What does that mean?"

"It means prior to my finding it, someone was reading every email you received, recording every website you visited, and possibly recording every keystroke. Someone went to a lot of trouble to record everything you do and have stored on this computer. Whoever did this have your passwords, screenshots, emails and anything else that might be on your hard drive."

"Oh my God," he gasped as he sat down in one of the leather chairs across the desk from David. "What am I going to do? Who did this?"

"You don't have to do anything. I took care of it. I removed all traces from your hard drive. The issue, and it's a big one, is finding out who did this and what they've done with the information. Who's been in this room?"

"Miriam, my maid, cleans in here once a week. But that twit doesn't have the brain or the know-how to do anything like this."

"Who else? One of your girlfriends?"

"It couldn't be Candace or any of the others. Their time spent in the house is mostly in my bedroom. I doubt if any of them even know how to use a computer. Their interest is my money and what it can do for them."

"So there's no one else who might have come into your office?"

"No, no one," he said as he smoothed back his hair with his hand. "Wait a minute. The night of my dinner party, I found Lane Henderson up here standing against the wall outside my office. I asked him what he was doing and he said he was waiting for his wife who was using the bathroom. I told him that he was standing near the wrong room and led him to the bathroom to wait for her. But when I came out of my bedroom, he was back outside the office door pressing his wife against the wall near my office door kissing her."

"And you didn't think that was odd?"

"Not at the time. I thought maybe she'd come out of the bathroom and the mood had hit him in the hallway and he'd backed her up against the wall to make out. I know I'd do the same thing every chance I got if she was mine."

"I think it'd be a good idea if I kept an eye on them —
especially her, due to the fact a lipstick container was used
to hide the flash drive. A man wouldn't do that."

Dr. Caine sat silent for a moment thinking about
Frankie Douglas and how much he wanted her. He didn't
want this sick freak to be anywhere near her. But then he
thought about the amount of potentially damaging
information on his computer. He'd be put away for a long,
long time.

"Do it."

CHAPTER NINE

"Just sit down, you have to have food. Besides, we can talk more about the case." Frankie had nagged her uncle until he agreed to go out with them for pizza. The Italian spices in the air had Frankie practically drooling. Lane held her chair out for her, and then sat down himself.

The waiter took their order for a large pepperoni and mushroom pizza with extra cheese and three cold Heinekens. They waited to talk until they were sure the waiter was out of earshot. Tim Brennan spoke first.

"Frankie, you can't breathe a word of this to your mother or anyone else in the family. We can't let your Aunt Megan find out about this yet. I don't know if her heart can take it."

Frankie watched him as he scrubbed his face with his hands. She knew he was struggling for control. The more calm he remained, the better for him think clearly and the better their chances of finding Jennifer.

Frankie simply nodded and looked down at her hands. They had to find Jennifer and take her home. They had to. She was still trying to wrap her mind around Jennifer's pregnancy. She hadn't realized how much she still thought of Jennifer as the child she used to carry around on her back. Now a baby was growing inside her — a baby that belonged to Paul Vance.

"What about Paul?" she asked. "Do you think he had anything to do with her disappearance?"

"Hell, yes, I do. You know as well as I do how these cases go. Isn't it usually the boyfriend or the husband who plays the major role in a woman's disappearance?"

He looked at Lane. "I want you to do a background check on Paul Vance. I want you to question him, then talk to his friends, neighbors, guys on the football team, and anyone else you can think of. I want his whereabouts for the last five days. I also want to know what he's told them about Jennifer and their relationship."

"Yes, sir," Lane said.

"Tomorrow I'll file the missing person report at the police station here in Bloomington."

"Why here? Why can't you process it back home?" asked Frankie.

"She was discovered missing in Bloomington, so here is where I have to file it."

He reached in the manila file he brought in with him and pulled out two slips of paper. He handed one to each of them. "Here is a photocopy of Jennifer's most recent picture. She drives a blue 2010 Honda Civic. I've listed her license number at the bottom of the page. If you need anything else, call me at the hotel."

"Are you going to release it to the media?" asked Lane.

"No, not yet. Let's see what our search efforts uncover. I hope there won't be a need for that. I still hope we find her." He paused as the waiter set a bottle of beer in front of each of them along with plates and silverware. "We'll follow our usual process for a missing person. I'll apply for a warrant for her cell phone call as well as cell tower history tomorrow."

Frankie looked down at her hands again. It would take too long for the warrant and time was of the essence. She and her partner, Ted had contacts at the cell phone company who would get her the information with a moment's notice. Every second counted. For every day Jennifer remained missing, the likelihood of finding her alive diminished.

"I want to go back and talk to her roommate again tomorrow. I want to look around her room to see if I can find anything that might help us find her. Frankie, I want you to check her bank account, both credit and debit activity."

She nodded as Tim scratched notes on the manila file. "After I do that, I'll do an Internet search and social media sites like Facebook and Twitter to see if and when she's visited and what she's communicated. I'll also be able to determine her circle of friends from these sites." Frankie made a mental note to also check the hospitals and mortuaries. It was something she didn't want her uncle to even have to think about.

"Lane, I'd like you to check the apartment and house rental agencies. There's a chance she moved to get away from Paul," said Tim. "I also want you to check for surveillance cameras on campus, especially near her dorm. I'll ask her friends where she liked to go and I'll email those locations to you tomorrow."

The pizza arrived and the three ate their meal in silence. Frankie wondered what the next day would bring.

They were ready to leave when Tim asked Lane to get the car. As soon as Lane left, he leaned in close to Frankie and whispered, "Remember all those times I told you to play by the rules? Well, forget I said that. I know your private investigative equipment is state of the art. Use anything you can think of to bring Jennifer home. Do you understand what I'm saying? Go as far out of the box as you need to. Just find her."

"So where's Jennifer Brennan?" David stretched his arms then folded them behind his head as he rocked in the desk chair in the doctor's home office. Dr. Caine sat behind the desk scrolling through his email messages.

"Not your concern, David." He glowered at him then went back to his computer screen.

"You're way out of your league here, doc. You don't know the first thing about getting rid of a problem."

"Look who's talking. Like you did such a bang-up job with the first two problems. You freaking idiot." Dr. Caine's accusing voice stabbed the air.

"Don't call me names," David said. "Where is she?"

"None of your business."

"Do you really think you're so clever that I don't know that she's in your basement in your new locked room?"

"Stay away from her. She's worth $100,000 to us if we wait until she gives birth. After that, you can do whatever you want. Just don't get caught." Dr. Caine glared at David Chambers. He was a loose cannon who would bring them both down if something wasn't done about him.

"Speaking of getting caught, where is her car, smart-guy? Did she have a cell phone? If so, where is it? The first thing the cops will do is look for her car and get her cell phone information. Hell, they can track her right to your front door with her cell tower history."

"Then they'll track her to the bottom of Monroe Lake."

"Are you kidding me? Did anyone see you?"

"Not a chance."

They'd dropped off Tim at the hotel and Frankie had moved back to the passenger seat when Lane said, "Frankie, I'm going to take you home, and then I have to run an errand."

"What errand?" she asked. He hesitated just long enough she knew he was about to lie.

"We need some groceries."

"What kind of groceries?"

"We need milk. We're almost out."

"No we're not. I just bought two gallons. What are you up to, Lane?"

He sighed with frustration and pulled into a shopping plaza and parked the car. He looked at Frankie for a long moment.

"Sweetheart, how close are you to Jennifer?"

"She's my cousin, but I think of her as my baby sister. We spent a lot of time together growing up because I babysat her. How could this have happened?" Tears streamed freely down her cheeks.

Lane put his arm around her. "You're too close to this, Frankie. So is your uncle. That's why I'm taking you home. There's something I need to do alone."

She twisted in her seat, surprised. "You know something, don't you? I thought you were acting odd back at the hotel room. What is it? Where are you going?"

"You're too emotionally involved right now. Trust me to do what I have to do."

"I thought you said partners weren't supposed to have secrets."

"That's a good one coming from you. Do you really want to have that conversation we started back at the house now? You know the one, where you were about to tell me about the surveillance you installed on Dr. Caine's computer. Now *that* was a secret."

She met his icy glare head-on. "We can discuss that later. For now, I'm going with you."

"No, you're not."

Frankie showed no signs of relenting. "Yes, I am. There is no way I'm getting out of this car unless you take me with you."

"Damn it, Frankie." He backed the car out of the parking space and back onto the road. "Just keep your hot temper in check."

The street was lined with cars but Lane finally found a space to park the car in front of an apartment building. Frankie watched him as he scanned the row of parked cars along the street. He acted as if he were looking for particular car that wasn't there. He led her to an outside staircase. Once up the stairs to the second floor, she followed him until he stopped in front of an apartment door and knocked. No one came to the door. He looked up and down the hallway before glancing over the railing to the first floor.

"Where are we? What are you doing?" she whispered.

Lane shushed her and pulled a credit card out of his wallet. He slid it against the inside of the doorframe and the door opened. Pulling her inside, he shut the door and turned on a small lamp.

"I don't believe what you just did. Talk about not following the rules."

"Not now."

Curious she watched him move around the room lifting sofa cushions, fanning magazines and thumbing through what looked like textbooks. "Lane, now would be a good time to tell me where we are and why."

He took her by the hand and led her to the sofa. He sat down beside her. "Will you promise me you'll stay calm and professional?"

"Yes, I promise."

"This is Ally Black's apartment. She shared it with a roommate. When I came here the other day, I bumped into a pregnant girl on the stairs who appeared to be in a hurry. One of the neighbors said the girl was Ally's roommate and she left in a blue Honda Civic like your uncle said Jennifer drives. The girl looked like Jennifer. I've never met her so I can't be sure. I thought I might find something here that identifies Jennifer as the woman living here with Ally."

"But you said Ally Black lived in the apartments where all the other pregnant girls live who are giving their babies up for adoptions — the apartment house that Dr. Caine owns." Then it hit her. Jennifer is pregnant. If she lives here, she must be involved with the adoption agency. No, she can't be thinking of giving her baby to him. "Lane, if it's Jennifer who lives here and has done something to cross Dr. Caine, he or David Chambers will kill her."

"We don't know for sure Jennifer lives here. Help me find something that we know belongs to her."

Frankie jumped to her feet. "I'll take her bedroom."

"Down the hall. It's the first room on the right."

Frankie entered her room and turned on a small lamp near the bed. She opened the first drawer of the dresser. It was filled with bikini panties and bras. The next drawer contained folded sweaters and shirts. There was nothing but clothing in the remaining drawers. Frankie hadn't seen Jennifer for months. She wouldn't be able to identify her clothing, especially since she probably was wearing maternity clothes.

She slid the closet door open and peered inside. The closet was filled with not only pregnancy clothing but regular clothes too. She spied something on the closet floor that made a chill slide up her spine. She lifted a pink leather jewelry case and carried it to the bed where she held it on her lap. She ran her hand over the top where there was scrollwork on the leather in gold. What were the chances this belonged to someone else? On Christmas day when she was sixteen, her grandmother had given as gifts a pink leather jewelry case to each of her granddaughters, including Jennifer. It was identical to this one. She slowly pushed open the lid. Inside a tiny plastic ballerina sprang to life and twirled as the song played. Lying on the top shelf was an engraved silver bracelet that bore Jennifer's name. Frankie had a matching bracelet.

With a heavy heart she carried the case to the kitchen where she found Lane. "Jennifer Brennan lives here."

For the fifth time, Jennifer jumped as high as she could but she could not reach the basement windows in her room. The glass was frosted with a swirly design that kept her from seeing the outside. If only she could find something to stand on. She looked at the bed and realized it was bolted to the floor.

Why on earth had Dr. Caine done this? How could she have so badly misjudged the man? And why in the hell was he keeping her captive? It made no sense. She hadn't done anything to him except tell him that one of his employees may have harmed his patient. Why wouldn't he want to know?

She sat back down on the bed. Maybe that was a very stupid question. Could he *and* David have done something to Ally Black? She leaned back on her pillow as she considered the question and heard a crackle as she moved. She patted her jean pocket then pulled out the piece of newspaper on which she'd written the directions to the doctor's house. She opened the paper to the directions. Then she turned it over. In the center of the piece of paper was a photograph of Ally Black. Under the photo were the words "Girl's Body Found in Woods".

Lane found Jennifer's laptop under a pile of books on a chair in the living room. He put it on the kitchen counter next to the jewelry case Frankie found. After they scoured Jennifer's apartment looking for clues for another hour, they drove home. Lane glanced at Frankie who sat frozen staring out the windshield. She was holding the jewelry case. They were almost home and she hadn't said a word the entire drive.

"You better not be thinking what I think you're thinking." He worried that Frankie's out-of-the-box ideas and attitude would one day get her into trouble.

"And what's that?"

He glanced at her, and said, "That you want to kick Eric Caine's ass and search his house looking for Jennifer."

"What's wrong with that idea?"

"For one thing it would land us both in jail."

"I can see why it would land *me* in jail, but why you?"

"Because if he laid a hand on you, I'd have to rip his head off."

"Well, don't call a bail bondsman. I don't plan on doing anything tonight that will land us in jail. I'm going to concentrate on what I do best."

"Really?" Lane asked as he ran his hand up her thigh.

"I don't mean *that*." She playfully slapped his arm. "I'm going to make some calls, pull some strings and then do some Internet research. I'll find Jennifer. I have to."

"Sounds like a plan. I can't check apartment and house rental agencies or check on campus surveillance cameras until morning, so I'll help."

"Actually, Lane, there is a little something I'd like you to do."

"Oh, yeah?"

"Would you bake some of those insanely good chocolate chunk cookies? All this stress has me craving them."

Jennifer heard a knock on the door; then someone slid a tray of food in the room through a small slot at the bottom of the door. Next came a bottle of water and a bottle of prenatal vitamins. She just stared at the food. Did he actually expect her to have an appetite?

She gazed at the basement windows. There had to be a way for her to reach them and escape.

David Chambers killed Ally Black with Dr. Caine's approval. She knew it. It was no accident that Dr. Caine imprisoned her shortly after she asked him to talk to the police. What a fool she'd been. She'd actually asked him to go to the police about a crime she was sure he helped commit. Why kill Ally? Was it the money he'd have to return to the adoptive parents if she backed out of the adoption? Was it so much money that he felt he had to take a life to prevent losing it?

What a horrible mess she was in, and she could see no way out of it. It was useless, but she thought about how things could have turned out so differently if Paul had really loved her. She replayed in her head the last night she'd seen him. Only this time when Paul heard about the baby, he cried out with joy. He threw his arms around her and said they'd have to look for a new place that was big enough for the three of them.

But that certainly was only a fantasy and not the reality. Paul had accused her of getting pregnant to trap him and then wanted her to kill their baby. Now that version of the story had no happy ending. Biting her lip, she cried as tears streamed down her cheeks and neck until she fell asleep.

Lane and Frankie sat behind their laptops, facing each other at the kitchen table.

"We can't review her banking documents until tomorrow, so I'll see if she's visited any of the social networks," said Lane.

"While you do that, I'll make a call outside on the patio."

He watched her pace back and forth on the patio through the window. He knew she was calling one of her contacts to get Jennifer's cell phone records. Did she really think he didn't know? He'd seen her face when Tim mentioned he was applying for a warrant.

He went back to his laptop and Googled Jennifer's name. He got hits on both Facebook and Twitter. On her Facebook page, the photo of Jennifer's smiling face haunted him. She looked incredibly happy. He went into her photo albums and discovered many of the photos included Jennifer and Paul Vance at various campus activities. There was one that looked like it was taken after a football game, with Paul still in his uniform, hugging Jennifer and laughing.

He was eager to question Paul. He wasn't as certain as his boss that Paul was involved with her disappearance. The guy looked frantic at the hotel earlier. He clearly wanted to find her.

Frankie slid open the glass door and came in from the patio. "Those cookies smell amazing."

"What did you find out? Spill it."

"My contact needs some time to get the call record and tower history. It shouldn't be long. Ted is calling his bank contact to get Jennifer's debit and credit records. How about you?"

"I'm on Jennifer's Facebook page and it looks to me like she and Paul Vance were crazy about each other. I'm not convinced he was involved. She hasn't communicated on Facebook since last month."

The oven timer went off and Lane pulled out the baking tray of cookies. He laid it on top of the stove and pulled a couple of dessert plates from the cabinet along with two glasses. He filled the glasses with milk from the refrigerator and used a spatula to place two warm cookies on each plate.

"I'd appreciate it if you didn't tell anyone that I was baking cookies in the middle of two murder investigations and a missing person case. I don't want to think about the ribbing I'd get, along with the blow to my reputation."

"My lips are sealed." She smiled at him as he pushed the plate of cookies and glass of milk in front of her. "At the moment, I'm thinking you're pretty darn amazing."

David Chambers sat in the Lincoln Town Car on the street where Frankie and Lane were living. He'd been watching their house for hours but no activity. Earlier, he'd crept around the house through the side yard and watched Frankie talking on her cell phone on the patio. He couldn't hear what she was saying but couldn't move any closer for fear of being discovered.

He'd noticed her early on and had decided he disliked her. She seemed like one of those women who thought she had the world by the balls with her hot body and good looks. Those were the type of women he liked the least. His wife was like that before he'd broken her in. All it took was a couple of beatings and the promise there'd be more. Then when the kids arrived, it was even easier to control her. All he had to do was threaten to beat one of them and his wish was her command.

He still couldn't believe she'd left him and taken his
kids. He'd look for her when things calmed down and
when he found her, she'd regret it. And heaven help them,
if he discovered anyone had helped her escape. They'd
pay big time.

But for now, he focused on Frankie Henderson. He
watched as one by one the lower lights went out in the
house. Then a light appeared in what was probably a
bedroom upstairs. He turned the ignition key, started the
car's motor, and eased down the road. Tomorrow was
another day. And if he discovered Frankie Henderson had
planted that computer surveillance software and knew
more than she should, it would be her last day.

Frankie awoke to sound of a cell phone and
instinctively patted the bedside table next to her for it. She
picked it up to look at the display. No call. She glanced at
the clock. Only six in the morning.

She pushed herself into a sitting position and
answered. "Hello?"

"Frankie, it's Ted. Sorry about the hour. I just heard
from my contact at the bank. It seems Jennifer used her
debit card two days ago. She bought some things at a
Target store and she got gas at a 7-Eleven on West 11th
Street. Those are the last times she's used her debit card.
She hasn't used her credit card at all. Do you want me to
come down there and get their surveillance tapes from
these stores?

"No, but thanks for the offer. Lane is tracking down
surveillance cameras and tapes today. I'll add these stores
to his list."

She ended the call and set the cell phone back on the table. She turned to look at Lane who was now yawning and stretching beside her.

"I heard. I'll visit Target and 7-Eleven this morning too. I don't think I can go back to sleep. I'm going downstairs to make coffee."

"I'm coming with you." She threw on her robe and followed Lane down the stairs. It was still dark out but she was wide awake. She'd gotten little sleep, tossing and turning all night as one nightmare about Jennifer after the other spun its web in her mind.

Once in the kitchen, Frankie pulled out the coffee canister and handed it to Lane who was washing the filter in the sink. She found a carton of blueberry muffins and brought them to the kitchen table. As she fired up her computer, she suddenly remembered they had Jennifer's laptop in their possession.

"Lane, where's Jennifer's laptop?"

He looked at her for a long moment. "Crap, I think I left it in the back seat of the car."

Frankie ran to the car and opened the back door. There was Jennifer's small black laptop on the seat. Pulling it out of the car, she tucked it under her arm and raced back into the house. She moved her own laptop to the kitchen counter and put Jennifer's in its place on the table. The first thing that appeared on Jennifer's laptop screen was a photo screensaver featuring Jennifer and Paul. She still loved him, Frankie thought. If a man had wronged her, a photo screensaver highlighting the two of them would be one of the first things to go. Why torture yourself like that?

Frankie accepted a hot mug of coffee from Lane as she surfed to Jennifer's Internet history. On the Google website, Jennifer had visited a couple of times using "Ally Black" as a search term. Checking the dates of the visits, she discovered each search occurred on the days immediately following the projected date of Ally's death. She was living with Ally. Of course, she'd be suspicious when Ally had her baby then never returned to the apartment. What worried Frankie was who Jennifer shared these suspicions with. Sharing them with the wrong person would land her in a lot of trouble. The kind of trouble that ends lives.

In addition to this search were some Internet searches for information on the stages of pregnancy as well as one using the search term "giving up baby". Was Jennifer having second thoughts? There was another search that caught Jennifer's attention. It was to the Indiana University Health contact information web page. Why did Jennifer need this information? Is this where Ally Black gave birth? Did Jennifer visit there? She intended to find out.

In Jennifer's email account, there were weekly emails to her mother that discussed her classes, the weather and family stuff. She frequently told her mother how much she missed her but term papers and course assignment prevented her from coming home.

Why on earth didn't Jennifer tell her parents about her pregnancy? Both her father and mother adored her. Did she think they wouldn't support her? Was she ashamed she'd gotten pregnant? What was she thinking?

She looked up as Lane walked into the room. She'd been so focused she hadn't even noticed he left. He was dressed in a gray suit and tie with a white shirt. He had his gun plastered to one hip; on the other was his badge. He looked all business, but handsome and sexy. Every time he got near her, she felt this buzz of sexual awareness.

"I'm going to the 7-Eleven and Target stores first since they're the most recent and may be the last sighting of Jennifer in a public place. After that, I'll check the hospitals and mortuaries." He pulled his travel mug out of the dishwasher and filled it with black coffee. Frankie rose from her chair and pulled him into a hug.

"Please get information that helps us find her."

"I'll do my best. Are you going to tell your uncle about where Jennifer was living and its connection to Forever Home Adoption Agency, or do you want me to do it?"

She thought for a moment, and then decided. "It's better he hears it from me, Lane. I'll talk to him this morning."

"One more thing, stay out of trouble, Frankie. Don't do anything stupid."

"I won't."

David Chambers, parked under a shade tree, watched Frankie Henderson as she backed her red Mazda Miata out of her garage. She was on the move. He followed her, staying back a safe distance so she wouldn't notice him. He watched as she pulled into the parking lot of the Courtyard by Marriott. She looked like she was in a hurry, her long ponytail bobbing back and forth as she dashed into the building. He didn't try to follow her inside. He backed into a parking space and watched the front of the building.

What was Frankie Henderson doing at a hotel in the middle of the morning? He wondered if she had a lover. He wouldn't doubt it. Women couldn't be trusted. That's why he kept his on a short leash. He thought of how the doc had talked about her. It was sickening to hear him talking like a schoolboy with a crush. He took a swig of his soda and looked around. Nothing much going on here except students cutting through the parking lot on their way to classes. A couple of retirees were at their car filling their trunk with their suitcases. He settled back in his seat to get comfortable. This could be a long wait.

Her uncle answered the door of his hotel room after just a couple of knocks. Tim let Frankie in then gave her a hug. It had been a rough morning so far. Reporting Jennifer missing at the police station then filing for a warrant to get her cell phone call and cell tower history made everything become reality. He would have never predicted this kind of thing would happen to him. Disappearances happened to other parents.

"After I filled the missing person report and a request for a warrant for her cell phone information, I visited Jennifer's dorm roommate, Tobi, again."

"Did you get any useful information?"

"Naw. I don't think she had a clue that Jennifer was pregnant. She told me that she thought Jennifer was gaining weight because she was stressed about something.

Guess she didn't recognize a baby bump when she saw one. She showed me Jennifer's closet and it was empty like Paul Vance said. She didn't have much to say about him either. The visit was a dead end."

Rays of sun streamed across them as they sat at the small round table near the window. What she was about to tell her uncle was one of the most difficult things she had ever had to say. But there was no getting around it. He had to know.

"Uncle Tim, we found where Jennifer was living."

"You did!"

A spark of hope came to her uncle's eyes that made her wish what she had to say was better news. "Lane had a hunch last night. You see, Ally Black had a roommate. It was Jennifer. We searched the apartment and I found the pink leather jewelry case Grandma got her that Christmas when she bought all her granddaughters the same gift. We also found her laptop."

"Why would she be rooming with Ally Black?"

"Well, the apartment is in a building owned by the Forever Home Adoption Agency run by Eric Caine."

"She was going to give the baby away? She was going to give away our grandchild?"

"We don't know that for sure."

"She's involved with Dr. Caine, isn't she? That and she roomed with one of the murdered girls?"

"Yes." She nodded.

"That son-of-a-bitch. I'll kill him if he's hurt her. I'll kill him."

"Uncle Tim, you can't talk like that. You're a county sheriff. Please."

Frankie's cell phone rang and she jerked it out of her purse. She walked into the hall to take the call and returned a few minutes later.

"That was my contact. She doesn't have Jennifer's call history yet, but she has the cell tower history. Jennifer's cell phone pinged for the last time near Monroe Lake. Do you know where that is?"

"Hell, yes. Jennifer, your aunt and I used to rent a cabin and come up here almost every summer to Monroe Lake. There are cabins all around the water. Jennifer is very familiar with that area. That's it! Maybe Jennifer rented a cabin to get away from it all. Living with a roommate who never came back from the hospital may have spooked her and she went to the lake." He pulled his suit jacket out of his closet and put it on. "I'm going back to the police station and talk to the chief. We need to start searching those cabins."

Lane took a deep breath and counted to ten. He needed to calm down before he punched the skinny, pimpled-face 7-Eleven clerk standing in front of him in the nose. Lane had waited patiently for the clerk to take care of a long line of customers before he asked him for the manager, who, he was told, was taking a vacation day. Then he showed the clerk his badge and asked to see the store's surveillance tapes for Sunday, the day Jennifer pumped gas.

"Well, that could be a problem," explained the clerk in a tone Lane classified as smartass. "For one thing, I'm too busy to help you with the tapes."

"I don't need your help. This is not my first time with surveillance tapes. I can see you're busy. I won't bother you."

"Well, there's another thing."

"Yeah, what's that?"

"We re-use the tapes so the one from Sunday is long gone. We've taped over it."

Lane marched to his SUV, got in, fastened his seat belt and headed to Target. Once he reached the store, he asked for the manager who approached him a short-time later dressed in a Target's signature red shirt.

"I'm looking for a missing person who was in your store last Sunday. I need to see your surveillance tapes from that day."

She nodded and led him behind the counter and up a narrow staircase to an office upstairs with one-way glass lining one wall that enabled their security officers to watch shoppers. The security officer at the desk across from him heard about his request from the manager and asked to see his badge, which Lane obliged.

"Sure, I have Sunday's taping." He pointed to an empty desk on which sat a computer monitor and hard drive. "Sit here and I'll set you up so you can see it."

Within fifteen minutes, Lane spotted Jennifer in the parking lot on the surveillance taping. Wearing a loose white blouse and a pair of jeans, she pushed a cart filled with bags toward her blue Honda Civic. Jennifer was alone. She placed the bags in the trunk of her car, returned the cart, and then drove off. There was nothing suspicious to note. Whatever had happened to Jennifer had not happened at the Target store.

David Chambers watched Frankie exit the hotel with an older guy wearing a suit. Once they reached the parking lot, they exchanged a few words, hugged, then headed toward their separate cars. He didn't know what their relationship was, but it didn't look like they were lovers. David switched on the ignition to start his car then followed Frankie as she left the parking lot heading west on Third Street. He let a farmer with a pickup truck filled with hay pass him, to ensure Frankie would not notice his car. She appeared to be talking on her cell phone. He continued to follow her until a short time later she reached her destination, Indiana University Health. His brows drew together in a suspicious expression. What the hell was Frankie Henderson doing here?

David waited until she entered the hospital then he emerged from his car and sprinted toward the door. He reached the lobby just as Frankie entered an elevator. He stood in the hall and waited until the elevator stopped on the third floor.

Frankie pulled out the photocopy of Jennifer's picture and showed it to a nurse at the nurses' station.

"Have you seen this young woman?"

"I don't recall seeing her."

Another nurse, returning from break, pushed her purse in a drawer and looked at the photo Frankie held out to her.

"Yeah, I remember her. She was in here about a week ago. She was looking for Carole and I think she talked to her, too."

"Who's Carole?" asked Frankie.

"She's one of our clinical assistants. I think she's at work today. Do you want to talk to her?"

"Yes, I'd love to talk to her."

Frankie leaned against the counter as the nurse buzzed Carole to come to the nurse's station. David took a nearby seat in the waiting room. He reached for a magazine that he pretended to read and deliberately let his hair fall in his face. The place was crazy busy and he took the last chair available. It was perfect for watching and listening to Frankie Henderson.

Carole appeared and Frankie showed her the photo of Jennifer.

"Yes, I talked to her last week. I remember her, so pretty with her long blonde hair. In fact she looked a lot like you."

"She's my cousin. Her name is Jennifer," Frankie explained.

"She asked me about a patient who'd had a baby recently. It seems this girl was worried because the patient was her roommate and she never came home. I told her not to worry because Ally Black left the hospital with her father. But she didn't believe me. She said that Ally Black didn't have a father. She came back a couple days later with a sketch she'd drawn and it was the splitting image of the father. She asked me to identify the sketch as the father and I did. It was him, clear as day."

David's expression darkened as he listened to the women talk. He held the magazine up higher to shield his face. When the conversation ended, he waited until Frankie boarded the elevator, then he headed for the stairs.

So the blonde bitch was Jennifer Brennan's cousin. He wondered if she knew how important the information she'd just received was. She was smart. She'd figure it out. But not before he got to her.

As for Carole, the Clinical Assistant, he'd get her, too. It was probably his likeness in the sketch. The woman had been in the room when he left with Ally that day. That made her a liability. But her time would have to wait. Frankie Henderson had just gone to the top of his hit list.

Frankie walked outside, slipping on her sunglasses to protect her eyes form the mid-day sun. She thought about the conversation she'd just had with Carole. Jennifer knew that Ally Black had not left the hospital with her father. But she had a good idea who Ally left with and she'd created a sketch of the man. Therefore, it was a man that Jennifer had seen or had known. Was it Dr. Caine?

Christ, Jennifer was in so much danger. She had to find her and fast. She drove the Miata out of the parking lot to head for home so she could do more research on her laptop. She wanted to get Jennifer's cell phone call history too. It could explain a lot. She prayed Lane was home so they could discuss what she'd just learned.

Frankie looked down at the speedometer. She was speeding, so lost in her thoughts she didn't realize it. Slowing down, she entered a paved stretch of rural road that led to their house. She pulled her cell phone out of her purse and called Lane.

"Hey, Frankie, I was just about to call you to see where you were. I'm fixing a late lunch."

"I'm on my way there. I just passed the Johnson farm. What's for lunch?" Suddenly she noticed a large black car appear in her rearview mirror. He was coming too fast. He was right on her bumper now. Crash! He hit her car with his. The jolt threw her against the steering wheel then back, punching the air out of her lungs.

"What was that noise? Frankie! Answer me."

"A car just hit me. He backed off, but here he comes again!" This time the impact caused her small car to spin like a top in the middle of the road. She screamed. She gripped the steering wheel and struggled for control of the car to no avail. When the spinning stopped, the car flipped once, landing upside down in the ditch. The black car sped away.

"Frankie! Frankie!" He screamed in the phone before the cell lost connection. He grabbed his keys and raced to his car.

Frankie hung by the seatbelt upside down like a bat. She pushed at the airbag that was suffocating her. If she could only get it out of the way. Something wet was on her face so she used the back of her hand to wipe it off. There was blood on her hand.

She had to get out of the car. She smelled the burning rubber of the tires. There was a good chance that gas and other automotive fluids were leaking onto hot surfaces like the exhaust pipe and the car could explode. In addition, this was no accident and the driver of the black car could return to finish the job.

Frankie braced one hand against the ceiling of the car, the other struggled with the clasp of the seatbelt. She pulled at the clasp so hard all four fingernails broke in unison. Struggling with it one more time, the metal clasp released and freed her. She flexed her body until she rolled right side up on the passenger seat ceiling. Frankie felt around until she located her purse and pulled it to her. Jerking out her Glock, she then pushed the purse aside. All of the windows were broken. This was a good thing. There was no way she could get the car door open at this angle. Frankie crawled through the window, biting her lip as a sharp shard of glass ripped at her skin beneath her blouse. Once she was out of the car, she struggled to get to her feet but her legs felt like rubber. She lifted her shirt to inspect the damage done to her by the glass. There was a long, jagged cut that ran from her waist to her right breast. It was bleeding but didn't look too deep.

She shoved the Glock in the back of her jeans and wiped the blood out of her eyes. Cursing, she braced herself against the car, trying to get her bearing until she could stand.

She heard the rumbling sound of tires in the distance. There was a car coming. The driver was coming back to finish the job — to kill her. Beside her was a stretch of woods. Across the road there was a cornfield. She chose the woods and climbed out of the ditch and ran until she reached a thicket of tall trees. Frankie stopped for a moment, listening. The car was getting closer. Dodging tall weeds and bushes that scratched at her legs, she raced into the trees. She ran until the pain at her side gnawed at her and her lungs burned like they were on fire. She took shelter behind the thick trunk of an ancient oak tree and willed her breathing to slow. Panic like she'd never known before welled in her throat.

Just as she'd decided she could move on, she heard the crunching of leaves and footsteps. She slid the Glock out from the back of her jeans and gripped it in her right hand. She was terrified but she was also confident. There was a move that she and Ted had practiced many times where they were in a hiding position, then jumped out to reveal themselves to an imaginary pursuer, aimed, and fired.

She froze so she'd make no sounds. The footsteps were getting louder now. He was getting closer, but not close enough for her to make her move. She waited until she thought he was four to five feet away, then she launched herself from behind the tree and took aim. At the last second, she lifted her gun toward the sky as she recognized it was Lane running toward her.

It was Lane. She went limp with relief. He rushed to her and threw his arms around her. It was then that it hit her. She'd almost killed Lane. At four to five feet away, there was little chance she would have miss the shot. Just thinking of it shattered her and she tightened her grip around his waist.

She heard sirens and looked up at Lane.

CHAPTER TEN

"I called the police. They're sending an ambulance, too." Lane pushed her to arm's length so he could get a good look. There were glistening pieces of glass in her hair. A cut was above her right eyebrow and a spreading blood stain ran the length of her white blouse. He lifted the fabric to see the bleeding cut running from her waist to her breast. His expression darkened with unreadable emotions. His jaw visibly tensed. The sirens of the emergency vehicles echoed through the trees.

"Can you walk, Frankie? The ambulance may be here and I want you checked out." He slipped his arm around her waist.

"I can walk, but I'll tell you right now, I'm not going to the hospital."

"Frankie..."

"I mean it. There's no time. The EMTs can check me over if they're quick about it, but there's no time to lose. I have to find Jennifer. I found out something."

He considered the uselessness of arguing with her about it, and then decided to say nothing. If anything was seriously wrong with her, he'd get her to the hospital if he had to carry her kicking and screaming. He held on to her forearm and walked with her out of the woods. He saw the ambulance as soon as he reached the clearing. The EMTs spotted them and ran toward them to help Frankie to the back of the vehicle where they'd already set up a gurney.

Lane watched them as they unbuttoned her blouse and laid it aside as they worked. They cleansed the jagged cut on her midsection and did the same with the cut above her eyebrow. She winced with pain a few times but didn't cry out. She still wore the determined don't-screw-with-me expression she'd had in the woods before.

He walked over to look at the Miata. It was upside down in the ditch surrounded by shards of glass, pieces of metal, and some of the contents from Frankie's purse. The smell of burning rubber from the tires mixed with automotive fluids permeated the air.

A couple of deputies were examining the car and taking notes. He moved to the back of the Miata. The car had hit the Miata with such force that the back end of the car was folded like an accordion. The sides were crumpled when it rolled before landing in the ditch. One of the only things left intact was the roll bar, which probably saved Frankie's life. One of the officers reached in the car and retrieved Frankie's purse. Lane picked up her things from the ground and threw them into her purse.

He overhead the EMTs talking with Frankie so he returned to the back of the ambulance. Frankie was sitting up now. A butterfly bandage covered the cut above her eyebrow and a whole series of them covered the long cut that started from her waist and ended just below her right breast.

One of the EMTs pulled him aside. "Listen, she insists she is not going to the hospital to get a doctor to check her out. We're okay with that, but make sure she rests. If she's too active, those cuts could reopen and then she'll need some stitches."

Right. Make Frankie rest. He had a track record for *not* being able to convince Frankie to do anything she didn't want to do. He glanced at her and she returned his gaze. Her nose was darkening with bruising and the areas under her eyes were swollen. She buttoned up her blouse as she headed toward his SUV. He helped her get into the car then placed her purse on the floor in the back seat. He rounded the vehicle and popped in the driver seat.

"Baby, you've got to rest when we get home."

"Stop babying me and start grilling me with questions."

"What are you talking about?" Lane quirked his eyebrow questioningly.

"You know as well as I do that the best information from a witness comes when the questions are asked immediately after the incident. So start asking me about the car that did this to me.

"Did you see who was behind the wheel?" He hoped she could recognize the driver so he could make him pay.

"No, he had tinted windows, but I could see his shadow and I know it was a male."

"Describe the car."

"It was a big car, as big as some of the used Caddies my dad used to sell at his dealership and it was black."

"What about the front of the car? What do you remember about that?"

She closed her eyes and concentrated. "I remember there was chrome work right in the center, but it didn't extend to the sides. The chrome work was vertical slats inside a frame of chrome that had a kind of semi-circle bottom and a horizontal line of chrome that joined the bottom at the top. It kind of looked like a smile. Does that make sense?"

He nodded and asked, "Do you remember the night you photographed the license plate of the car David Chambers had driven to Dr. Caine's place?"

"Yes."

"Did you see the front of the car that night?"

"No, I was aiming for the back of the car where I knew the license plate would be."

"I'm asking because your description of the size of the car along with the distinctive chrome grill sounds like a Lincoln Town Car. That's the kind of car that David Chambers drives for Dr. Caine."

Frankie paled and Lane felt her fingernails embedded in his forearm. "What?"

"What if one of them followed me to the hospital? What if he overheard the conversation?"

"Baby, I don't know what you're talking about." He pulled her fingers from his arm and held her hand.

"Before the accident that wasn't an *accident*, I was at the hospital where Ally Black had her baby."

"Why were you there?"

"On Jennifer's laptop this morning, I searched her Internet history to see which websites she'd visited. There were a couple of Google searches using "Ally Black" as the search term done within days of when we think Ally disappeared. She was living with Ally at the time. Of course, she'd be concerned when she didn't return home from the hospital."

"Did you find anything else?"

"Yes, I also found a Google search she did for contact information for Indiana University Health. I had a hunch Ally had her baby there so after I met with Uncle Tim, I went to the hospital and talked to a Clinical Assistant named Carole who identified Jennifer's photo. She told me that Jennifer talked to her two times. The first time was the day after Ally Black gave birth. When she was told that Ally left the hospital with her father, Jennifer refused to believe it. She told Carole that neither Ally nor her mother knew who Ally's father was. It seems Jennifer visited this Clinical Assistant again last week. This time she asked Carole if a man she'd sketched was the man who said he was Ally's father. Carole confirmed the sketch was Ally's father."

"So what are you thinking?"

"I think the man in the sketch was someone Jennifer knew. I think it was Dr. Caine or David Chambers. If Jennifer shared her suspicions that either of them was involved with Ally's disappearance or murder and it got back to either man, then she's in more danger than I thought."

"If the car that hit you was a Lincoln Town Car driven by Dr. Caine or David Chambers, then you're in danger, too, Frankie."

It was seven freaking o'clock before Sheriff Tim Brennan could inspire the city police chief to get a search party out to Monroe Lake. He was frustrated and pissed. Tim bet if it was the police chief's daughter who was missing, he'd move his ass faster.

Tim sat in his car and watched a uniformed deputy go house-to-house, showing occupants a picture of Jennifer. He still couldn't fully grasp that his daughter was missing. Yes, he'd been worried about her living on campus a couple of hours away from home. But never in his worst nightmare would he have thought she'd become a missing person.

His attention went back to the deputy who was to be in a lengthy conversation with the home owner. At first, he thought there might be some information the deputy was gleaning about Jennifer. But then he heard laughter and realized they were not talking about his missing daughter.

Furious, he got out of the car and slammed the door so hard he was surprised the window glass didn't break. He pulled Jennifer's photo and his badge out of his pocket and started the process of going house-to-house on the opposite side of the road. At the fifth house he visited, no one was home. The house had a wide view of Monroe Lake. He walked through the backyard of the house to a wooden boat ramp. Standing on the ramp, he looked across the glistening lake and thought. If this were a missing person in his county and the last ping on the cell tower was near a lake, one of his first orders would be to get scuba divers into the lake. He jerked his cell phone out of his pocket to call his county scuba diving team leader, Blake Stone. Fuck protocol. He didn't care whose jurisdiction it was. He was going to find his daughter. If there was something in that lake that would lead him to Jennifer, he had to find it. He prayed to God it wouldn't be her body.

David Chambers sat in the shade of a huge oak tree in the black Lincoln Town Car, five houses up from where Lane and Frankie lived. He'd been there at least an hour and was getting more tense by the minute. He'd checked the front of the car and the damage wasn't as bad as he thought it would be considering what he'd done. To the average person, it looked like he'd been in a fender-bender. No big deal.

That bitch, Frankie Henderson, had to be dead. Hell, her car spun three or four times before it flipped. Being hit like he rammed her in a tiny car with a convertible top like that, there was little chance she made it out alive. But he had to make sure. That's why he was watching the house.

He drummed his fingers on the steering wheel. He hadn't told Dr. Caine about what he'd overheard in the hospital nor had he told him about ramming Frankie's car. The wimp-ass doctor would probably tell him not to hurt his precious Frankie Henderson. Like he'd listen to that advice, especially after he'd overheard that Frankie was related to Jennifer Brennan. Shit. And now she also knew that Jennifer suspected the man Ally Black left with was not her father. What was the deal about the sketch? Whose likeness did she sketch? He was willing to bet it was him.

It was highly unlikely Frankie and Lane Henderson had come to the Forever Home Adoption Agency by chance. Hell, the likelihood of it being a coincidence was as likely as him becoming the next pope. That bitch, Frankie was looking for her cousin, Jennifer Brennan.

A car appeared down the street moving in his direction. It was a black Cadillac Escalade like the one he knew Lane Henderson drove. The SUV drew closer then turned into the Henderson's driveway. David eased the car up the road closer to the house so he could see better. Lane got out of the driver's side, walked around the vehicle, and opened the passenger door to help Frankie Henderson out of the car. Damn! He slammed his hands down on the steering wheel. How the hell did she survive?! Now what was he going to do? He had to get rid of the bitch before his world exploded around him. He'd find a way, too. Nothing stood in his way in the past when he needed to take care of a problem and nothing would this time. She'd better enjoy her final hours alive because if he had anything to do with it, they'd be her last.

Lane led Frankie upstairs, his large hand protectively rested against the small of her back. But instead of heading toward his room where he wanted her to take a nap, she headed for the shower in her suite.

"Frankie, are you sure a shower is a good idea?"

"I feel disgusting. I'm sweaty and dirtier than I want to think about. I'm taking a shower." Lane stood in her bathroom as she tore off her bloodstained white blouse and pitched it toward a waste basket. She pulled off her jeans and threw them in the laundry basket. Wearing only her bra and panties, she put her hands on her hips and said, "Are you just going to stand there and watch or can you give me some privacy? I know I must look like crap."

"Baby, you look beautiful to me no matter what."

"That's sweet of you to say, but I would really like to be alone for a while."

Making no move to leave, Lane turned on the shower and watched as steam filled the room. He looked down at the butterfly bandages that ran up her mid-section. "I forgot about these bandages. They're going to get wet. "I'll go downstairs and look in the first aid kit," said Lane as he slowly closed the door. He was worried about her, and hesitant to leave her in the shower alone. He raced down the stairs taking the steps two at a time. He went into the kitchen where he kept the first aid kit. He grabbed it and ran back upstairs. When he got to the closed bathroom door, he knocked.

"Frankie, are you okay?"

"Yes."

"Can I come in?"

"Can I stop you?" she asked sarcastically.

He took that as a "yes" and pushed the bathroom door open. Then he stood at the shower door watching Frankie's silhouette in the etched glass. "You're so hot, Frankie. Want me to join you?" he teased.

"What part of 'I want to be alone' do you not understand?"

He leaned against the shower door as he opened the first aid kit. "Do you want the good news or the bad news?"

"Both."

"The good news is we have a well-stocked first aid kit. The bad news is there are no butterfly bandages. I'll run down to the drug store and get them. When I get back we can play doctor."

"Just go. Get out of my hair for a while."

"I'm not going anywhere until you get out of the shower. People fall in showers all the time and you were in a major accident today. You may think you're fine, but you're not super-human, Frankie. You need to rest."

Frankie sighed and turned off the water. She grabbed the fluffy white towel Lane offered and wrapped it around her body. She got another towel to dry her hair, and then slipped into her terrycloth robe. She looked at Lane, "Okay, I'm out of the shower. You can go now."

He kissed her forehead and closed the bathroom door behind him. In a few moments, motor of Lane's SUV revved up, then he back out of the driveway.

She wiped the steam from the mirror and gazed at her reflection. There was a strip of bluish green bruising across her nose and swelling beneath each of her eyes. It could have been worse, Frankie thought. She could have lost her life when that car flipped so a little bruising, swelling and cuts were nothing.

Frankie used a wide-tooth comb to rake through her hair, and then she brushed her teeth. Walking into her bedroom, she pulled a white knit tank and a pair of purple cotton pajama shorts out of a dresser drawer and slipped them on. She pulled down the comforter on her bed and fluffed the pillows. Suddenly a nap sounded very, very good. She lay down on the bed and rested her head against the pillows.

The front door of the house had a distinctive squeak when opened. She heard that sound and opened her eyes. Someone was in the house. She'd heard the motor of Lane's SUV as he left for the drug store. Frankie heard the faint sound of footsteps in the foyer as if someone were trying to be especially quiet. She reached for her bedside table drawer and quietly pulled it open to get her Glock. But it wasn't there. Then she remembered she'd left it in her purse that was still in Lane's car.

Frankie heard the footsteps again, this time on the steps of the staircase. Someone was headed upstairs. She looked into the drawer again for her stun gun, pepper spray, or knife. Anything! Then she remembered she'd put these things in her backpack the last time they did surveillance. Damn it. Why didn't she put something back in the drawer?

She listened to the sound of footsteps in the hallway as the intruder headed for Lane's room. Lane's bedroom door opened, and then a second later, it closed. The footsteps were now coming toward *her* room. She froze. Time had run out to do anything but pretend she was asleep until she could make a move. She closed her eyes. She hadn't turned on a lamp so the only light came from the bathroom. The footsteps drew closer and closer, until in the slits of her eyes she could see David Chambers standing in her doorframe holding a revolver in his hand.

Still pretending to be asleep, peeking through the slits of her eyes, she watched him cross the room to the end of her bed. As he slowly moved to the side of the bed and moved closer to her, she mentally prepared to fight. A couple more steps and she'd make her move.

David was so close she could hear him breathing, when she quickly kicked her long leg and sent the gun flying to the other side of the room. Surprised, he staggered backward. She jumped to her feet to kick him again, but he grabbed her left arm. Swiftly, she brought her right fist down and delivered a hard blow to the bridge of his nose. He howled as blood sprayed all over her and the wall. She didn't stop. She spun and kicked but missed his groin. He pushed her away, crashing her against the wall. He raced toward her and tried to get a grip on her throat, but she fisted her hand, brought up her arm and slammed her fist into a cluster of nerves she knew resided in the side of his neck. He dropped his hands and looked confused. She then brought her fist up and smashed into the same area of his neck again. He staggered back, got his balance and headed for her again. This time she tightened her fist and hammered his ear and watched as he slumped to the floor, slipping into unconsciousness.

She was breathing hard, her adrenalin at full speed. She dove across the bed and found his gun lying on the floor on the other side. She got to her feet and pointed the gun at him. He lay motionless on the floor, clearly unconscious.

David Chambers was here to kill her. Now she was certain he was driving the black car that rammed her Miata. He was undoubtedly sent here to finish the job by Dr. Eric Caine, who was his employer and directed his every move. She nudged at David's leg to ensure he was still unconscious, and then she searched his pockets and found his car keys. She grabbed her Reeboks out of the closet and ran down the stairs. In the coat closet in the foyer, she grabbed her backpack, flung open the front door and ran.

She didn't stop running until she got to the Lincoln Town Car. She dived inside, locked the doors and turned the ignition. She put David's gun, her shoes, and backpack on the passenger seat. The good doctor was about to get an uninvited visitor.

Three policemen and Tim Brennan stood in a huddle discussing the results of their house search for Jennifer. Not one had a thing to add to the discussion. They'd found no one who had seen Jennifer, nor was she in any of the homes that the residents freely agreed to have them search.

Frustrated, Tim walked back to his car to call Blake Stone to see when his county's scuba diver team would arrive, and to tell him he'd made reservations for them in the same hotel where he was staying. They'd start out early the next morning to search the lake.

Paul Vance watched the scene as he sat in his car that was parked in the driveway of an empty house down the road. He couldn't get too close but he could see enough to let him figure out what was going on. For some reason, her father and the police had targeted this area to do a house to house search for Jennifer. And judging from the body language and gestures of the cops in the huddle, they didn't find her or information that would help them locate her.

Paul slumped down in his seat so Tim Brennan wouldn't notice him as he drove past to get to the main road. He fired up his car and followed.

Jennifer Brennan had spent the day concentrating on how she could escape. She'd spent a lot time considering the basement windows. They were too high up for her to reach by jumping, so she tried the dresser. First she pulled out each drawer and set it aside. Standing on one side of it, she tried to shove it toward the high wall lined with windows at the top. She pushed and then stopped to rest. Then she pushed again as hard as she could, throwing her body against the dresser. A sharp pain ripped through her midsection making her gasp. She bent, holding herself, riding out the pain until finally she was able to get to the bed to sit down. Jennifer cried as she held herself and rocked, terrified now that she may have hurt the baby.

The pain stopped and she noticed the gap left by the now removed drawer. There was something metallic on the floor of the dresser. She moved closer to see and discovered four large screws bolted the piece of furniture to the floor.

She thought about the planning that went into her abduction and imprisonment. Obviously, Dr. Caine had put a lot of thought into the room where he'd keep her. Soundproofing foam lined the walls so no one would hear her cries for help. Every piece of furniture was bolted to the floor so it could not be moved.

Why was he keeping her alive? They'd killed Ally Black. Jennifer was sure of it. So why was she still alive? She knew too much and she'd stupidly gone to Dr. Caine's office and shared with him just how much she knew and suspected. She should have gone to the police. But then, how could she have done that and kept her pregnancy a secret from her father?

It was then she felt a flutter. She moved her hand down to cover her baby bump. There it was again, a flicker of movement within her as light as the brushing of butterfly wings. Her baby had moved. Filled with wonder, she stared at her tummy. The wonder was swiftly replaced with terror as the realization hit her. He was keeping her alive for her *baby*.

In his hotel room, Tim Brennan tossed his cell phone on the bed and slumped into one of the chairs at the round table. He'd just called his wife, Megan, and lied to her yet again. She sensed something was wrong. He could hear it in her voice. They'd known and loved each other for a long time. She knew him.

At one point, she'd asked him where he was staying and he'd almost blurted out Bloomington, but stopped himself and said Indianapolis. Telling her he was in Bloomington would have been a huge mistake that would have led to her questions about Jennifer. She would have known that he'd never have stayed in Bloomington without seeing his daughter. So he'd lied.

He wouldn't be able to keep this secret much longer. He would have to tell her that the daughter they adored was missing and that he could not find her. The police chief had promised to keep it under wraps for a few more days before they'd go to the media with Jennifer's photo.

He thought of the next day's activities. He'd meet with his four scuba divers for breakfast in the cafe downstairs. They'd plan how they'd conduct their search of the lake, and then they'd head out to Monroe Lake. He hoped they'd find something that would lead them to Jennifer. He prayed it would not be her body.

Tim's cell phone sounded and he plucked it from the bed. "Sheriff Brennan."

"Sir, this is Deputy Tammy Short. I have the cell phone information you requested for Jennifer Brennan."

"Let's hear it."

"For the call history, the last call to the subject occurred at 5:25 p.m. on Sunday. The call was from E. Caine from Bloomington."

"Are you sure that's the name?"

"Yes, sir. E. Caine. For the cell tower history..."

"I don't need that. Thank you, Deputy Short."

Alarm and anger ripped up his spine. Jennifer's last call was from Eric Fucking Caine, owner and operator of the adoption agency from hell. He pulled his badge out of his pocket and threw it on the bed. It was time for him to act like a father of a missing daughter, *not* a sheriff. He pulled his holster from the closet and strapped it on. He pushed his revolver in the holster and threw on a denim jacket to cover it.

He sat at the table, opened the manila folder and flipped through the file until he found a piece of paper that held the one thing he needed — Dr. Eric Caine's home address.

Paul Vance sat in the hotel parking lot having already decided he'd spend another night there sleeping in his car. He glanced up at the full moon. The sky was clear and glittering with stars. He was parked several rows over from Tim Brennan's car and periodically glanced in that direction, although he didn't think the car would be moving anymore today. Mr. Brennan was probably upstairs in his room preparing for bed.

Paul slid his seat back so he could stretch his legs as he prepared for the long night ahead. He grabbed a red plaid football blanket from the back seat and put it on the passenger seat. With the warm June weather, it was unlikely he'd need it for warmth until the early hours of morning.

He closed his eyes for a second, but was too anxious to sleep. Where was Jennifer? If it was the last thing he did in his lifetime, he had to find her and make things right. If he had to walk on fiery coals to get to her, he'd do it. He had to make her believe he was still the man she thought he was before that night she told him she was pregnant.

He opened his eyes and noticed a man leave the hotel building. As he neared his car in the parking lot, he realized the man was Tim Brennan. He adjusted his seat, turned on his car's ignition and prepared to follow him.

Jennifer heard the sound of footsteps outside her door. The metal slot at the bottom of the door opened as someone slid a tray of food into the room. It was time.

Sitting at the end of the bed, she began rocking back and forth as she moaned. She heard movement and then the sound of someone pressing himself on the door as if bracing himself as he looked through the peep hole. She moaned louder and kept rocking.

"What's wrong?" It was Dr. Caine's voice. She'd recognize it anywhere.

"I'm having these horrible pains that started an hour ago," she cried.

"It's too early for contractions."

She cried out in pain as she doubled over. "The pain is excruciating. You have to help me."

She held her breath as he hesitated. She filled a long minute with more groaning and cries for help. She heard the key twist in the lock. Then Dr. Caine entered the room. She stood and moved toward him still moaning.

He reached out to take her wrist to check her pulse. The second he took her wrist, she slammed her knee into his groin. He crumbled at her feet, writhing in pain. She raced out the door and into the basement toward the staircase. She sprinted up the stairs until she reached the kitchen. There was a sliding glass door that led to the terrace. She ripped the door open and ran across the backyard.

Jennifer saw beams of headlights wash over the side yard and she halted, trying not to panic. A car was coming down the doctor's driveway. David Chambers could be behind the wheel of that car. She froze until the light beams disappeared. Then she headed toward the woods where she worked her way through the thick undergrowth, until she reached a cluster of trees, where she hid while trying to catch her breath. Jennifer looked back toward the house and saw no movement so she walked farther, trying to find her way to the road and help.

Lane pulled his SUV into his driveway and immediately noticed something he thought was odd. The front lights were off and the house was dark. The only light that was on in the entire house was the one in Frankie's bathroom window upstairs. He couldn't think of a reason why Frankie would shut off the front lights, and he was certain he turned them on before he left for the drug store.

Thanks to long lines of sick customers, the drug store errand to buy butterfly bandages took a lot longer than he thought it would. Then once he got out of there, he was in his car when he noticed the gas gauge was on empty so he pulled into a gas station and filled up the tank.

He pulled his vehicle up to the garage, stopped and turned off the ignition. He opened his car door, and then turned to retrieve the bag of butterfly bandages from the passenger seat.

Suddenly a sharp, agonizing pain shot through his neck. Just before he lost consciousness, he saw David Chambers standing in front of him holding a hypodermic needle.

David watched with satisfaction as Lane slumped in the driver's seat. He raced to the passenger side and grabbed hold of Lane's arm and dragged him across the console until he could prop his body up with the seat belt of the passenger seat. He then slammed the door shut and went to the driver side of the vehicle. Jumping in, he fired up the vehicle and backed out of the driveway then headed toward Dr. Caine's house.

If anyone knew where that bitch Frankie went, it was Lane. Once he got him to Dr. Caine's house, there were all kinds of unpleasant things he'd do to him to get him to give her up. Once Lane gave him the information he wanted, he'd be eliminated, just as Frankie would be when he found her.

Frankie backed the Lincoln Town Car on the dirt road Lane had shown her that was located directly in front of Dr. Caine's home but across the road. She turned off the car and put her shoes on. Then she picked up David's revolver along with her backpack and got out of the car. Frankie pulled out a pair of sweatpants from the backpack and pulled them on. She tucked the revolver in the right deep pocket of her sweatpants and placed a small stun gun in her left pocket. She mounted the backpack on her back then crossed the road and set off through the woods toward Caine's house, avoiding the security gate in his driveway.

Frankie moved through the thicket of trees as quietly as she could, heading toward the house. Once she passed the security gate, she walked into the front yard and made a beeline for the front door.

She leaned against the door and listened for sounds from inside the house. It was very quiet. Frankie knocked softly on the door because she only wanted the door answered if someone was close by. No one answered so she pulled her lock pick tool kit out of her backpack. She jiggled the door with a tool and it opened easily. She shoved the tool in the kit which she placed in the backpack.

Frankie entered the house, glanced up the staircase then into the massive living area. Seeing no one, she walked quietly toward the kitchen. It, too, was empty. If she were going to hide someone in this house, it would be in the basement, so that was the area she wanted to search first for Jennifer. She remembered from the house tour given to her by Dr. Caine at the party that the door leading to the basement was in the kitchen.

Once she reached the kitchen, she opened the door and went down the basement steps taking them slowly one at a time as she listened for sounds. On the landing, she scanned the basement and noted it was very long and probably ran the length of the house. The laundry room with a washer, dryer and ironing setup was to her left. To her right was a sitting area with a sofa and two chairs along with a small flat-screen television that was mounted on the wall. Moving forward she noticed a small room that looked like it was built recently. Some of the sheetrock was exposed and looked new. She moved closer, but froze when she heard what sounded like a man moaning.

"You bitch, Jennifer! Do you really think I won't find you? Wait until I get a hold of you. If I'm permanently injured, you're dead. Do you hear me? You're dead, baby or not!"

It was Dr. Caine. She could hear him as he used the door knob to pull himself up. He cursed and stumbled into the room. She reached inside her pocket and pulled the revolver out, took the stance and aimed at him. He stopped and looked confused, as if he needed to gather his thoughts to say the most convincing thing.

"Frankie, what are you doing in my house? Why do you have a gun?"

"Where is Jennifer?" Her voice was low, filled with anger.

"Jennifer? I don't know a Jennifer."

"You're lying. I just heard you say her name. Try again."

"I'm sorry, Frankie. You must be confused. I really don't know what you're talking about."

"You're a freaking liar. One more time. Where is Jennifer?" she shouted.

Tim Brennan stopped his car after he pulled off the road not far from Dr. Caine's house. He could see the house clearly and noted there were lights on but not much activity. Was Jennifer inside? There were no cars in the driveway but lights were on in a couple of the lower level rooms. He took a deep breath and considered a bit more about what he was going to do. His first thought was to ring the doorbell and confront Dr. Caine when he answered the door, pushing past him into the house if he had to. But the doctor would undoubtedly call the police and he might get arrested before he was able to thoroughly search the house. Another idea was to watch the house until two or three in the morning then break in and search the lower levels of the house while Caine slept. He decided to get closer to the house to do surveillance.

Tim pulled a small flashlight from the glove compartment of his car and entered the woods. The moonlight was so bright he ended up not having to use it. He maneuvered the weeds and bushes as he walked at a right angle to the house guided by the light of the full moon. Deep into the woods, he stopped, leaned on a tree and stared at the doctor's house. The house was a huge brick structure and must have cost a fortune. It sickened him that the money used to buy such an expensive home was from the sale of innocent babies born into the worst of circumstances. He vowed his grandchild would not be sold by a maniac. He had to find Jennifer. He had to find her alive.

He moved forward, deeper into the woods. Suddenly he heard footsteps, and with each step there was crunching of leaves and vegetation that echoed through the woods. He was not alone. The footsteps had to be a human, because animals don't make the kind of noise that's made by someone wearing shoes. The person was moving toward him. Remembering this was the wooded area where someone shot at Lane, he pulled his revolver out of its holster and moved behind the thick trunk of a tree.

About twenty yards away now, he heard the snap of branches, then a startled cry, and a crash as someone slammed to the ground. He whipped out from behind the tree.

"Freeze!" he shouted. "I'm a law enforcement officer and I'm armed. Stand with your hands up!"

"Dad?" The word was carried on a whisper and he thought he was hearing things.

"Dad," she said it louder and moved toward him.

Shock and disbelief rippled through his body when he saw her

He threw his arms around Jennifer and held her close. Both sobbing, they held each other for a long moment, until she spoke.

"Daddy, we have to get out of here. These men are dangerous. We have to get out of here."

"You're safe now, Jennifer. No one is going to hurt you."

"There are things I need to tell you."

"Not now, honey. Not now."

Guided by the moonlight, he led her toward the road. They'd gone about twenty-five feet when they heard a gunshot in the distance. Tim pulled out his revolver again, and pushed Jennifer behind him. When they travelled further, Tim saw a man in a light colored shirt lying on the ground in a fetal position. Tim put the revolver back in the holster, and pulled out a flashlight that he aimed toward the figure.

"He's hurt. Jennifer, stay back." He moved closer to the man, not realizing that his daughter was close behind him.

Suddenly she rushed forward and screamed, "It's Paul!"

CHAPTER ELEVEN

"Doc, have I ever told you about all those medals I earned as an Army Sharpshooter?" Frankie asked as she held the gun, aiming it toward Dr. Caine's chest.

"Impressive, and here I thought you were just a horny little housewife."

"One of us was horny, but it sure wasn't me for *you*. Again, where is Jennifer?"

"Like I said before, I don't know a Jennifer."

"When you gave me the extensive tour of your home, I don't recall seeing the room you just came out of. Let's take a look. Back up to the room and if you try anything, you're a dead man."

She held the gun on him as he took backward steps until he reached the room where Jennifer was held. She motioned him to the wall at the right side of the door. "Put your hands up high and face the wall. Closer. Press yourself against it. Good, boy."

She moved to a position so she could see inside the room. Inside was the twin bed bolted to the floor, a small dresser with four drawers, a toilet and a sink. The walls were covered with blue foam soundproofing.

"You bastard. You kept her locked in there like an animal? What have you done to her? Where is she?" She was close to losing it and struggled to keep her temper in check. Still pointing the gun at him, she ordered him to turn around. Frankie noticed a subtle change in his expression. Gone was the haughty, smug look he had before. Replacing it was alarm. Finally, he seemed to realize how much trouble he was in.

"Look, I didn't hurt her. I swear. I took good care of her. I brought her healthy meals and plenty of water and milk. I even gave her pre-natal vitamins. I swear I didn't hurt her."

"Where is Jennifer?"

"She pretended to have labor pains and when I went in to check on her she kicked me and ran. I don't know where she is. I just know she's ..." The rumbling of a garage door opening above them broke his train of thought.

"Who uses your garage besides you?"

"Fuck you." His fear dissipated. "That's David. You're dead now. Once he takes care of you, he'll find Jennifer and kill her, too."

"Wrong answer." She jerked her small stun gun out of her pocket and jabbed him in the neck. His head bounced against the wall, and then he slid to the floor as he lost consciousness.

She slipped to the wall next to the staircase to listen and wait. It wasn't long before she heard the house door to the garage open, then slam shut. She heard a dragging sound, and grunting as David dragged something down the steps. When he reached the landing and walked into the room, she greeted him with her gun drawn.

He dragged Lane's limp body into the room, his gun pointed at Lane's head. "Drop it, bitch, or he gets it now instead of later."

She slowly lowered the gun, and then placed it on the floor near the staircase. "What's wrong with Lane? What did you do to him?"

Wordlessly, David drug Lane over to a chair, then pulled some rope out of his pocket and held it out to her. "Get over here and tie him to the chair. And do a good job because I'm watching you."

Taking the rope from David, she leaned down to wrap it around Lane's waist. Frankie held Lane's wrist to check his pulse. It was a little slow. She then tied his hands behind his back, as David directed. God, how she wanted to get Lane out of there and fast.

"Tighter. Tie the rope tighter," David shouted.

She pulled at the rope. If she pulled on it any tighter, it would cut off the blood flow to his hands.

She didn't know what she would do if anything happened to Lane. Why hadn't she told him she loved him? How many times had they made love and the words were on the tip of her tongue, but she lacked the courage to say them? Was she so afraid of getting hurt that she'd missed her chance to tell him?

Frankie pretended to adjust the rope as she leaned in close to Lane's ear. "I love you, Lane. I love you so much, baby."

"Move away from him." He sent her an icy glare and then noticed for the first time that Dr. Caine lay unconscious by the room where Jennifer was kept. "What the hell happened to him?"

"It was his naptime."

"Smartass, where is Jennifer? Or should I say, where is your *cousin*? Isn't that what you called her at the hospital?"

"You might want to reconsider the eavesdropping thing. In most circles, it's considered to be pretty rude," said Frankie. She backed up a step when his hand fisted, his face a glowering mask of rage.

"You're going to find out how very rude I can be. Let's go check on the good doc. You go first." He pushed her toward the other end of the room where the doctor still lay on the floor.

Behind them, Lane moved. He shook his head back and forth as he fought the grogginess. What the hell did Chambers have in that hypodermic? He blinked several times, trying to focus. Whatever the drug was, it was wearing off. He looked around. Where was he?

It was then he noticed Frankie at the far end of the room with David Chambers who was holding a gun on her. Dr. Caine was slumped on the floor and David was checking his wrist.

Lane quietly pulled at his arms, and then realized he was tied to the chair with rope. Stretching his hands, he tried to loosen the rope around his wrists. It stretched a bit, but not enough to free him. He kept working at it. Lane watched as David brought Frankie back to the sitting area near him. He shoved Frankie onto the sofa, and then he glanced at Lane.

"Well, look who's conscious, Mr. Lane Henderson. Did anyone ever tell you that you needed to exhibit some control over your bitch of a wife?"

Lane returned his glare and said nothing. A muscle clenched along his jaw. He wanted to kill him. If he hurt Frankie, he would.

"I bet I could teach you a thing or two about breaking in the little woman. A couple of good beatings and the promise of more can work miracles to improve a wife's behavior."

"Yeah, you're a big man, David Chambers. I saw up close and personal what you did to those two little girls. You're such a big man, you pick on little girls." Lane taunted him to get his attention away from Frankie.

"Shut up. You don't know what you're talking about." Provoked, he shifted toward Lane and moved in front of him.

"Let me introduce myself to you. My name is Lane Hansen and I'm a detective who knows you're guilty of at least two murders, maybe more. Any minute the county sheriff I work for, who was supposed to meet with me an hour ago, is going to storm this house with the SWAT Team. What do you think about that, big guy?"

"You're a liar!" He swung his arm wide and back-handed Lane hard. Blood sprayed from Lane's nose and mouth. Frankie jumped to her feet. David spun around to face her and screamed, "Sit down, bitch!"

Lane spit blood at David and jerked against the rough rope that bound his wrists. He gritted his teeth and pulled at the rope until it cut into his flesh. He had to get free before David hurt Frankie.

Frankie glared at David defiantly, and hissed, "Any wimp can hit a man who's tied up. Just like a sissy who beats up little girls. That's you, David. You're a bully who targets little girls." She purposely taunted him to distract him from Lane, who now strained at his bindings, his arm and chest muscles bulging.

David raced to the sofa. The second he swung his arm at her, she ducked, then popped up into position and kicked the gun out of his hand. It landed on the floor and slid under a chair. Stunned, he grabbed for her but she moved. He caught her by her ponytail and knocked her to her knees and held her there.

Lane roared at David, "You son-of-a-bitch, leave her alone. Fight me like a man!" Hurling insults as he rocked back and forth in the chair, Lane twisted his wrists until the blood slickened and loosened the rope.

"Shut up!" screamed David, who was still holding Frankie by her hair.

"Come fight *me*, big guy. What's the matter, are you afraid? You chicken shit! Are you scared I'll kick your sissy ass?" As he shouted, Lane twisted and turned his wrists to free himself from the rope. It was loosening. He was almost there. Lane clenched his jaw, made fists with his hands and made a fierce pull at the rope. It broke!

David's attention shifted from Frankie to Lane. This was a mistake. She used the opportunity to slam her elbow upward into his groin. He screamed and clutched himself. She didn't stop there. She knew she couldn't. He could recover and kill her and Lane.

Frankie grabbed David's thumb, bending back his wrist until he howled in pain. Jerking his arm behind his back, she dropped him to the floor. Still gripping his arm, she pushed her knee into his back as he struggled beneath her. But he was too strong. He struggled and got his wrist out of her grip, then flipped over on his back, wielding a powerful punch to her face. He sat on top of her, pinning her to the floor.

Lane flew across the room, slamming into David with such force; it hurled them both across the room. Lane threw a punch and heard a satisfying crunch that was the sound of David's nose breaking. When David's hand instinctively went to his face, Lane locked his wrist behind his back and twisted until David screamed in pain. Lane shoved his weight into his knee that was now pinning David to the floor.

"Baby, are you okay?" Lane called to Frankie who was now at his side.

They heard sirens then the front door slammed open. Three members of the SWAT Team followed by Sheriff Tim Brennan flew down the stairs.

"So you were telling the truth about the SWAT Team?" Frankie asked.

"Actually, I was bluffing. But I can't say I'm unhappy about handing these two bastards over to them."

A large man dressed in a SWAT uniform relieved Lane and soon had David in handcuffs.

Tim looked them both over, noting the blood spreading across Frankie's white tank top and Lane's wrists that were raw and bleeding.

"There are a couple of ambulances outside. You and Frankie *both*, go get checked out. And that's an order." He watched them climb the stairs, then walked the extent of the room and looked into the room where his daughter was held. He said a silent grateful prayer that she was safe.

Outside, the road was filled with emergency vehicles with bright flashing lights. Officers were using the SWAT vehicle to ram the security gate open. A deputy waited to stretch yellow crime scene tape across the opening at the end of the driveway.

Lane held Frankie close to him as they walked toward the ambulances. As they neared the first vehicle, they overheard two EMTs talking. "This guy got very lucky. Guess he was holding his gun as he entered the woods. He tripped over a tree root and involuntarily pulled the trigger as he was going down. Looks like a through-and-through wound."

Once they were close enough, they noticed there were people inside the ambulance. A man was lying on a gurney as an EMT tended to him, a young woman with long blonde hair sat on another gurney next to him.

"Oh, my God. That's Jennifer!" Frankie ran to the ambulance and jumped inside. She pulled her cousin to her and stroked her hair. "I can't tell you how glad I am to see you."

"Me, too. I'm sorry about all of this, Frankie."

"Your dad and I were so worried about you. Seeing you here alive and healthy is such a blessing."

The EMT asked Frankie to get out of the ambulance so he'd have more room to help Paul who had an oxygen mask on his face and tubing in his arm leading to a bag of blood dangling overhead. Frankie kissed Jennifer on the cheek and got out of the vehicle.

Paul reached for Jennifer's hand and squeezed. "Jennifer, I'm the one who should be sorry. If I'd been the man I should've been when you told me you were having my baby, none of this would have happened. I just hope you'll let me make everything up to you and the baby."

Paul was interrupted with the news they needed to leave for the hospital.

"Are you going with us?" The EMT directed the question to Jennifer.

"Please stay with me, Jennifer," begged Paul.

"I'll see you at the hospital, Paul. I need some time with my dad."

Lane was waiting for Frankie at the second ambulance, his wrists already treated and wrapped in gauze and white tape. He noticed the blood was spreading across the front of her white tank as she rounded the corner of the open vehicle door.

"Holy shit, Frankie. Come here." He lifted her shirt to reveal the long cut on her midsection was missing several butterfly bandages and some sections were bleeding profusely. He shouted for an EMT. One came running and helped Lane get Frankie into the ambulance and on a gurney.

The EMT took one look at Frankie and said, "Didn't I just treat you? Weren't you the one driving that red Mazda Miata that flipped over in the ditch?"

"Great memory. Just fix me up. And one more thing — I'm *not* going to the hospital."

Lane waited outside the ambulance and watched as two members of the SWAT Team hauled David and Dr. Caine to waiting patrol cars. Though it was the end of a chapter, it was not the end of their work.

Everyone knew how thorough Michael Brandt was when he prepared a prosecution case. Every single piece of evidence must align until he had a slam dunk. That meant Lane would have to make sure Michael had all he needed to put these two away. More evidence to support the baby trafficking charge against the doctor would have to be found. He prayed that the forensic evidence that was collected from the two crime scenes would nail David

Chambers. That guy was too dangerous to be roaming this earth.

He heard arguing inside the ambulance, and stepped back to have a look.

"Are you nuts? I don't care what kind of a bad-ass cop you think you are, you need stitches and you're going to the hospital!"

"No, I'm not." Frankie said as she climbed out of the vehicle.

"I've got this," said Lane as he scooped her up in his arms, noticing how she grimaced and bit her lip. Typically, she was in pain but wanted no one to know about it.

As he headed across the yard, he shouted at the cop who'd just put David Chambers in the back of his car. "Hey, that perp has my car keys."

"I've got them." The cop pulled the keys out of his pocket and ran to hand them to Lane.

Lane carried Frankie inside the garage and deposited her on the passenger seat of his black Cadillac Escalade. He rounded the SUV and popped into the driver's seat and turned his key in the ignition. He watched in his rearview mirror as the two police officers turned their cars around, and then headed down the driveway. He backed out and turned his vehicle around, too.

"You're quiet, Frankie. What are you thinking?"

"I'm thinking how good it will be to get home."

Lane grinned as he drove down the driveway, and then turned left and headed toward the hospital.

Jennifer waited in her dad's car as he tied up some loose ends. She wondered how she would explain everything that had happened. If there was anyone she owed an explanation to, it was her dad. She felt a kick and smiled. The baby was moving again. Or maybe, she thought, the baby was communicating to her, so she spoke out loud.

"Sweetie, you're staying with your mom. After all we've been through; I could never give you up. Your mom is much stronger than she thought she was when this misadventure began. She knows that no matter what, she's going to protect you, love you, and give you the best home she can. That's a promise."

Jennifer heard the twist of the door handle then saw her father get into the car. As soon as he sat down, she said, "Dad, we need to talk."

"Yes, we do."

She reached across the console and pulled her father's hand until it was stretched flat against her baby bump. She felt the baby kick again and so did her father. Quick tears glistened in his eyes.

"There's plenty of room in our big old house for you and the baby. What your mother wouldn't give to fill that place up again. It'd be a wonderful place to raise a child, Jennifer. Please tell me you don't still plan to give it away."

"No chance, Dad." She squeezed his hand and lifted it to her lips. "No chance."

"Why did you go to such lengths to hide your pregnancy from us? As parents, what did we do wrong?"

"You and Mom did nothing wrong. I want you to be proud of me, Dad. Getting pregnant like I did brought shame to our family. You are such a public person and you've worked so hard to get to where you are in your career. I didn't want my mistake to hurt you." Her heart squeezed as she felt her dad tighten his grip on her hand.

"Jennifer, don't you know I've been proud of you since the day you were born? The public person people are going to see in our county is a sheriff who is so damn proud to have a wonderful daughter and brand-new grandchild that he can't stop boasting about either of them."

"I love you, Dad."

"Love you, too. Don't ever forget it." He pulled his daughter to him and kissed her forehead. "It's going to be a long night at the police station making statements. I'll drive there and you take the car so you can rest in my hotel room until I get there."

"I think I'll drive to the hospital to see Paul first."

By the time she got to Paul's room in the hospital, his wound had been treated and he was sitting up watching television. As soon as he noticed her in the doorway, he flipped off the TV.

Jennifer eased into the room and sat in a chair next to his bed. She felt awkward in his presence. Scenes of their last night together flashed through her mind. He was staring at her and she had to say something. "What did the doctors say?"

"They said the bullet went clear through and didn't hit anything important so I'll be fine."

"That's good."

"Jennifer, I am so sorry for the way I acted the night you told me you were pregnant. Please forgive me."

"Honestly, I don't know if I can do that." It was the truth. She couldn't forget that he wanted her to kill their baby.

"Marry me, Jennifer. We can fly to Vegas. Let's leave tomorrow and get married."

"Yeah, that will solve everything. Let's run off and get married because I'm pregnant."

"I'm not looking at it like that."

"Yes, you are. The topic wouldn't have come up if I wasn't pregnant. You've had two years to ask me to marry you, but you didn't. You barely had time for me with all the football practices and games."

"You said you understood how important football was to me."

"I know how important football *is* to you. I also know how much it means to you to have a chance at pro ball."

"Marry me."

"The answer is no. I think this pregnancy was a test of our relationship and we failed miserably. You freaked, and I made the stupid decision to hide it from my parents. Even worse was the decision I made to give the baby away."

"Honey, you have to reconsider. I looked everywhere for you."

"I don't trust you to be there when the going gets tough, Paul. I'm sorry, but I don't. Things may change in the future, but right now I can't see me being with you any time soon. I'm taking my dad up on his offer to move home, have the baby and possibly raise him or her there. If you want to see the baby and have a relationship, I'm all for that. It's up to you."

It was six o'clock the next morning and Jennifer was fast asleep when her dad crept into the hotel room. Tim took off his jacket, put his revolver in a drawer, and hung up his holster. He looked at her and thought of how angelic she looked in sleep, just as she had as a child. His baby was all grown up now and soon would have a baby of her own.

Suddenly his cell phone sounded, piercing through the quiet room. Jennifer stirred and opened her eyes and watched him as he answered.

"Shit, I forgot all about you guys. Are you at the lake? No kidding. Did you call a tow truck yet? Okay, I'll be right there."

"What was that about, Dad?"

"I forgot all about the scuba team searching for evidence in Monroe Lake this morning. They just found your car. I'm going out to meet them."

"No you're not." She pulled herself out of bed, still dressed in the jeans and shirt from the night before. "It's my car they found and I'm going. I know exactly where the lake is. Besides, you better get some sleep. Sometime later today, we need to tell Mom about my pregnancy."

"Talked me into it," he said as he headed for the shower.

At Monroe Lake, bright beams of sunlight cut through the trees surrounding the sparkling blue lake. It was a beautiful morning for being outside doing anything besides looking for evidence that might lead to a missing person — alive or not.

Blake Stone stood watching the rest of his team walking out of the water toward the shore and didn't notice Jennifer pulling in a parking space near the boat dock. The men pulled off their diving suits as he had done and threw them on the shore.

Blake reached down in the water for the rope tied to their boat and looped it around a wooden dock post.

Jennifer watched Blake from the distance as she walked toward him on the dock. He was obviously the one in charge. He carried himself with a commanding air of self-confidence. She watched his powerful, well-muscled body move with grace as he helped a man in a scuba suit out of the boat.

"I can't tell you how freaking glad I was that we found her car but didn't find Jennifer Brennan down there," Blake said to the man standing next to him.

"And *I* can't tell you how freaking glad *I* am that you found her car but didn't find Jennifer Brennan down there."

Hearing the feminine voice, he spun around and at first thought he was seeing things. Standing in front of him, very much alive, was the young woman in the photo his sheriff had given to him.

Blake put his hands on his hips and said, "You're alive. And you're even more beautiful than your photo, Jennifer Brennan."

Michael Brandt called an emergency meeting for one o'clock and his office soon filled as Tim, Frankie and Lane arrived and took their seats at his conference table.

Michael started the meeting. "The three of you did an outstanding job apprehending two men who would have taken more lives and sold more babies, if you hadn't. I can't thank you enough."

Frankie swelled with pride, as she smiled at Lane.

But there is additional work to be done if we want to successfully prosecute them and keep their asses in jail where they belong," Michael began. "I want this case tied up with a neat little bow. I want the evidence to be so air-tight they have no defense. So while we're waiting for the rest of the forensic evidence to come in, there are some things that need to be done."

The sheriff nodded in agreement and turned to Frankie. "Frankie, I'd like you to stay on the op for a while. I know how good you are at finding people. Find David Chamber's wife. She's disappeared, undoubtedly trying to get away from him since he put her in the hospital a couple of times. Find her and discover what she knows about David's whereabouts and behavior the day of both murders."

Frankie nodded. Of course she'd stay on the op until David Chambers and Dr. Caine received the punishments they deserved.

"Another one for you, Frankie, is to interview every employee of the Forever Home Adoption Agency, as well as the pregnant women living in his apartment house. See if they have some valuable information for our case."

"Will do," Frankie responded.

"Just one more thing. If you don't already have cell records for David Chambers on the day of each of the murders, get them. Check his cell tower history to pinpoint his whereabouts." She made a mental note to call her contacts as soon as she could. If the cell tower showed David's location to be in or near Kramer the days of the murder, it was strong evidence for the prosecution.

Tim looked across the table at Lane. "Lane, I know this was your first big case. I want you to know I'm proud of the way you handled yourself. I know Michael is too. We have one more important thing for you to take care of. Follow the money to the Caymans. The bank there is not being very cooperative. We need you there in person. Follow the money so we can make a connection between the selling of the babies and the money the doctor received."

"Yes, sir," said Lane.

"I also want you to look for banking records that show Dr. Caine putting large sums of money in David's account following each murder. Take as long as you need in the Caymans. I have money in my budget for the trip."

Frankie's heart sunk at this news. Depending on how cooperative the bank would be, Lane could be away for weeks.

The group was standing up, ready to leave, when Michael's desk phone rang.

"Are you serious? Damn it, I didn't know Anne was having contractions or I never would have scheduled this meeting here. Is the ambulance just leaving? Okay. I'll meet her at the hospital!"

"Anne? Is she having the baby?" asked Frankie.

"Make that — babies. She's been on bed rest the last two weeks and didn't want you to know.

"Why not?" She was incredulous. Frankie didn't think she and Anne had secrets from each other.

"She said you wouldn't let her continue with the computer work she was doing for your company while you were gone. She said she'd go insane on bed rest with nothing to do."

"It just hit me. Did you say 'babies', as in plural?"

"Yes, there are two of them." He smiled at her as he hurried to the door.

"Michael, wait up. I've got a deputy downstairs to take you!" Tim said as he ran after him.

Hours later, Lane and Frankie walked into Anne's hospital room with a pink gift bag along with a blue one filled with baby presents. Anne was holding their baby girl, Melissa Anne, while Michael held his namesake, Michael Jr.

Frankie crept up to Anne, hugged her neck and kissed her cheek. "Wow! They are so beautiful." She stroked the baby in Anne's arm across her cheek.

Anne held the tiny infant girl wrapped in a soft pink blanket out to Frankie. "Please hold her. Melissa wants to meet her God-Mom."

"God-Mom, are you serious? Daisy will kill me."

"No chance," said Michael. "Daisy is on cloud nine and hasn't come down since we asked her to be 'Grammy'."

Frankie took the small bundle from Anne's arms and sat in a nearby chair to cuddle her, inhaling the sweet baby smell of her hair.

Lane watched Frankie. She was glowing and was definitely a woman who was meant to hold babies. And if he had his way, she'd be holding as many of his as she wanted.

On the way to the airport, there were so many things Lane wanted to say to Frankie, but they were rushing like crazy to make his flight. It didn't seem like the right time. In the driver's seat, Frankie raced to the departure curb and skidded to a stop. She jumped out to help with his luggage. He grabbed his heavy suitcase before she could and placed it on the curb.

He gathered her up in his arms. "Back there in the doctor's basement, I forgot to tell you something."

Frankie was confused. "What?"

"I love you back." With that he raced inside to catch his flight.

Lane was in the Caymans for two weeks. They were two *long* weeks for Frankie. Each night seemed worse than the last. She couldn't seem to sleep without Lane's warm body next to hers. She tossed and turned, until she finally gave up and read a book or watched television.

She'd moved her things out of the house in Bloomington. Tim hired people to thoroughly clean the house, especially her bedroom where she fought with David. She boxed the few things left by Lane and put the boxes in her guest room.

Frankie had travelled to Bloomington almost every day to interview Forever Homes Adoption Agency employees. A couple of nurses who had important knowledge agreed to testify as long as they wouldn't be prosecuted for their involvement.

She searched for David's wife and couldn't find her. She came to a dead end at the Nashville hotel. The great difficulty she was having finding her made Frankie think the woman had professional help and was in hiding.

With each day that passed, her confidence in her relationship with Lane slipped. She had not heard from him. If he was going to back out of their relationship, now was as good a time as ever. She was beginning to wonder if she'd ever see him again.

Fifteen days had passed and she was in the kitchen making a pitcher of iced tea when she heard her doorbell.

She swung open the door and found Lane holding a very large black puppy in his arms. Surprised and filled with joy, she moved aside for him to enter.

"How did you get here from the airport? And is that my Giant Schnauzer puppy you're holding?"

Lane wrapped his one free arm around her neck and kissed her soundly.

"Michael picked me up at the airport. I asked him to bring this little buddy with him so I could give him to you."

He put the puppy on the floor and it bounded to Frankie and gave her puppy kisses all over her face when she bent down to him. She laughed with delight. "Isn't he beautiful?"

"Yes, and he likes to ride in the car," said Lane. "I bought him a collar. Baby, you might want to check to see if it is too tight."

Frankie inserted her finger between the collar and the puppy's fur, sliding it completely around the collar until she stopped. She had touched a cold, metallic object dangling from the buckle. She bent down to look closer. Fastened to the collar was the most beautiful diamond engagement ring she'd ever seen.

Unable to speak, she threw herself into Lane's arms. He held her so close, it was hard to breathe.

"So you're saying 'yes', right? Because if you're not, I've got a whole lot of persuading to do, and we can get started right now in your bedroom."

"Yes, Lane. Yes. Forever. Yes."

Dear Reader:

If you liked *Deadly Deception*, I would appreciate it if you would help others enjoy this book too by recommending it to your friends on Goodreads or by writing a positive review on Amazon.

If you do write a review, please send me an email at alexagrace@cfl.rr.com. I'd like to give you a free copy of *Deadly Offerings* or my next book *Deadly Relations* as a way of thanking you.

Thank you.

Alexa Grace

Turn the page for more sizzling romantic suspense from

Alexa Grace

Deadly

Offerings

Book One in the Deadly Trilogy

Available now on Amazon.

Deadly Offerings

Book One in the Deadly Trilogy

He may offer her only chance at survival.
But will she survive the passion
that rages between them?

Anne Mason thinks she'll be safe living in the Midwest building a wind farm. She may be dead wrong. Someone is dumping bodies in her corn field and telling Anne they are gifts—for her!

As the body count rises, Anne realizes a cold-blooded serial killer is patiently waiting and watching her every move. And he won't stop until he ends her life. It is clear there are no limits to this killer's thirst for revenge or how far he will go to get it.

Anne is not at all pleased to learn that her new next-door neighbor is county prosecutor Michael Brandt — the same man who represented her ex in her divorce proceedings. He is the last person Anne can trust, but may offer her only chance at survival from a psychopathic killer. But will she survive the passion that rages between them?

Excerpt from *Deadly Offerings*

Anne grabbed a shopping basket and strode down an aisle of the store picking up Reese's Peanut Butter Cups, Butterfinger candy bars, tortilla chips, a jar of salsa, and a quart of soda as she went. She moved to the refrigerator case and eyed the selection of ice cream. She pulled out a couple of cartons of Ben & Jerry's Red Velvet Cake then headed to the teenaged cashier whose eyes were plastered on her long legs.

She paid for the items, whirled around and slammed into the hard chest of a tall man entering the store. Her items tumbled from the bag. The salsa jar rolled across the store as did the bottle of soda. The man uttered "sorry" as he bent to help her pick up the items. He picked up the salsa and put it in her bag. He moved down the aisle to get the soda that had rolled under a freezer then turned toward her. In a black leather jacket and snug faded jeans, he was one of those men that radiated testosterone. And wasn't it just her luck, or lack of, that Michael Brandt, her jerk ex-husband's attorney was heading toward her holding her soda, sending her a dazzling smile that sent her stupid heart racing. She yanked the soda bottle out of his hand, thanked him and resisted the childish urge to kick him in the shin. Instead, she rushed out of the store.

She opened the back of the car to place the groceries inside. She pulled a Butterfinger bar out of one of the bags and got into the front seat. As she opened the candy bar, she glanced at Michael Brandt, still inside the store, who was now staring at her with an odd expression on his face, hands on his hips. She heard movement in the back seat then felt something hard slam against her face. The candy bar flew out of her hand and landed on the floorboard.

"Drive."

She looked in the rearview mirror and gasped; a sliver of panic cut through her. A man in a black ski mask was slammed against her seat thrusting a gun in her face.

Coming Soon — *Deadly Relations*

Book Three in the Deadly Trilogy

She races against time to find a serial killer

before he strikes again.

The most important case of her career could be her last.

A serial killer of young women hides in plain sight in a quiet county in the Midwest. He hides behind a friendly face that inspires trust, a personality that is charming and persuasive, and a rage to kill.

Detective Jennifer Brennan knows from personal experience that an abduction is the equivalent of a nuclear blast to a family. So when three young women go missing and are found murdered on her watch, she vows to find the killer — or die trying.

Detective Blake Stone has been looking for a woman like Jennifer Brennan his entire life. Now that he's found her, can he convince her to trust again?

Two detectives race against time to find a deadly serial killer before he strikes again. It is the most important case of their careers. It could be their last.

About the Author
Alexa Grace

Alexa's journey started in March 2011 when the Sr. Director of Training & Development position she'd held for thirteen years was eliminated. A door closed but another one opened. She finally had the time to pursue her dream of writing books — her dream since childhood. Her focus is now on writing riveting romantic suspense novels.

Alexa earned two degrees from Indiana State University and currently lives in Florida. She's a member of Romance Writers of America (national) as well as the Florida Chapter. Her first book *Deadly Offerings* has consistently been on Amazon's Top 100 Bestselling Romantic Suspense Books. She was recently named one of the top 100 Indie authors by *Kindle Review*.

Her writing support team includes five Miniature Schnauzers, three of which are rescues. As a writer, she is fueled by Starbucks lattes, chocolate and emails from readers.

For more information on her upcoming releases:

Check out her website at:

http://www.alexa-grace.net/

Visit on Facebook at:
https://www.facebook.com/AuthorAlexaGrace

Email her at: **www.alexagrace@cfl.rr.com**

Follow her at: **http://twitter.com/#!/AlexaGrace2**

20238726R00167

Made in the USA
Lexington, KY
01 February 2013